The Paradise Mystery

J. S. Fletcher

Table of Contents

The Paradise Mystery

J. S. Fletcher

CHAPTER I. ONLY THE GUARDIAN

American tourists, sure appreciators of all that is ancient and picturesque in England, invariably come to a halt, holding their breath in a sudden catch of wonder, as they pass through the half–ruinous gateway which admits to the Close of Wrychester. Nowhere else in England is there a fairer prospect of old–world peace. There before their eyes, set in the centre of a great green sward, fringed by tall elms and giant beeches, rises the vast fabric of the thirteenth–century Cathedral, its high spire piercing the skies in which rooks are for ever circling and calling. The time–worn stone, at a little distance delicate as lacework, is transformed at different hours of the day into shifting shades of colour, varying from grey to purple: the massiveness of the great nave and transepts contrasts impressively with the gradual tapering of the spire, rising so high above turret and clerestory that it at last becomes a mere line against the ether. In morning, as in afternoon, or in evening, here is a perpetual atmosphere of rest; and not around the great church alone, but in the quaint and ancient houses which fence in the Close. Little less old than the mighty mass of stone on which their ivy–framed windows look, these houses make the casual observer feel that here, if anywhere in the world, life must needs run smoothly. Under those high gables, behind those mullioned windows, in the beautiful old gardens lying between the stone porches and the elm–shadowed lawn, nothing, one would think, could possibly exist but leisured and pleasant existence: even the busy streets of the old city, outside the crumbling gateway, seem, for the moment, far off.

In one of the oldest of these houses, half hidden behind trees and shrubs in a corner of the Close, three people sat at breakfast one fine May morning. The room in which they sat was in keeping with the old house and its surroundings—a long, low–ceilinged room, with oak panelling around its walls, and oak beams across its roof—a room of old furniture, and, old pictures, and old books, its antique atmosphere relieved by great masses of flowers, set here and there in old china bowls: through its wide windows, the—casements of which were thrown wide open, there was an inviting prospect of a high–edged flower garden, and, seen in vistas through the trees and shrubberies, of patches of the west front of the Cathedral, now sombre and grey in shadow. But on the garden and into this flower–scented room the sun was shining gaily through the trees, and making gleams of light on the silver and china on the table and on the faces of the three people who sat around it.

Of these three, two were young, and the third was one of those men whose age it is never easy to guess—a tall, clean–shaven, bright–eyed, alert–looking man, good–looking in a clever, professional sort of way, a man whom no one could have taken for anything but a member of one of the learned callings. In some lights he looked no more than forty: a strong light betrayed the fact that his dark hair had a streak of grey in it, and was showing a tendency to whiten about the temples. A strong, intellectually superior man, this, scrupulously groomed and well–dressed, as befitted what he really was—a medical practitioner with an excellent connection amongst the exclusive society of a cathedral town. Around him hung an undeniable air of content and prosperity —as he turned over a pile of letters which stood by his plate, or glanced at the morning newspaper which lay at his elbow, it was easy to see that he had no cares beyond those of the day, and that they—so far as he knew then—were not likely to affect him greatly. Seeing him in these pleasant domestic circumstances, at the head of his table, with abundant evidences of comfort and refinement and modest luxury about him, any one would have said, without hesitation, that Dr. Mark Ransford was undeniably one of the fortunate folk of this world.

The second person of the three was a boy of apparently seventeen—a well–built, handsome lad of the senior schoolboy type, who was devoting himself in business–like fashion to two widely–differing pursuits—one, the consumption of eggs and bacon and dry toast; the other, the study of a Latin textbook, which he had propped up in front of him against the old–fashioned silver cruet. His quick eyes wandered alternately between his book and his plate; now and then he muttered a line or two to himself. His companions took no notice of these combinations of eating and learning: they knew from experience that it was his way to make up at breakfast–time for the moments he had stolen from his studies the night before.

It was not difficult to see that the third member of the party, a girl of nineteen or twenty, was the boy's sister. Each had a wealth of brown hair, inclining, in the girl's case to a shade that had tints of gold in it; each had grey eyes, in which there was a mixture of blue; each had a bright, vivid colour; each was undeniably good–looking and eminently healthy. No one would have doubted that both had lived a good deal of an open–air existence: the boy was already muscular and sinewy: the girl looked as if she was well acquainted with the tennis racket and the golf–stick. Nor would any one have made the mistake of thinking that these two were blood relations of the man at the head of the table—between them and him there was not the least resemblance of feature, of colour, or of manner.

While the boy learnt the last lines of his Latin, and the doctor turned over the newspaper, the girl read a letter —evidently, from the large sprawling handwriting, the missive of some girlish correspondent. She was deep in it when, from one of the turrets of the Cathedral, a bell began to ring. At that, she glanced at her brother.

"There's Martin, Dick!" she said. "You'll have to hurry."

Many a long year before that, in one of the bygone centuries, a worthy citizen of Wrychester, Martin by name, had left a sum of money to the Dean and Chapter of the Cathedral on condition that as long as ever the Cathedral stood, they should cause to be rung a bell from its smaller bell–tower for three minutes before nine o'clock every morning, all the year round. What Martin's object had been no one now knew—but this bell served to remind young gentlemen going to offices, and boys going to school, that the hour of their servitude was near. And Dick Bewery, without a word, bolted half his coffee, snatched up his book, grabbed at a cap which lay with more books on a chair close by, and vanished through the open window. The doctor laughed, laid aside his newspaper, and handed his cup across the table.

"I don't think you need bother yourself about Dick's ever being late, Mary," he said. "You are not quite aware of the power of legs that are only seventeen years old. Dick could get to any given point in just about one–fourth of the time that I could, for instance—moreover, he has a cunning knowledge of every short cut in the city."

Mary Bewery took the empty cup and began to refill it.

"I don't like him to be late," she remarked. "It's the beginning of bad habits."

"Oh, well!" said Ransford indulgently. "He's pretty free from anything of that sort, you know. I haven't even suspected him of smoking, yet."

"That's because he thinks smoking would stop his growth and interfere with his cricket," answered Mary. "He would smoke if it weren't for that."

"That's giving him high praise, then," said Ransford. "You couldn't give him higher! Know how to repress his inclinations. An excellent thing—and most unusual, I fancy. Most people—don't!"

He took his refilled cup, rose from the table, and opened a box of cigarettes which stood on the mantelpiece. And the girl, instead of picking up her letter again, glanced at him a little doubtfully.

"That reminds me of—of something I wanted to say to you," she said. "You're quite right about people not repressing their inclinations. I—I wish some people would!"

Ransford turned quickly from the hearth and gave her a sharp look, beneath which her colour heightened. Her eyes shifted their gaze away to her letter, and she picked it up and began to fold it nervously. And at that Ransford rapped out a name, putting a quick suggestion of meaning inquiry into his voice.

"Bryce?" he asked.

The girl nodded her face showing distinct annoyance and dislike. Before saying more, Ransford lighted a cigarette.

"Been at it again?" he said at last. "Since–last time?"

"Twice," she answered. "I didn't like to tell you—I've hated to bother you about it. But—what am I to do? I dislike him intensely—I can't tell why, but it's there, and nothing could ever alter the feeling. And though I told him—before—that it was useless—he mentioned it again—yesterday—at Mrs. Folliot's garden-party."

"Confound his impudence!" growled Ransford. "Oh, well!—I'll have to settle with him myself. It's useless trifling with anything like that. I gave him a quiet hint before. And since he won't take it—all right!"

"But—what shall you do?" she asked anxiously. "Not—send him away?"

"If he's any decency about him, he'll go—after what I say to him," answered Ransford. "Don't you trouble yourself about it—I'm not at all keen about him. He's a clever enough fellow, and a good assistant, but I don't like him, personally—never did."

"I don't want to think that anything that I say should lose him his situation—or whatever you call it," she remarked slowly. "That would seem—"

"No need to bother," interrupted Ransford. "He'll get another in two minutes—so to speak. Anyway, we can't have this going on. The fellow must be an ass! When I was young—"

He stopped short at that, and turning away, looked out across the garden as if some recollection had suddenly struck him.

"When you were young—which is, of course, such an awfully long time since!" said the girl, a little teasingly. "What?"

"Only that if a woman said No—unmistakably—once, a man took it as final," replied Ransford. "At least—so I was always given to believe. Nowadays—"

"You forget that Mr. Pemberton Bryce is what most people would call a very pushing young man," said Mary. "If he doesn't get what he wants in this world, it won't be for not asking for it. But—if you must speak to him—and I really think you must!—will you tell him that he is not going to get—me? Perhaps he'll take it finally from you—as my guardian."

"I don't know if parents and guardians count for much in these degenerate days," said Ransford. "But—I won't have him annoying you. And—I suppose it has come to annoyance?"

"It's very annoying to be asked three times by a man whom you've told flatly, once for all, that you don't want him, at any time, ever!" she answered. "It's—irritating!"

"All right," said Ransford quietly. "I'll speak to him. There's going to be no annoyance for you under this roof."

The girl gave him a quick glance, and Ransford turned away from her and picked up his letters.

"Thank you," she said. "But—there's no need to tell me that, because I know it already. Now I wonder if you'll tell me something more?"

Ransford turned back with a sudden apprehension.

"Well?" he asked brusquely. "What?"

"When are you going to tell me all about—Dick and myself?" she asked. "You promised that you would, you know, some day. And—a whole year's gone by since then. And—Dick's seventeen! He won't be satisfied always—just to know no more than that our father and mother died when we were very little, and that you've been guardian—and all that you have been!—to us. Will he, now?"

Ransford laid down his letters again, and thrusting his hands in his pockets, squared his shoulders against the mantelpiece. "Don't you think you might wait until you're twenty-one?" he asked.

"Why?" she said, with a laugh. "I'm just twenty—do you really think I shall be any wiser in twelve months? Of course I shan't!"

"You don't know that," he replied. "You may be—a great deal wiser."

"But what has that got to do with it?" she persisted. "Is there any reason why I shouldn't be told—everything?"

She was looking at him with a certain amount of demand—and Ransford, who had always known that some moment of this sort must inevitably come, felt that she was not going to be put off with ordinary excuses. He hesitated—and she went on speaking.

"You know," she continued, almost pleadingly. "We don't know anything—at all. I never have known, and until lately Dick has been too young to care—"

"Has he begun asking questions?" demanded Ransford hastily.

"Once or twice, lately—yes," replied Mary. "It's only natural." She laughed a little—a forced laugh. "They say," she went on, "that it doesn't matter, nowadays, if you can't tell

7

who your grandfather was—but, just think, we don't know who our father was—except that his name was John Bewery. That doesn't convey much."

"You know more," said Ransford. "I told you—always have told you—that he was an early friend of mine, a man of business, who, with your mother, died young, and I, as their friend, became guardian to you and Dick. Is—is there anything much more that I could tell?"

"There's something I should very much like to know —personally," she answered, after a pause which lasted so long that Ransford began to feel uncomfortable under it. "Don't be angry—or hurt—if I tell you plainly what it is. I'm quite sure it's never even occurred to Dick—but I'm three years ahead of him. It's this—have we been dependent on you?"

Ransford's face flushed and he turned deliberately to the window, and for a moment stood staring out on his garden and the glimpses of the Cathedral. And just as deliberately as he had turned away, he turned back.

"No!" he said. "Since you ask me, I'll tell you that. You've both got money—due to you when you're of age. It—it's in my hands. Not a great lot—but sufficient to—to cover all your expenses. Education—everything. When you're twenty–one, I'll hand over yours—when Dick's twenty–one, his. Perhaps I ought to have told you all that before, but—I didn't think it necessary. I—I dare say I've a tendency to let things slide."

"You've never let things slide about us," she replied quickly, with a sudden glance which made him turn away again. "And I only wanted to know—because I'd got an idea that—well, that we were owing everything to you."

"Not from me!" he exclaimed.

"No—that would never be!" she said. "But—don't you understand? I—wanted to know—something. Thank you. I won't ask more now."

"I've always meant to tell you—a good deal," remarked Ransford, after another pause. "You see, I can scarcely—yet —realize that you're both growing up! You were at school a year ago. And Dick is still very young. Are—are you more satisfied now?" he went on anxiously. "If not—"

8

"I'm quite satisfied," she answered. "Perhaps—some day —you'll tell me more about our father and mother?—but never mind even that now. You're sure you haven't minded my asking —what I have asked?"

"Of course not—of course not!" he said hastily. "I ought to have remembered. And—but we'll talk again. I must get into the surgery—and have a word with Bryce, too."

"If you could only make him see reason and promise not to offend again," she said. "Wouldn't that solve the difficulty?"

Ransford shook his head and made no answer. He picked up his letters again and went out, and down a long stone–walled passage which led to his surgery at the side of the house. He was alone there when he had shut the door—and he relieved his feelings with a deep groan.

"Heaven help me if the lad ever insists on the real truth and on having proofs and facts given to him!" he muttered. "I shouldn't mind telling her, when she's a bit older—but he wouldn't understand as she would. Anyway, thank God I can keep up the pleasant fiction about the money without her ever knowing that I told her a deliberate lie just now. But —what's in the future? Here's one man to be dismissed already, and there'll be others, and one of them will be the favoured man. That man will have to be told! And—so will she, then. And—my God! she doesn't see, and mustn't see, that I'm madly in love with her myself! She's no idea of it —and she shan't have; I must—must continue to be—only the guardian!"

He laughed a little cynically as he laid his letters down on his desk and proceeded to open them—in which occupation he was presently interrupted by the opening of the side-door and the entrance of Mr. Pemberton Bryce.

CHAPTER II. MAKING AN ENEMY

It was characteristic of Pemberton Bryce that he always walked into a room as if its occupant were asleep and he was afraid of waking him. He had a gentle step which was soft without being stealthy, and quiet movements which brought him suddenly to anybody's side before his presence was noticed. He was by Ransford's desk ere Ransford knew he was in the surgery—and Ransford's sudden realization of his presence roused a certain feeling of irritation in his mind, which he instantly endeavoured to suppress—it was no use getting cross with a man of whom you were about to rid yourself, he said to himself. And for the moment, after replying to his assistant's greeting—a greeting as quiet as his entrance—he went on reading his letters, and Bryce turned off to that part of the surgery in which the drugs were kept, and busied himself in making up some prescription. Ten minutes went by in silence; then Ransford pushed his correspondence aside, laid a paper-weight on it, and twisting his chair round, looked at the man to whom he was going to say some unpleasant things. Within himself he was revolving a question—how would Bryce take it?

He had never liked this assistant of his, although he had then had him in employment for nearly two years. There was something about Pemberton Bryce which he did not understand and could not fathom. He had come to him with excellent testimonials and good recommendations; he was well up to his work, successful with patients, thoroughly capable as a general practitioner—there was no fault to be found with him on any professional grounds. But to Ransford his personality was objectionable—why, he was not quite sure. Outwardly, Bryce was rather more than presentable—a tall, good-looking man of twenty-eight or thirty, whom some people—women especially—would call handsome; he was the sort of young man who knows the value of good clothes and a smart appearance, and his professional manner was all that could be desired. But Ransford could not help distinguishing between Bryce the doctor and Bryce the man—and Bryce the man he did not like. Outside the professional part of him, Bryce seemed to him to be undoubtedly deep, sly, cunning—he conveyed the impression of being one of those men whose ears are always on the stretch, who take everything in and give little out. There was a curious air of watchfulness and of secrecy about him in private matters which was as repellent—to Ransford's thinking—as it was hard to explain. Anyway, in private affairs, he did not like his assistant, and he liked him less than ever as he glanced at him on this particular occasion.

"I want a word with you," he said curtly. "I'd better say it now."

Bryce, who was slowly pouring some liquid from one bottle into another, looked quietly across the room and did not interrupt himself in his work. Ransford knew that he must have recognized a certain significance in the words just addressed to him—but he showed no outward sign of it, and the liquid went on trickling from one bottle to the other with the same uniform steadiness.

"Yes?" said Bryce inquiringly. "One moment."

He finished his task calmly, put the corks in the bottles, labelled one, restored the other to a shelf, and turned round. Not a man to be easily startled—not easily turned from a purpose, this, thought Ransford as he glanced at Bryce's eyes, which had a trick of fastening their gaze on people with an odd, disconcerting persistency.

"I'm sorry to say what I must say," he began. "But—you've brought it on yourself. I gave you a hint some time ago that your attentions were not welcome to Miss Bewery."

Bryce made no immediate response. Instead, leaning almost carelessly and indifferently against the table at which he had been busy with drugs and bottles, he took a small file from his waistcoat pocket and began to polish his carefully cut nails.

"Yes?" he said, after a pause. "Well?"

"In spite of it," continued Ransford, "you've since addressed her again on the matter—not merely once, but twice."

Bryce put his file away, and thrusting his hands in his pockets, crossed his feet as he leaned back against the table —his whole attitude suggesting, whether meaningly or not, that he was very much at his ease.

"There's a great deal to be said on a point like this," he observed. "If a man wishes a certain young woman to become his wife, what right has any other man—or the young woman herself, for that matter to say that he mustn't express his desires to her?"

"None," said Ransford, "provided he only does it once—and takes the answer he gets as final."

"I disagree with you entirely," retorted Bryce. "On the last particular, at any rate. A man who considers any word of a woman's as being final is a fool. What a woman thinks on Monday she's almost dead certain not to think on Tuesday. The whole history of human relationship is on my side there. It's no opinion—it's a fact."

Ransford stared at this frank remark, and Bryce went on, coolly and imperturbably, as if he had been discussing a medical problem.

"A man who takes a woman's first answer as final," he continued, "is, I repeat, a fool. There are lots of reasons why a woman shouldn't know her own mind at the first time of asking. She may be too surprised. She mayn't be quite decided. She may say one thing when she really means another. That often happens. She isn't much better equipped at the second time of asking. And there are women—young ones—who aren't really certain of themselves at the third time. All that's common sense."

"I'll tell you what it is!" suddenly exclaimed Ransford, after remaining silent for a moment under this flow of philosophy. "I'm not going to discuss theories and ideas. I know one young woman, at any rate, who is certain of herself. Miss Bewery does not feel any inclination to you—now, nor at any time to be! She's told you so three times. And—you should take her answer and behave yourself accordingly!"

Bryce favoured his senior with a searching look.

"How does Miss Bewery know that she mayn't be inclined to—in the future?" he asked. "She may come to regard me with favour."

"No, she won't!" declared Ransford. "Better hear the truth, and be done with it. She doesn't like you—and she doesn't want to, either. Why can't you take your answer like a man?"

"What's your conception of a man?" asked Bryce.

"That!—and a good one," exclaimed Ransford.

"May satisfy you—but not me," said Bryce. "Mine's different. My conception of a man is of a being who's got some perseverance. You can get anything in this world—anything! —by pegging away for it."

"You're not going to get my ward," suddenly said Ransford. "That's flat! She doesn't want you—and she's now said so three times. And—I support her."

"What have you against me?" asked Bryce calmly. "If, as you say, you support her in her resolution not to listen to my proposals, you must have something against me. What is it?"

"That's a question you've no right to put," replied Ransford, "for it's utterly unnecessary. So I'm not going to answer it. I've nothing against you as regards your work—nothing! I'm willing to give you an excellent testimonial."

"Oh!" remarked Bryce quietly. "That means—you wish me to go away?"

"I certainly think it would be best," said Ransford.

"In that case," continued Bryce, more coolly than ever, "I shall certainly want to know what you have against me—or what Miss Bewery has against me. Why am I objected to as a suitor? You, at any rate, know who I am—you know that my father is of our own profession, and a man of reputation and standing, and that I myself came to you on high recommendation. Looked at from my standpoint, I'm a thoroughly eligible young man. And there's a point you forget—there's no mystery about me!"

Ransford turned sharply in his chair as he noticed the emphasis which Bryce put on his last word.

"What do you mean?" he demanded.

"What I've just said," replied Bryce. "There's no mystery attaching to me. Any question about me can be answered. Now, you can't say that as regards your ward. That's a fact, Dr. Ransford."

Ransford, in years gone by, had practised himself in the art of restraining his temper—naturally a somewhat quick one. And he made a strong effort in that direction now, recognizing that there was something behind his assistant's last remark, and that Bryce meant him to know it was there.

"I'll repeat what I've just said," he answered. "What do you mean by that?"

"I hear things," said Bryce. "People will talk—even a doctor can't refuse to hear what gossiping and garrulous patients say. Since she came to yon from school, a year ago, Wrychester people have been much interested in Miss Bewery, and in her brother, too. And there are a good many residents of the Close—you know their nice, inquisitive ways!—who want to know who the sister and brother really are—and what your relationship is to them!"

"Confound their impudence!" growled Ransford.

"By all means," agreed Bryce. "And—for all I care—let them be confounded, too. But if you imagine that the choice and select coteries of a cathedral town, consisting mainly of the relicts of deceased deans, canons, prebendaries and the like, and of maiden aunts, elderly spinsters, and tea–table–haunting curates, are free from gossip—why, you're a singularly innocent person!"

"They'd better not begin gossiping about my affairs," said Ransford. "Otherwise—"

"You can't stop them from gossiping about your affairs," interrupted Bryce cheerfully. "Of course they gossip about your affairs; have gossiped about them; will continue to gossip about them. It's human nature!"

"You've heard them?" asked Ransford, who was too vexed to keep back his curiosity. "You yourself?"

"As you are aware, I am often asked out to tea," replied Bryce, "and to garden–parties, and tennis–parties, and choice and cosy functions patronized by curates and associated with crumpets. I have heard—with these ears. I can even repeat the sort of thing I have heard. 'That dear, delightful Miss Bewery—what a charming girl! And that good–looking boy, her brother—quite a dear! Now I wonder who they really are? Wards of Dr. Ransford, of course! Really, how very romantic! —and just a little—eh?—unusual? Such a comparatively young man to have such a really charming girl as his ward! Can't be more than forty–five himself, and she's twenty—how very, very romantic! Really, one would think there ought to be a chaperon!'"

"Damn!" said Ransford under his breath.

"Just so," agreed Bryce. "But—that's the sort of thing. Do you want more? I can supply an unlimited quantity in the piece if you like. But it's all according to sample."

"So—in addition to your other qualities," remarked Ransford, "you're a gossiper?"

Bryce smiled slowly and shook his head.

"No," he replied. "I'm a listener. A good one, too. But do you see my point? I say—there's no mystery about me. If Miss Bewery will honour me with her hand, she'll get a man whose antecedents will bear the strictest investigation."

"Are you inferring that hers won't?" demanded Ransford.

"I'm not inferring anything," said Bryce. "I am speaking for myself, of myself. Pressing my own claim, if you like, on you, the guardian. You might do much worse than support my claims, Dr. Ransford."

"Claims, man!" retorted Ransford. "You've got no claims! What are you talking about? Claims!"

"My pretensions, then," answered Bryce. "If there is a mystery—as Wrychester people say there is—about Miss Bewery, it would be safe with me. Whatever you may think, I'm a thoroughly dependable man—when it's in my own interest."

"And—when it isn't?" asked Ransford. "What are you then?—as you're so candid."

"I could be a very bad enemy," replied Bryce.

There was a moment's silence, during which the two men looked attentively at each other.

"I've told you the truth," said Ransford at last. "Miss Bewery flatly refuses to entertain any idea whatever of ever marrying you. She earnestly hopes that that eventuality may never be mentioned to her again. Will you give me your word of honour to respect her wishes?"

"No!" answered Bryce. "I won't!"

"Why not?" asked Ransford, with a faint show of anger. "A woman's wishes!"

"Because I may consider that I see signs of a changed mind in her," said Bryce. "That's why."

"You'll never see any change of mind," declared Ransford. "That's certain. Is that your fixed determination?"

"It is," answered Bryce. "I'm not the sort of man who is easily repelled "

"Then, in that case," said Ransford, "we had better part company." He rose from his desk, and going over to a safe which stood in a corner, unlocked it and took some papers from an inside drawer. He consulted one of these and turned to Bryce. "You remember our agreement?" he continued. "Your engagement was to be determined by a three months' notice on either side, or, at my will, at any time by payment of three months' salary?"

"Quite right," agreed Bryce. "I remember, of course."

"Then I'll give you a cheque for three months' salary—now," said Ransford, and sat down again at his desk. "That will settle matters definitely—and, I hope, agreeably."

Bryce made no reply. He remained leaning against the table, watching Ransford write the cheque. And when Ransford laid the cheque down at the edge of the desk he made no movement towards it.

"You must see," remarked Ransford, half apologetically, "that it's the only thing I can do. I can't have any man who's not —not welcome to her, to put it plainly—causing any annoyance to my ward. I repeat, Bryce—you must see it!"

"I have nothing to do with what you see," answered Bryce. "Your opinions are not mine, and mine aren't yours. You're really turning me away—as if I were a dishonest foreman! —because in my opinion it would be a very excellent thing for her and for myself if Miss Bewery would consent to marry me. That's the plain truth."

Ransford allowed himself to take a long and steady look at Bryce. The thing was done now, and his dismissed assistant seemed to be taking it quietly—and Ransford's curiosity was aroused.

"I can't make you out!" he exclaimed. "I don't know whether you're the most cynical young man I ever met, or whether you're the most obtuse—"

"Not the last, anyway," interrupted Bryce. "I assure you of that!"

"Can't you see for yourself, then, man, that the girl doesn't want you!" said Ransford. "Hang it!—for anything you know to the contrary, she may have—might have–other ideas!"

Bryce, who had been staring out of a side window for the last minute or two, suddenly laughed, and, lifting a hand, pointed into the garden. And Ransford turned—and saw Mary Bewery walking there with a tall lad, whom he recognized as one Sackville Bonham, stepson of Mr. Folliot, a wealthy resident of the Close. The two young people were laughing and chatting together with evident great friendliness.

"Perhaps," remarked Bryce quietly, "her ideas run in—that direction? In which case, Dr. Ransford, you'll have trouble. For Mrs. Folliot, mother of yonder callow youth, who's the apple of her eye, is one of the inquisitive ladies of whom I've just told you, and if her son unites himself with anybody, she'll want to know exactly who that anybody is. You'd far better have supported me as an aspirant! However —I suppose there's no more to say."

"Nothing!" answered Ransford. "Except to say good–day—and good–bye to you. You needn't remain—I'll see to everything. And I'm going out now. I think you'd better not exchange any farewells with any one."

Bryce nodded silently, and Ransford, picking up his hat and gloves, left the surgery by the side door. A moment later, Bryce saw him crossing the Close.

CHAPTER III. ST. WRYTHA'S STAIR

The summarily dismissed assistant, thus left alone, stood for a moment in evident deep thought before he moved towards Ransford's desk and picked up the cheque. He looked at it carefully, folded it neatly, and put it away in his pocket—book; after that he proceeded to collect a few possessions of his own, instruments, hooks from various drawers and shelves. He was placing these things in a small hand—bag when a gentle tap sounded on the door by which patients approached the surgery.

"Come in!" he called.

There was no response, although the door was slightly ajar; instead, the knock was repeated, and at that Bryce crossed the room and flung the door open.

A man stood outside—an elderly, slight—figured, quiet—looking man, who looked at Bryce with a half—deprecating, half—nervous air; the air of a man who was shy in manner and evidently fearful of seeming to intrude. Bryce's quick, observant eyes took him in at a glance, noting a much worn and lined face, thin grey hair and tired eyes; this was a man, he said to himself, who had seen trouble. Nevertheless, not a poor man, if his general appearance was anything to go by—he was well and even expensively dressed, in the style generally affected by well—to—do merchants and city men; his clothes were fashionably cut, his silk hat was new, his linen and boots irreproachable; a fine diamond pin gleamed in his carefully arranged cravat. Why, then, this unmistakably furtive and half—frightened manner—which seemed to be somewhat relieved at the sight of Bryce?

"Is this—is Dr. Ransford within?" asked the stranger. "I was told this is his house."

"Dr. Ransford is out," replied Bryce. "Just gone out—not five minutes ago. This is his surgery. Can I be of use?"

The man hesitated, looking beyond Bryce into the room.

"No, thank you," he said at last. "I—no, I don't want professional services—I just called to see Dr. Ransford—I —the fact is, I once knew some one of that name. It's no matter—at present."

Bryce stepped outside and pointed across the Close.

"Dr. Ransford," he said, "went over there—I rather fancy he's gone to the Deanery—he has a case there. If you went through Paradise, you'd very likely meet him coming back—the Deanery is the big house in the far corner yonder."

The stranger followed Bryce's outstretched finger.

"Paradise?" he said, wonderingly. "What's that?"

Bryce pointed to a long stretch of grey wall which projected from the south wall of the Cathedral into the Close.

"It's an enclosure—between the south porch and the transept," he said. "Full of old tombs and trees—a sort of wilderness —why called Paradise I don't know. There's a short cut across it to the Deanery and that part of the Close—through that archway you see over there. If you go across, you're almost sure to meet Dr. Ransford."

"I'm much obliged to you," said the stranger. "Thank you."

He turned away in the direction which Bryce had indicated, and Bryce went back—only to go out again and call after him.

"If you don't meet him, shall I say you'll call again?" he asked. "And—what name?"

The stranger shook his head.

"It's immaterial," he answered. "I'll see him—somewhere—or later. Many thanks."

He went on his way towards Paradise, and Bryce returned to the surgery and completed his preparations for departure. And in the course of things, he more than once looked through the window into the garden and saw Mary Bewery still walking and talking with young Sackville Bonham.

"No," he muttered to himself. "I won't trouble to exchange any farewells—not because of Ransford's hint, but because there's no need. If Ransford thinks he's going to drive me out of Wrychester before I choose to go he's badly mistaken —it'll be time enough to say farewell when I take my departure—and that won't be just yet. Now I wonder who that old chap was? Knew some one of Ransford's name once, did he? Probably Ransford himself—in which case he knows more of Ransford than anybody in Wrychester knows—for nobody in Wrychester knows anything beyond a few years back. No, Dr. Ransford!—no farewells—to anybody! A mere departure—till I turn up again."

But Bryce was not to get away from the old house without something in the nature of a farewell. As he walked out of the surgery by the side entrance, Mary Bewery, who had just parted from young Bonham in the garden and was about to visit her dogs in the stable yard, came along: she and Bryce met, face to face. The girl flushed, not so much from embarrassment as from vexation; Bryce, cool as ever, showed no sign of any embarrassment. Instead, he laughed, tapping the hand–bag which he carried under one arm.

"Summarily turned out—as if I had been stealing the spoons," he remarked. "I go—with my, small belongings. This is my first reward—for devotion."

"I have nothing to say to you," answered Mary, sweeping by him with a highly displeased lance. "Except that you have brought it on yourself."

"A very feminine retort!" observed Bryce. "But—there is no malice in it? Your anger won't last more than—shall we say a day?"

"You may say what you like," she replied. "As I just said, I have nothing to say—now or at any time."

"That remains to be proved," remarked Bryce. "The phrase is one of much elasticity. But for the present—I go!"

He walked out into the Close, and without as much as a backward look struck off across the sward in the direction in which, ten minutes before, he had sent the strange man. He had rooms in a quiet lane on the farther side of the Cathedral precinct, and his present intention was to go to them to leave his bag and make some further arrangements. He had no idea of leaving Wrychester—he knew of another doctor in the city who was badly in need of help: he would go to him—would tell him, if need be, why he had left Ransford. He had a multiplicity of schemes and ideas in his head, and he began to consider some of them as he stepped out of the Close into the ancient enclosure which all Wrychester folk knew by its time—honoured name of Paradise. This was really an outer court of the old cloisters; its high walls, half—ruinous, almost wholly covered with ivy, shut in an expanse of turf, literally furnished with yew and cypress and studded with tombs and gravestones. In one corner rose a gigantic elm; in another a broken stairway of stone led to a doorway set high in the walls of the nave; across the enclosure itself was a pathway which led towards the houses in the south—east corner of the Close. It was a curious, gloomy spot, little frequented save by people who went across it rather than follow the gravelled paths outside, and it was untenanted when Bryce stepped into it. But just as he walked through the archway he saw Ransford. Ransford was emerging hastily from a postern door in the west porch—so hastily that Bryce checked himself to look at him. And though they were twenty yards apart, Bryce saw that Ransford's face was very pale, almost to whiteness, and that he was unmistakably agitated. Instantly he connected that agitation with the man who had come to the surgery door.

"They've met!" mused Bryce, and stopped, staring after Ransford's retreating figure. "Now what is it in that man's mere presence that's upset Ransford? He looks like a man who's had a nasty, unexpected shock—a bad 'un!"

He remained standing in the archway, gazing after the retreating figure, until Ransford had disappeared within his own garden; still wondering and speculating, but not about his own affairs, he turned across Paradise at last and made his way towards the farther corner. There was a little wicket—gate there, set in the ivied wall; as Bryce opened it, a man in the working dress of a stone—mason, whom he recognized as being one of the master—mason's staff, came running out of the bushes. His face, too, was white, and his eyes were big with excitement. And recognizing Bryce, he halted, panting.

"What is it, Varner?" asked Bryce calmly. "Something happened?"

The man swept his hand across his forehead as if he were dazed, and then jerked his thumb over his shoulder.

"A man!" he gasped. "Foot of St. Wrytha's Stair there, doctor. Dead—or if not dead, near it. I saw it!"

Bryce seized Varner's arm and gave it a shake.

The Paradise Mystery

"You saw—what?" he demanded.

"Saw him—fall. Or rather—flung!" panted Varner. "Somebody—couldn't see who, nohow—flung him right through yon doorway, up there. He fell right over the steps—crash!" Bryce looked over the tops of the yews and cypresses at the doorway in the clerestory to which Varner pointed—a low, open archway gained by the half–ruinous stair. It was forty feet at least from the ground.

"You saw him—thrown!" he exclaimed. "Thrown—down there? Impossible, man!"

"Tell you I saw it!" asserted Varner doggedly. "I was looking at one of those old tombs yonder—somebody wants some repairs doing—and the jackdaws were making such a to–do up there by the roof I glanced up at them. And I saw this man thrown through that door—fairly flung through it! God!—do you think I could mistake my own eyes?"

"Did you see who flung him?" asked Bryce.

"No; I saw a hand—just for one second, as it might be—by the edge of the doorway," answered Varner. "I was more for watching him! He sort of tottered for a second on the step outside the door, turned over and screamed—I can hear it now!—and crashed down on the flags beneath."

"How long since?" demanded Bryce.

"Five or six minutes," said Varner. "I rushed to him—I've been doing what I could. But I saw it was no good, so I was running for help—"

Bryce pushed him towards the bushes by which they were standing.

"Take me to him," he said. "Come on!"

Varner turned back, making a way through the cypresses. He led Bryce to the foot of the great wall of the nave. There in the corner formed by the angle of nave and transept, on a broad pavement of flagstones, lay the body of a man crumpled up in a curiously twisted position. And with one glance, even before he reached it, Bryce knew what body it was—that of the man who had come, shyly and furtively, to Ransford's door.

The Paradise Mystery

"Look!" exclaimed Varner, suddenly pointing. "He's stirring!"

Bryce, whose gaze was fastened on the twisted figure, saw a slight movement which relaxed as suddenly as it had occurred. Then came stillness. "That's the end!" he muttered. "The man's dead! I'll guarantee that before I put a hand on him. Dead enough!" he went on, as he reached the body and dropped on one knee by it. "His neck's broken."

The mason bent down and looked, half–curiously, half–fearfully, at the dead man. Then he glanced upward—at the open door high above them in the walls.

"It's a fearful drop, that, sir," he said. "And he came down with such violence. You're sure it's over with him?"

"He died just as we came up," answered Bryce. "That movement we saw was the last effort—involuntary, of course. Look here, Varner!—you'll have to get help. You'd better fetch some of the cathedral people—some of the vergers. No!" he broke off suddenly, as the low strains of an organ came from within the great building. "They're just beginning the morning service—of course, it's ten o'clock. Never mind them—go straight to the police. Bring them back—I'll stay here."

The mason turned off towards the gateway of the Close, and while the strains of the organ grew louder, Bryce bent over the dead man, wondering what had really happened. Thrown from an open doorway in the clerestory over St. Wrytha's Stair?—it seemed almost impossible! But a sudden thought struck him supposing two men, wishing to talk in privacy unobserved, had gone up into the clerestory of the Cathedral—as they easily could, by more than one door, by more than one stair—and supposing they had quarrelled, and one of them had flung or pushed the other through the door above—what then? And on the heels of that thought hurried another—this man, now lying dead, had come to the surgery, seeking Ransford, and had subsequently gone away, presumably in search of him, and Bryce himself had just seen Ransford, obviously agitated and pale of cheek, leaving the west porch; what did it all mean? what was the apparently obvious inference to be drawn? Here was the stranger dead—and Varner was ready to swear that he had seen him thrown, flung violently, through the door forty feet above. That was—murder! Then—who was the murderer?

23

The Paradise Mystery

Bryce looked carefully and narrowly around him. Now that Varner had gone away, there was not a human being in sight, nor anywhere near, so far as he knew. On one side of him and the dead man rose the grey walls of nave and transept; on the other, the cypresses and yews rising amongst the old tombs and monuments. Assuring himself that no one was near, no eye watching, he slipped his hand into the inner breast pocket of the dead man's smart morning coat. Such a man must carry papers—papers would reveal something. And Bryce wanted to know anything—anything that would give information and let him into whatever secret there might be between this unlucky stranger and Ransford.

But the breast pocket was empty; there was no pocket–book there; there were no papers there. Nor were there any papers elsewhere in the other pockets which he hastily searched: there was not even a card with a name on it. But he found a purse, full of money—banknotes, gold, silver—and in one of its compartments a scrap of paper folded curiously, after the fashion of the cocked–hat missives of another age in which envelopes had not been invented. Bryce hurriedly unfolded this, and after one glance at its contents, made haste to secrete it in his own pocket. He had only just done this and put back the purse when he heard Varner's voice, and a second later the voice of Inspector Mitchington, a well–known police official. And at that Bryce sprang to his feet, and when the mason and his companions emerged from the bushes was standing looking thoughtfully at the dead man. He turned to Mitchington with a shake of the head.

"Dead!" he said in a hushed voice. "Died as we got to him. Broken—all to pieces, I should say—neck and spine certainly. I suppose Varner's told you what he saw."

Mitchington, a sharp–eyed, dark–complexioned man, quick of movement, nodded, and after one glance at the body, looked up at the open doorway high above them.

"That the door" he asked, turning to Varner. "And—it was open?"

"It's always open," answered Varner. "Least–ways, it's been open, like that, all this spring, to my knowledge."

"What is there behind it?" inquired Mitchington.

"Sort of gallery, that runs all round the nave," replied Varner. "Clerestory gallery–that's what it is. People can go up there and walk around—lots of 'em do—tourists, you know.

There's two or three ways up to it—staircases in the turrets."

Mitchington turned to one of the two constables who had followed him.

"Let Varner show you the way up there," he said. "Go quietly —don't make any fuss—the morning service is just beginning. Say nothing to anybody—just take a quiet look around, along that gallery, especially near the door there—and come back here." He looked down at the dead man again as the mason and the constable went away. "A stranger, I should think, doctor —tourist, most likely. But—thrown down! That man Varner is positive. That looks like foul play."

"Oh, there's no doubt of that!" asserted Bryce. "You'll have to go into that pretty deeply. But the inside of the Cathedral's like a rabbit—warren, and whoever threw the man through that doorway no doubt knew how to slip away unobserved. Now, you'll have to remove the body to the mortuary, of course—but just let me fetch Dr. Ransford first. I'd like some other medical man than myself to see him before he's moved—I'll have him here in five minutes."

He turned away through the bushes and emerging upon the Close ran across the lawns in the direction of the house which he had left not twenty minutes before. He had but one idea as he ran—he wanted to see Ransford face to face with the dead man —wanted to watch him, to observe him, to see how he looked, how he behaved. Then he, Bryce, would know—something.

But he was to know something before that. He opened the door of the surgery suddenly, but with his usual quietness of touch. And on the threshold he paused. Ransford, the very picture of despair, stood just within, his face convulsed, beating one hand upon the other.

CHAPTER IV. THE ROOM AT THE MITRE

In the few seconds which elapsed before Ransford recognized Bryce's presence, Bryce took a careful, if swift, observation of his late employer. That Ransford was visibly upset by something was plain enough to see; his face was still pale, he was muttering to himself, one clenched fist was pounding the open palm of the other hand—altogether, he looked like a man who is suddenly confronted with some fearful difficulty. And when

Bryce, having looked long enough to satisfy his wishes, coughed gently, he started in such a fashion as to suggest that his nerves had become unstrung.

"What is it?—what are you doing there?" he demanded almost fiercely. "What do you mean by coming in like that?"

Bryce affected to have seen nothing.

"I came to fetch you," he answered. "There's been an accident in Paradise—man fallen from that door at the head of St. Wrytha's Stair. I wish you'd come—but I may as well tell you that he's past help—dead!"

"Dead! A man?" exclaimed Ransford. "What man? A workman?"

Bryce had already made up his mind about telling Ransford of the stranger's call at the surgery. He would say nothing—at that time at any rate. It was improbable that any one but himself knew of the call; the side entrance to the surgery was screened from the Close by a shrubbery; it was very unlikely that any passer–by had seen the man call or go away. No—he would keep his knowledge secret until it could be made better use of.

"Not a workman—not a townsman—a stranger," he answered. "Looks like a well–to–do tourist. A slightly–built, elderly man—grey–haired."

Ransford, who had turned to his desk to master himself, looked round with a sudden sharp glance—and for the moment Bryce was taken aback. For he had condemned Ransford—and yet that glance was one of apparently genuine surprise, a glance which almost convinced him, against his will, against only too evident facts, that Ransford was hearing of the Paradise affair for the first time.

"An elderly man—grey–haired—slightly built?" said Ransford. "Dark clothes—silk hat?"

"Precisely," replied Bryce, who was now considerably astonished. "Do you know him?"

"I saw such a man entering the Cathedral, a while ago," answered Ransford. "A stranger, certainly. Come along, then."

The Paradise Mystery

He had fully recovered his self–possession by that time, and he led the way from the surgery and across the Close as if he were going on an ordinary professional visit. He kept silence as they walked rapidly towards Paradise, and Bryce was silent, too. He had studied Ransford a good deal during their two years' acquaintanceship, and he knew Ransford's power of repressing and commanding his feelings and concealing his thoughts. And now he decided that the look and start which he had at first taken to be of the nature of genuine astonishment were cunningly assumed, and he was not surprised when, having reached the group of men gathered around the body, Ransford showed nothing but professional interest.

"Have you done anything towards finding out who this unfortunate man is?" asked Ransford, after a brief examination, as he turned to Mitchington. "Evidently a stranger—but he probably has papers on him."

"There's nothing on him—except a purse, with plenty of money in it," answered Mitchington. "I've been through his pockets myself: there isn't a scrap of paper—not even as much as an old letter. But he's evidently a tourist, or something of the sort, and so he'll probably have stayed in the city all night, and I'm going to inquire at the hotels."

"There'll be an inquest, of course," remarked Ransford mechanically. "Well—we can do nothing, Mitchington. You'd better have the body removed to the mortuary." He turned and looked up the broken stairway at the foot of which they were standing. "You say he fell down that?" he asked. "Whatever was he doing up there?"

Mitchington looked at Bryce.

"Haven't you told Dr. Ransford how it was?" he asked.

"No," answered Bryce. He glanced at Ransford, indicating Varner, who had come back with the constable and was standing by. "He didn't fall," he went on, watching Ransford narrowly. "He was violently flung out of that doorway. Varner here saw it."

Ransford's cheek flushed, and he was unable to repress a slight start. He looked at the mason.

"You actually saw it!" he exclaimed. "Why, what did you see?"

"Him!" answered Varner, nodding at the dead man. "Flung, head and heels, clean through that doorway up there. Hadn't a chance to save himself, he hadn't! Just grabbed at —nothing!—and came down. Give a year's wages if I hadn't seen it—and heard him scream."

Ransford was watching Varner with a set, concentrated look.

"Who—flung him?" he asked suddenly. "You say you saw!"

"Aye, sir, but not as much as all that!" replied the mason. "I just saw a hand—and that was all. But," he added, turning to the police with a knowing look, "there's one thing I can swear to—it was a gentleman's hand! I saw the white shirt cuff and a bit of a black sleeve!"

Ransford turned away. But he just as suddenly turned back to the inspector.

"You'll have to let the Cathedral authorities know, Mitchington," he said. "Better get the body removed, though, first—do it now before the morning service is over. And—let me hear what you find out about his identity, if you can discover anything in the city."

He went away then, without another word or a further glance at the dead man. But Bryce had already assured himself of what he was certain was a fact—that a look of unmistakable relief had swept across Ransford's face for the fraction of a second when he knew that there were no papers on the dead man. He himself waited after Ransford had gone; waited until the police had fetched a stretcher, when he personally superintended the removal of the body to the mortuary outside the Close. And there a constable who had come over from the police-station gave a faint hint as to further investigation.

"I saw that poor gentleman last night, sir," he said to the inspector. "He was standing at the door of the Mitre, talking to another gentleman—a tallish man."

"Then I'll go across there," said Mitchington. "Come with me, if you like, Dr. Bryce."

This was precisely what Bryce desired—he was already anxious to acquire all the information he could get. And he walked over the way with the inspector, to the quaint old-world inn which filled almost one side of the little square known as Monday Market, and in at the courtyard, where, looking out of the bow window which had served as an outer bar in the coaching days, they found the landlady of the Mitre, Mrs. Partingley. Bryce saw at once that she had heard the news.

"What's this, Mr. Mitchington?" she demanded as they drew near across the cobble–paved yard. "Somebody's been in to say there's been an accident to a gentleman, a stranger—I hope it isn't one of the two we've got in the house?"

"I should say it is, ma'am," answered the inspector. "He was seen outside here last night by one of our men, anyway."

The landlady uttered an expression of distress, and opening a side–door, motioned them to step into her parlour.

"Which of them is it?" she asked anxiously. "There's two —came together last night, they did—a tall one and a short one. Dear, dear me!—is it a bad accident, now, inspector?"

"The man's dead, ma'am," replied Mitchington grimly. "And we want to know who he is. Have you got his name   and the other gentleman's?"

Mrs. Partingley uttered another exclamation of distress and astonishment, lifting her plump hands in horror. But her business faculties remained alive, and she made haste to produce a big visitors' book and to spread it open before her callers.

"There it is!" she said, pointing to the two last entries. "That's the short gentleman's name—Mr. John Braden, London. And that's the tall one's—Mr. Christopher Dellingham—also London. Tourists, of course—we've never seen either of them before."

"Came together, you say, Mrs. Partingley?" asked Mitchington. "When was that, now?",

"Just before dinner, last night," answered the landlady. "They'd evidently come in by the London train—that gets in at six–forty, as you know. They came here together, and they'd dinner together, and spent the evening together. Of course, we took them for friends. But they didn't go out together this morning, though they'd breakfast together. After breakfast, Mr. Dellingham asked me the way to the old Manor Mill, and he went off there, so I concluded. Mr. Braden, he hung about a bit, studying a local directory I'd

29

lent him, and after a while he asked me if he could hire a trap to take him out to Saxonsteade this afternoon. Of course, I said he could, and he arranged for it to be ready at two–thirty. Then he went out, and across the market towards the Cathedral. And that," concluded Mrs. Partingley, "is about all I know, gentlemen."

"Saxonsteade, eh?" remarked Mitchington. "Did he say anything about his reasons for going there?"

"Well, yes, he did," replied the landlady. "For he asked me if I thought he'd be likely to find the Duke at home at that time of day. I said I knew his Grace was at Saxonsteade just now, and that I should think the middle of the afternoon would be a good time."

"He didn't tell you his business with the Duke?" asked Mitchington.

"Not a word!" said the landlady. "Oh, no!—just that, and no more. But—here's Mr. Dellingham."

Bryce turned to see a tall, broad–shouldered, bearded man pass the window—the door opened and he walked in, to glance inquisitively at the inspector. He turned at once to Mrs. Partingley.

"I hear there's been an accident to that gentleman I came in with last night?" he said. "Is it anything serious? Your ostler says—"

"These gentlemen have just come about it, sir," answered the landlady. She glanced at Mitchington. "Perhaps you'll tell—" she began.

"Was he a friend of yours, sir?" asked Mitchington. "A personal friend?"

"Never saw him in my life before last night!" replied the tall man. "We just chanced to meet in the train coming down from London, got talking, and discovered we were both coming to the same place—Wrychester. So—we came to this house together. No—no friend of mine—not even an acquaintance—previous, of course, to last night. Is—is it anything serious?"

"He's dead, sir," replied Mitchington. "And now we want to know who he is."

The Paradise Mystery

"God bless my soul! Dead? You don't say so!" exclaimed Mr. Dellingham. "Dear, dear! Well, I can't help you—don't know him from Adam. Pleasant, well-informed man—seemed to have travelled a great deal in foreign countries. I can tell you this much, though," he went on, as if a sudden recollection had come to him; "I gathered that he'd only just arrived in England—in fact, now I come to think of it, he said as much. Made some remark in the train about the pleasantness of the English landscape, don't you know?—I got an idea that he'd recently come from some country where trees and hedges and green fields aren't much in evidence. But—if you want to know who he is, officer, why don't you search him? He's sure to have papers, cards, and so on about him."

"We have searched him," answered Mitchington. "There isn't a paper, a letter, or even a visiting card on him."

Mr. Dellingham looked at the landlady.

"Bless me!" he said. "Remarkable! But he'd a suit-case, or something of the sort—something light—which he carried up from the railway station himself. Perhaps in that—"

"I should like to see whatever he had," said Mitchington. "We'd better examine his room, Mrs. Partingley."

Bryce presently followed the landlady and the inspector upstairs—Mr. Dellingham followed him. All four went into a bedroom which looked out on Monday Market. And there, on a side-table, lay a small leather suit-case, one which could easily be carried, with its upper half thrown open and back against the wall behind.

The landlady, Mr. Dellingham and Bryce stood silently by while the inspector examined the contents of this the only piece of luggage in the room. There was very little to see—what toilet articles the visitor brought were spread out on the dressing-table—brushes, combs, a case of razors, and the like. And Mitchington nodded side-wise at them as he began to take the articles out of the suit-case.

"There's one thing strikes me at once," he said. "I dare say you gentlemen notice it. All these things are new! This suit-case hasn't been in use very long—see, the leather's almost unworn—and those things on the dressing-table are new. And what there is here

31

looks new, too. There's not much, you see—he evidently had no intention of a long stop. An extra pair of trousers—some shirts—socks—collars—neckties —slippers—handkerchiefs—that's about all. And the first thing to do is to see if the linen's marked with name or initials."

He deftly examined the various articles as he took them out, and in the end shook his head.

"No name—no initials," he said. "But look here—do you see, gentlemen, where these collars were bought? Half a dozen of them, in a box. Paris! There you are—the seller's name, inside the collar, just as in England. Aristide Pujol, 82, Rue des Capucines. And—judging by the look of 'em—I should say these shirts were bought there, too—and the handkerchiefs and the neckwear—they all have a foreign look. There may be a clue in that—we might trace him in France if we can't in England. Perhaps he is a Frenchman."

"I'll take my oath he isn't!" exclaimed Mr. Dellingham. "However long he'd been out of England he hadn't lost a North-Country accent! He was some sort of a North-Countryman —Yorkshire or Lancashire, I'll go bail. No Frenchman, officer—not he!"

"Well, there's no papers here, anyway," said Mitchington, who had now emptied the suit-case. "Nothing to show who he was. Nothing here, you see, in the way of paper but this old book—what is it'd' History of Barthorpe."

"He showed me that in the train," remarked Mr. Dellingham. "I'm interested in antiquities and archaeology, and anybody who's long in my society finds it out. We got talking of such things, and he pulled out that book, and told me with great pride, that he'd picked it up from a book-barrow in the street, somewhere in London, for one-and-six. I think," he added musingly, "that what attracted him in it was the old calf binding and the steel frontispiece—I'm sure he'd no great knowledge of antiquities."

Mitchington laid the book down, and Bryce picked it up, examined the title-page, and made a mental note of the fact that Barthorpe was a market-town in the Midlands. And it was on the tip of his tongue to say that if the dead man had no particular interest in antiquities and archaeology, it was somewhat strange that he should have bought a book which was mainly antiquarian, and that it might be that he had so bought it because of a connection between Barthorpe and himself. But he remembered that it was his own policy to keep pertinent facts for his own private consideration, so he said nothing. And Mitchington presently remarking that there was no more to be done there, and ascertaining from Mr. Dellingham that it was his intention to remain in Wrychester for at any rate a few days, they went downstairs again, and Bryce and the inspector crossed over to the police–station.

The news had spread through the heart of the city, and at the police station doors a crowd had gathered. Just inside two or three principal citizens were talking to the Superintendent —amongst them was Mr. Stephen Folliot, the stepfather of young Bonham—a big, heavy–faced man who had been a resident in the Close for some years, was known to be of great wealth, and had a reputation as a grower of rare roses. He was telling the Superintendent something—and the Superintendent beckoned to Mitchington.

"Mr. Folliot says he saw this gentleman in the Cathedral," he said. "Can't have been so very long before the accident happened, Mr. Folliot, from what you say."

"As near as I can reckon, it would be five minutes to ten," answered Mr. Folliot. "I put it at that because I'd gone in for the morning service, which is at ten. I saw him go up the inside stair to the clerestory gallery—he was looking about him. Five minutes to ten—and it must have happened immediately afterwards."

Bryce heard this and turned away, making a calculation for himself. It had been on the stroke of ten when he saw Ransford hurrying out of the west porch. There was a stairway from the gallery down to that west porch. What, then, was the inference? But for the moment he drew none—instead, he went home to his rooms in Friary Lane, and shutting himself up, drew from his pocket the scrap of paper he had taken from the dead man.

CHAPTER V. THE SCRAP OF PAPER

When Bryce, in his locked room, drew that bit of paper from his pocket, it was with the conviction that in it he held a clue to the secret of the morning's adventure. He had only taken a mere glance at it as he withdrew it from the dead man's purse, but he had seen enough of what was written on it to make him certain that it was a document—if such a mere fragment could be called a document—of no ordinary importance. And now be unfolded and laid it flat on his table and looked at it carefully, asking himself what was the real meaning of what he saw.

There was not much to see. The scrap of paper itself was evidently a quarter of a leaf of old-fashioned, stoutish notepaper, somewhat yellow with age, and bearing evidence of having been folded and kept flat in the dead man's purse for some time—the creases were well-defined, the edges were worn and slightly stained by long rubbing against the leather. And in its centre were a few words, or, rather abbreviations of words, in Latin, and some figures:

> In Para. Wrycestr. juxt. tumb.
> Ric. Jenk. ox cap xxiii. xv.

Bryce at first sight took them to be a copy of some inscription but his knowledge of Latin told him, a moment later; that instead of being an inscription, it was a direction. And a very plain direction, too!—he read it easily. In Paradise, at Wrychester, next to, or near, the tomb of Richard Jenkins, or, possibly, Jenkinson, from, or behind, the head, twenty-three, fifteen—inches, most likely. There was no doubt that there was the meaning of the words. What, now, was it that lay behind the tomb of Richard Jenkins, or Jenkinson, in Wrychester Paradise?—in all probability twenty-three inches from the head-stone, and fifteen inches beneath the surface. That was a question which Bryce immediately resolved to find a satisfactory answer to; in the meantime there were other questions which he set down in order on his mental tablets. They were these:

1. Who, really, was the man who had registered at the
   Mitre under the name of John Braden?

2. Why did he wish to make a personal call on the
   Duke of Saxonsteade?

3. Was he some man who had known Ransford in time
   past—and whom Ransford had no desire to meet again?

4. Did Ransford meet him—in the Cathedral?

5. Was it Ransford who flung him to his death down St. Wrytha's Stair?

6. Was that the real reason of the agitation in which he, Bryce, had found Ransford a few moments after the discovery of the body?

There was plenty of time before him for the due solution of these mysteries, reflected Bryce—and for solving another problem which might possibly have some relationship to them —that of the exact connection between Ransford and his two wards. Bryce, in telling Ransford that morning of what was being said amongst the tea–table circles of the old cathedral city, had purposely only told him half a tale. He knew, and had known for months, that the society of the Close was greatly exercised over the position of the Ransford menage. Ransford, a bachelor, a well–preserved, active, alert man who was certainly of no more than middle age and did not look his years, had come to Wrychester only a few years previously, and had never shown any signs of forsaking his single state. No one had ever heard him mention his family or relations; then, suddenly, without warning, he had brought into his house Mary Bewery, a handsome young woman of nineteen, who was said to have only just left school, and her brother Richard, then a boy of sixteen, who had certainly been at a public school of repute and was entered at the famous Dean's School of Wrychester as soon as he came to his new home. Dr. Ransford spoke of these two as his wards, without further explanation; the society of the Close was beginning to want much more explanation. Who were they—these two young people? Was Dr. Ransford their uncle, their cousin—what was he to them? In any case, in the opinion of the elderly ladies who set the tone of society in Wrychester, Miss Bewery was much too young, and far too pretty, to be left without a chaperon. But, up to then, no one had dared to say as much to Dr. Ransford—instead, everybody said it freely behind his back.

Bryce had used eyes and ears in relation to the two young people. He had been with Ransford a year when they arrived; admitted freely to their company, he had soon discovered that whatever relationship existed between them and Ransford, they had none with anybody else—that they knew of. No letters came for them from uncles, aunts, cousins, grandfathers, grandmothers. They appeared to have no memories or reminiscences of relatives, nor of father or mother; there was a curious atmosphere of isolation about them. They had plenty of talk about what might be called their present—their recent schooldays, their youthful experiences, games, pursuits—but none of what, under any circumstances, could have been a very far–distant past. Bryce's quick and attentive ears discovered things—for instance that for many years past Ransford had been in the habit of spending his annual two months' holiday with these two. Year after year—at any rate since the boy's tenth year—he had taken them travelling; Bryce heard scraps of reminiscences of tours in France, and in Switzerland, and in Ireland, and in Scotland—even as far afield as the far north of Norway. It was easy to see that both boy and girl had a mighty veneration for Ransford; just as easy to see that Ransford took infinite pains to make life something more than happy and comfortable for both. And Bryce, who was one of those men who firmly believe that no man ever does anything for nothing and that self–interest is the mainspring of Life, asked himself over and over again the question which agitated the ladies of the Close: Who are these two, and what is the bond between them and this sort of fairy–godfather–guardian?

And now, as he put away the scrap of paper in a safely–locked desk, Bryce asked himself another question: Had the events of that morning anything to do with the mystery which hung around Dr. Ransford's wards? If it had, then all the more reason why he should solve it. For Bryce had made up his mind that, by hook or by crook, he would marry Mary Bewery, and he was only too eager to lay hands on anything that would help him to achieve that ambition. If he could only get Ransford into his power—if he could get Mary Bewery herself into his power—well and good. Once he had got her, he would be good enough to her—in his way.

Having nothing to do, Bryce went out after a while and strolled round to the Wrychester Club—an exclusive institution, the members of which were drawn from the leisured, the professional, the clerical, and the military circles of the old city. And there, as he expected, he found small groups discussing the morning's tragedy, and he joined one of them, in which was Sackville Bonham, his presumptive rival, who was busily telling three or four other young men what his stepfather, Mr. Folliot, had to say about the event.

"My stepfather says—and I tell you he saw the man," said Sackville, who was noted in Wrychester circles as a loquacious and forward youth; "he says that whatever happened must have happened as soon as ever the old chap got up into that clerestory gallery. Look here!—it's like this. My stepfather had gone in there for the morning service—strict old church–goer he is, you know—and he saw this stranger going up the stairway. He's positive, Mr. Folliot, that it was then five minutes to ten. Now, then, I ask you—isn't he right, my stepfather, when he says that it must have happened at once—immediately?

"Because that man, Varner, the mason, says he saw the man fall before ten. What?"

One of the group nodded at Bryce.

"I should think Bryce knows what time it happened as well as anybody," he said. "You were first on the spot, Bryce, weren't you?"

"After Varner," answered Bryce laconically. "As to the time —I could fix it in this way—the organist was just beginning a voluntary or something of the sort."

"That means ten o'clock—to the minute—when he was found!" exclaimed Sackville triumphantly. "Of course, he'd fallen a minute or two before that—which proves Mr. Folliot to be right. Now what does that prove? Why, that the old chap's assailant, whoever he was, dogged him along that gallery as soon as he entered, seized him when he got to the open doorway, and flung him through! Clear as—as noonday!"

One of the group, a rather older man than the rest, who was leaning back in a tilted chair, hands in pockets, watching Sackville Bonham smilingly, shook his head and laughed a little.

"You're taking something for granted, Sackie, my son!" he said. "You're adopting the mason's tale as true. But I don't believe the poor man was thrown through that doorway at all —not I!"

Bryce turned sharply on this speaker—young Archdale, a member of a well-known firm of architects.

"You don't?" he exclaimed. "But Varner says he saw him thrown!"

"Very likely," answered Archdale. "But it would all happen so quickly that Varner might easily be mistaken. I'm speaking of something I know. I know every inch of the Cathedral fabric—ought to, as we're always going over it, professionally. Just at that doorway, at the head of St. Wrytha's Stair, the flooring of the clerestory gallery is worn so smooth that it's like a piece of glass—and it slopes! Slopes at a very steep angle, too, to the doorway itself. A stranger walking along there might easily slip, and if the door was open, as it was, he'd be shot out and into space before he knew what was happening."

This theory produced a moment's silence—broken at last by Sackville Bonham.

"Varner says he saw—saw!—a man's hand, a gentleman's hand," insisted Sackville. "He saw a white shirt cuff, a bit of the sleeve of a coat. You're not going to get over that, you know. He's certain of it!"

"Varner may be as certain of it as he likes," answered Archdale, almost indifferently, "and still he may be mistaken. The probability is that Varner was confused by what he saw. He may have had a white shirt cuff and the sleeve of a black coat impressed upon him, as in a flash—and they were probably those of the man who was killed. If, as I suggest, the man slipped, and was shot out of that open doorway, he would execute some violent and curious movements in the effort to save himself in which his arms would play an important part. For one thing, he would certainly throw out an arm—to clutch at anything. That's what Varner most probably saw. There's no evidence whatever that the man was flung down."

Bryce turned away from the group of talkers to think over Archdale's suggestion. If that suggestion had a basis of fact, it destroyed his own theory that Ransford was responsible for the stranger's death. In that case, what was the reason of Ransford's unmistakable agitation on leaving the west porch, and of his attack—equally unmistakable—of nerves in the surgery? But what Archdale had said made him inquisitive, and after he had treated himself—in celebration of his freedom—to an unusually good lunch at the Club, he went round to the Cathedral to make a personal inspection of the gallery in the clerestory.

There was a stairway to that gallery in the corner of the south transept, and Bryce made straight for it—only to find a policeman there, who pointed to a placard on the turret door. "Closed, doctor—by order of the Dean and Chapter," he announced. "Till further orders. The fact was, sir," he went on confidentially, "after the news got out, so many people came crowding in here and; up to that gallery that the Dean ordered all the entrances to be shut up at once—nobody's been allowed up since noon."

"I suppose you haven't heard anything of any strange person being seen lurking about up there this morning?" asked Bryce.

"No, sir. But I've had a bit of a talk with some of the vergers," replied the policeman, "and they say it's a most extraordinary thing that none of them ever saw this strange gentleman go up there, nor even heard any scuffle. They say—the vergers—that they were all about at the time, getting ready for the morning service, and they neither saw nor heard. Odd, air, ain't it?"

"The whole thing's odd," agreed Bryce, and left the Cathedral. He walked round to the wicket gate which admitted to that side of Paradise—to find another policeman posted there. "What! —is this closed, too?" he asked.

"And time, sir," said the man. "They'd ha' broken down all the shrubs in the place if orders hadn't been given! They were mad to see where the gentleman fell—came in crowds at dinnertime."

Bryce nodded, and was turning away, when Dick Bewery came round a corner from the Deanery Walk, evidently keenly excited. With him was a girl of about his own age—a certain characterful young lady whom Bryce knew as Betty Campany, daughter of the librarian to the Dean and Chapter and therefore custodian of one of the most famous cathedral libraries in the country. She, too, was apparently brimming with excitement, and her pretty and vivacious face puckered itself into a frown as the policeman smiled and shook his head.

"Oh, I say, what's that for?" exclaimed Dick Bewery. "Shut up?—what a lot of rot! I say!—can't you let us go in—just for a minute?"

"Not for a pension, sir!" answered the policeman good–naturedly. "Don't you see the notice? The Dean 'ud have me out of the force by tomorrow if I disobeyed orders. No admittance, nowhere, nohow! But lor' bless yer!" he added, glancing at the two young people. "There's nothing to see—nothing!—as Dr. Bryce there can tell you."

Dick, who knew nothing of the recent passages between his guardian and the dismissed assistant, glanced at Bryce with interest.

"You were on the spot first, weren't you?" he asked: "Do you think it really was murder?"

"I don't know what it was," answered Bryce. "And I wasn't first on the spot. That was Varner, the mason—he called me." He turned from the lad to glance at the girl, who was peeping curiously over the gate into the yews and cypresses. "Do you think your father's at the Library just now?" he asked. "Shall I find him there?"

"I should think he is," answered Betty Campany. "He generally goes down about this time." She turned and pulled Dick Bewery's sleeve. "Let's go up in the clerestory," she said. "We can see that, anyway."

"Also closed, miss," said the policeman, shaking his head. "No admittance there, neither. The public firmly warned off—so to speak. 'I won't have the Cathedral turned into a peepshow!' that's precisely what I heard the Dean say with my own ears. So—closed!"

The boy and the girl turned away and went off across the Close, and the policeman looked after them and laughed.

"Lively young couple, that, sir!" he said. "What they call healthy curiosity, I suppose? Plenty o' that knocking around in the city today."

Bryce, who had half-turned in the direction of the Library, at the other side of the Close, turned round again.

"Do you know if your people are doing anything about identifying the dead man?" he asked. "Did you hear anything at noon?"

"Nothing but that there'll be inquiries through the newspapers, sir," replied the policeman. "That's the surest way of finding something out. And I did hear Inspector Mitchington say that they'd have to ask the Duke if he knew anything about the poor man—I suppose he'd let fall something about wanting to go over to Saxonsteade."

Bryce went off in the direction of the Library thinking. The newspapers?—yes, no better channel for spreading the news. If Mr. John Braden had relations and friends, they would learn of his sad death through the newspapers, and would come forward. And in that case—"

"But it wouldn't surprise me," mused Bryce, "if the name given at the Mitre is an assumed name. I wonder if that theory of Archdale's is a correct one?—however, there'll be more of that at the inquest tomorrow. And in the meantime—let me find out something about the tomb of Richard Jenkins, or Jenkinson—whoever he was."

The famous Library of the Dean and Chapter of Wrychester was housed in an ancient picturesque building in one corner of the Close, wherein, day in and day out, amidst priceless volumes and manuscripts, huge folios and weighty quartos, old prints, and relics of the mediaeval ages, Ambrose Campany, the librarian, was pretty nearly always to be found, ready to show his treasures to the visitors and tourists who came from all parts of the world to see a collection well known to bibliophiles. And Ambrose Campany, a cheery-faced, middle-aged man, with booklover and antiquary written all over him, shockheaded, blue-spectacled, was there now, talking to an old man whom Bryce knew as a neighbour of his in Friary Lane—one Simpson Barker, a quiet, meditative old fellow, believed to be a retired tradesman who spent his time in gentle pottering about the city. Bryce, as he entered, caught what Campany was just then saying.

"The most important thing I've heard about it," said Campany, "is—that book they found in the man's suitcase at the Mitre. I'm not a detective—but there's a clue!"

CHAPTER VI. BY MISADVENTURE

Old Simpson Harker, who sat near the librarian's table, his hands folded on the crook of his stout walking stick, glanced out of a pair of unusually shrewd and bright eyes at Bryce as he crossed the room and approached the pair of gossipers.

"I think the doctor was there when that book you're speaking of was found," he remarked. "So I understood from Mitchington."

"Yes, I was there," said Bryce, who was not unwilling to join in the talk. He turned to Campany. "What makes you think there's a clue—in that?" he asked.

"Why this," answered the librarian. "Here's a man in possession of an old history of Barthorpe. Barthorpe is a small market-town in the Midlands—Leicestershire, I believe, of no particular importance that I know of, but doubtless with a story of its own. Why should any one but a Barthorpe man, past or present, be interested in that story so far as to carry an old account of it with him? Therefore, I conclude this stranger was a Barthorpe man. And it's at Barthorpe that I should make inquiries about him."

Simpson Harker made no remark, and Bryce remembered what Mr. Dellingham had said when the book was found.

"Oh, I don't know!" he replied carelessly. "I don't see that that follows. I saw the book—a curious old binding and queer old copper–plates. The man may have picked it up for that reason—I've bought old books myself for less."

"All the same," retorted Campany, "I should make inquiry at Barthorpe. You've got to go on probabilities. The probabilities in this case are that the man was interested in the book because it dealt with his own town."

Bryce turned away towards a wall on which hung a number of charts and plans of Wrychester Cathedral and its precincts —it' was to inspect one of these that he had come to the Library. But suddenly remembering that there was a question which he could ask without exciting any suspicion or surmise, he faced round again on the librarian.

"Isn't there a register of burials within the Cathedral?" he inquired. "Some book in which they're put down? I was looking in the Memorials of Wrychester the other day, and I saw some names I want to trace."

Campany lifted his quill pen and pointed to a case of big leather–bound volumes in a far corner of the room.

"Third shelf from the bottom, doctor," he replied. "You'll see two books there—one's the register of all burials within the Cathedral itself up to date: the other's the register of those in Paradise and the cloisters. What names are you wanting to trace?"

But Bryce affected not to hear the last question; he walked over to the place which Campany had indicated, and taking down the second book carried it to an adjacent table. Campany called across the room to him.

The Paradise Mystery

"You'll find useful indexes at the end," he said. "They're all brought up to the present time—from four hundred years ago, nearly."

Bryce turned to the index at the end of his book—an index written out in various styles of handwriting. And within a minute he found the name he wanted—there it was plainly before him—Richard Jenkins, died March 8th, 1715: buried, in Paradise, March 10th. He nearly laughed aloud at the ease with which he was tracing out what at first had seemed a difficult matter to investigate. But lest his task should seem too easy, he continued to turn over the leaves of the big folio, and in order to have an excuse if the librarian should ask him any further questions, he memorized some of the names which he saw. And after a while he took the book back to its shelf, and turned to the wall on which the charts and maps were hung. There was one there of Paradise, whereon was marked the site and names of all the tombs and graves in that ancient enclosure; from it he hoped to ascertain the exact position and whereabouts of Richard Jenkins's grave.

But here Bryce met his first check. Down each side of the old chart—dated 1850—there was a tabulated list of the tombs in Paradise. The names of families and persons were given in this list—against each name was a number corresponding with the same number, marked on the various divisions of the chart. And there was no Richard Jenkins on that list—he went over it carefully twice, thrice. It was not there. Obviously, if the tomb of Richard Jenkins, who was buried in Paradise in 1715, was still there, amongst the cypresses and yew trees, the name and inscription on it had vanished, worn away by time and weather, when that chart had been made, a hundred and thirty-five years later. And in that case, what did the memorandum mean which Bryce had found in the dead man's purse?

He turned away at last from the chart, at a loss—and Campany glanced at him.

"Found what you wanted?" he asked.

"Oh, yes!" replied Bryce, primed with a ready answer. "I just wanted to see where the Spelbanks were buried—quite a lot of them, I see."

"Southeast corner of Paradise," said Campany. "Several tombs. I could have spared you the trouble of looking."

"You're a regular encyclopaedia about the place," laughed Bryce. "I suppose you know every spout and gargoyle!"

"Ought to," answered the librarian. "I've been fed on it, man and boy, for five—and—forty years."

Bryce made some fitting remark and went out and home to his rooms—there to spend most of the ensuing evening in trying to puzzle out the various mysteries of the day. He got no more light on them then, and he was still exercising his brains on them when he went to the inquest next morning—to find the Coroner's court packed to the doors with an assemblage of townsfolk just as curious as he was. And as he sat there, listening to the preliminaries, and to the evidence of the first witnesses, his active and scheming mind figured to itself, not without much cynical amusement, how a word or two from his lips would go far to solve matters. He thought of what he might tell—if he told all the truth. He thought of what he might get out of Ransford if he, Bryce, were Coroner, or solicitor, and had Ransford in that witness—box. He would ask him on his oath if he knew that dead man—if he had had dealings with him in times past—if he had met and spoken to him on that eventful morning he would ask him, point—blank, if it was not his hand that had thrown him to his death. But Bryce had no intention of making any revelations just then—as for himself he was going to tell just as much as he pleased and no more. And so he sat and heard—and knew from what he heard that. everybody there was in a hopeless fog, and that in all that crowd there was but one man who had any real suspicion of the truth, and that that man was himself.

The evidence given in the first stages of the inquiry was all known to Bryce, and to most people in the court, already. Mr. Dellingham told how he had met the dead man in the train, journeying from London to Wrychester. Mrs. Partingley told how he had arrived at the Mitre, registered in her book as Mr. John Braden, and had next morning asked if he could get a conveyance for Saxonsteade in the afternoon, as he wished to see the Duke. Mr. Folliot testified to having seen him in the Cathedral, going towards one of the stairways leading to the gallery. Varner—most important witness of all up to that point—told of what he had seen. Bryce himself, followed by Ransford, gave medical evidence; Mitchington told of his examination of the dead man's clothing and effects in his room at the Mitre. And Mitchington added the first information which was new to Bryce.

"In consequence of finding the book about Barthorpe in the suit−case," said Mitchington, "we sent a long telegram yesterday to the police there, telling them what had happened, and asking them to make the most careful inquiries at once about any townsman of theirs of the name of John Braden, and to wire us the result of such inquiries this morning. This is their reply, received by us an hour ago. Nothing whatever is known at Barthorpe—which is a very small town—of any person of that name."

So much for that, thought Bryce. He turned with more interest to the next witness—the Duke of Saxonsteade, the great local magnate, a big, bluff man who had been present in court since the beginning of the proceedings, in which he was manifestly highly interested. It was possible that he might be able to tell something of moment—he might, after all, know something of this apparently mysterious stranger, who, for anything that Mrs. Partingley or anybody else could say to the contrary, might have had an appointment and business with him.

But his Grace knew nothing. He had never heard the name of John Braden in his life—so far as he remembered. He had just seen the body of the unfortunate man and had looked carefully at the features. He was not a man of whom he had any knowledge whatever—he could not recollect ever having seen him anywhere at any time. He knew literally nothing of him —could not think of any reason at all why this Mr. John Braden should wish to see him.

"Your Grace has, no doubt, had business dealings with a good many people at one time or another," suggested the Coroner. "Some of them, perhaps, with men whom your Grace only saw for a brief space of time—a few minutes, possibly. You don't remember ever seeing this man in that way?"

"I'm credited with having an unusually good memory for faces," answered the Duke. "And—if I may say so—rightly. But I don't remember this man at all—in fact, I'd go as far as to say that I'm positive I've never—knowingly—set eyes on him in my life."

"Can your Grace suggest any reason at all why he should wish to call on you?" asked the Coroner.

"None! But then," replied the Duke, "there might be many reasons—unknown to me, but at which I can make a guess. If he was an antiquary, there are lots of old things at

Saxonsteade which he might wish to see. Or he might be a lover of pictures—our collection is a bit famous, you know. Perhaps he was a bookman—we have some rare editions. I could go on multiplying reasons—but to what purpose"

"The fact is, your Grace doesn't know him and knows nothing about him," observed the Coroner.

"Just no—nothing!" agreed the Duke and stepped down again.

It was at this stage that the Coroner sent the jurymen away in charge of his officer to make a careful personal inspection of the gallery in the clerestory. And while they were gone there was some commotion caused in the court by the entrance of a police official who conducted to the Coroner a middle–aged, well–dressed man whom Bryce at once set down as a London commercial magnate of some quality. Between the new arrival and the Coroner an interchange of remarks was at once made, shared in presently by some of the officials at the table. And when the jury came back the stranger was at once ushered into the witness–box, and the Coroner turned to the jury and the court.

"We are unexpectedly able to get some evidence of identity, gentlemen," he observed. "The gentleman who has just stepped into the witness–box is Mr. Alexander Chilstone, manager of the London Colonies Bank, in Threadneedle Street. Mr. Chilstone saw particulars of this matter in the newspapers this morning, and he at once set off to Wrychester to tell us what he knows of the dead man. We are very much obliged to Mr. Chilstone—and when he has been sworn he will perhaps kindly tell us what he can."

In the midst of the murmur of sensation which ran round the court, Bryce indulged himself with a covert look at Ransford who was sitting opposite to him, beyond the table in the centre of the room. He saw at once that Ransford, however strenuously he might be fighting to keep his face under control, was most certainly agitated by the Coroner's announcement. His cheeks had paled, his eyes were a little dilated, his lips parted as he stared at the bank–manager —altogether, it was more than mere curiosity that was indicated on his features. And Bryce, satisfied and secretly elated, turned to hear what Mr. Alexander Chilstone had to tell.

That was not much—but it was of considerable importance. Only two days before, said Mr. Chilstone—that was, on the day previous to his death—Mr. John Braden had called at the London Colonies Bank, of which he, Mr. Chilstone, was manager, and introducing himself as having just arrived in England from Australia, where, he said, he had been living for some years, had asked to be allowed to open an account. He produced some references from agents of the London Colonies Bank, in Melbourne, which were highly satisfactory; the account being opened, he paid into it a sum of ten thousand pounds in a draft at sight drawn by one of those agents. He drew nothing against this, remarking casually that he had plenty of money in his pocket for the present: he did not even take the cheque–book which was offered him, saying that he would call for it later.

"He did not give us any address in London, nor in England," continued the witness. "He told me that he had only arrived at Charing Cross that very morning, having travelled from Paris during the night. He said that he should settle down for a time at some residential hotel in London, and in the meantime he had one or two calls, or visits, to make in the country: when he returned from them, he said, he would call on me again. He gave me very little information about himself: it was not necessary, for his references from our agents in Australia were quite satisfactory. But he did mention that he had been out there for some years, and had speculated in landed property—he also said that he was now going to settle in England for good. That," concluded Mr. Chilstone, "is all I can tell of my own knowledge. But," he added, drawing a newspaper from his pocket, "here is an advertisement which I noticed in this morning's Times as I came down. You will observe," he said, as he passed it to the Coroner, "that it has certainly been inserted by our unfortunate customer."

The Coroner glanced at a marked passage in the personal column of the Times, and read it aloud:

"The advertisement is as follows," he announced. "'If this meets the eye of old friend Marco, he will learn that Sticker wishes to see him again. Write J. Braden, a/o London Colonies Bank, Threadneedle Street, London.'"

Bryce was keeping a quiet eye on Ransford. Was he mistaken in believing that he saw him start; that he saw his cheek flush as he heard the advertisement read out? He believed he was not mistaken—but if he was right, Ransford the next instant regained full control of himself and made no sign. And Bryce turned again to Coroner and witness.

But the witness had no more to say—except to suggest that the bank's Melbourne agents should be cabled to for information, since it was unlikely that much more could be got in England. And with that the middle stage of the proceedings ended—and the last one came, watched by Bryce with increasing anxiety. For it was soon evident, from certain remarks made by the Coroner, that the theory which Archdale had put forward at the club in Bryce's hearing the previous day had gained favour with the authorities, and that the visit of the jurymen to the scene of the disaster had been intended by the Coroner to predispose them in behalf of it. And now Archdale himself, as representing the architects who held a retaining fee in connection with the Cathedral, was called to give his opinion —and he gave it in almost the same words which Bryce had heard him use twenty–four hours previously. After him came the master–mason, expressing the same decided conviction—that the real truth was that the pavement of the gallery had at that particular place become so smooth, and was inclined towards the open doorway at such a sharp angle, that the unfortunate man had lost his footing on it, and before he could recover it had been shot out of the arch and over the broken head of St. Wrytha's Stair. And though, at a juryman's wish, Varner was recalled, and stuck stoutly to his original story of having seen a hand which, he protested, was certainly not that of the dead man, it soon became plain that the jury shared the Coroner's belief that Varner in his fright and excitement had been mistaken, and no one was surprised when the foreman, after a very brief consultation with his fellows, announced a verdict of death by misadventure.

"So the city's cleared of the stain of murder!" said a man who sat next to Bryce. "That's a good job, anyway! Nasty thing, doctor, to think of a murder being committed in a cathedral. There'd be a question of sacrilege, of course—and all sorts of complications."

Bryce made no answer. He was watching Ransford, who was talking to the Coroner. And he was not mistaken now —Ransford's face bore all the signs of infinite relief. From—what? Bryce turned, to leave the stuffy, rapidly–emptying court. And as he passed the centre table he saw old Simpson Harker, who, after sitting in attentive silence for three hours had come up to it, picked up the "History of Barthorpe" which had been found in Braden's suit–case and was inquisitively peering at its title–page.

CHAPTER VII. THE DOUBLE TRAIL

Pemberton Bryce was not the only person in Wrychester who was watching Ransford with keen attention during these events. Mary Bewery, a young woman of more than usual powers of observation and penetration, had been quick to see that her guardian's distress over the affair in Paradise was something out of the common. She knew Ransford for an exceedingly tender-hearted man, with a considerable spice of sentiment in his composition: he was noted for his more than professional interest in the poorer sort of his patients and had gained a deserved reputation in the town for his care of them. But it was somewhat surprising, even to Mary, that he should be so much upset by the death of a total stranger as to lose his appetite, and, for at any rate a couple of days, be so restless that his conduct could not fail to be noticed by herself and her brother. His remarks on the tragedy were conventional enough—a most distressing affair—a sad fate for the poor fellow—most unexplainable and mysterious, and so on—but his concern obviously went beyond that. He was ill at ease when she questioned him about the facts; almost irritable when Dick Bewery, schoolboy-like, asked him concerning professional details; she was sure, from the lines about his eyes and a worn look on his face, that he had passed a restless night when he came down to breakfast on the morning of the inquest. But when he returned from the inquest she noticed a change—it was evident, to her ready wits, that Ransford had experienced a great relief. He spoke of relief, indeed, that night at dinner, observing that the verdict which the jury had returned had cleared the air of a foul suspicion; it would have been no pleasant matter, he said, if Wrychester Cathedral had gained an unenviable notoriety as the scene of a murder.

"All the same," remarked Dick, who knew all the talk of the town, "Varner persists in sticking to what he's said all along. Varner says—said this afternoon, after the inquest was over—that he's absolutely certain of what he saw, and that he not only saw a hand in a white cuff and black coat sleeve, but that he saw the sun gleam for a second on the links in the cuff, as if they were gold or diamonds. Pretty stiff evidence that, sir, isn't it?"

"In the state of mind in which Varner was at that moment," replied Ransford, "he wouldn't be very well able to decide definitely on what he really did see. His vision would retain confused images. Probably he saw the dead man's hand—he was wearing a black coat and white linen. The verdict was a most sensible one."

No more was said after that, and that evening Ransford was almost himself again. But not quite himself. Mary caught him looking very grave, in evident abstraction, more than once; more than once she heard him sigh heavily. But he said no more of the matter until two days later, when, at breakfast, he announced his intention of attending John Braden's funeral, which was to take place that morning.

"I've ordered the brougham for eleven," he said, "and I've arranged with Dr. Nicholson to attend to any urgent call that comes in between that and noon—so, if there is any such call, you can telephone to him. A few of us are going to attend this poor man's funeral—it would be too bad to allow a stranger to go to his grave unattended, especially after such a fate. There'll be somebody representing the Dean and Chapter, and three or four principal townsmen, so he'll not be quite neglected. And"—here he hesitated and looked a little nervously at Mary, to whom he was telling all this, Dick having departed for school—" there's a little matter I wish you'd attend to—you'll do it better than I should. The man seems to have been friendless; here, at any rate—no relations have come forward, in spite of the publicity—so—don't you think it would be rather—considerate, eh?—to put a wreath, or a cross, or something of that sort on his grave—just to show—you know?"

"Very kind of you to think of it," said Mary. "What do you wish me to do?"

"If you'd go to Gardales', the florists, and order—something fitting, you know," replied Ransford, "and afterwards—later in the day—take it to St. Wigbert's Churchyard he's to be buried there—take it—if you don't mind—yourself, you know."

"Certainly," answered Mary. "I'll see that it's done."

She would do anything that seemed good to Ransford—but all the same she wondered at this somewhat unusual show of interest in a total stranger. She put it down at last to Ransford's undoubted sentimentality—the man's sad fate had impressed him. And that afternoon the sexton at St. Wigbert's pointed out the new grave to Miss Bewery and Mr. Sackville Bonham, one carrying a wreath and the other a large bunch of lilies. Sackville, chancing to encounter Mary at the florist's, whither he had repaired to execute a commission for his mother, had heard her business, and had been so struck by the notion—or by a desire to ingratiate himself with Miss Bewery—that he had immediately bought flowers himself—to be put down to her account—and insisted on accompanying Mary to the churchyard.

Bryce heard of this tribute to John Braden next day—from Mrs. Folliot, Sackville Bonham's mother, a large lady who dominated certain circles of Wrychester society in several senses. Mrs. Folliot was one of those women who have been gifted by nature with

50

capacity—she was conspicuous in many ways. Her voice was masculine; she stood nearly six feet in her stoutly-soled shoes; her breadth corresponded to her height; her eyes were piercing, her nose Roman; there was not a curate in Wrychester who was not under her thumb, and if the Dean himself saw her coming, he turned hastily into the nearest shop, sweating with fear lest she should follow him. Endued with riches and fortified by assurance, Mrs. Folliot was the presiding spirit in many movements of charity and benevolence there were people in Wrychester who were unkind enough to say—behind her back —that she was as meddlesome as she was most undoubtedly autocratic, but, as one of her staunchest clerical defenders once pointed out, these grumblers were what might be contemptuously dismissed as five-shilling subscribers. Mrs. Folliot, in her way, was undoubtedly a power—and for reasons of his own Pemberton Bryce, whenever he met her—which was fairly often—was invariably suave and polite.

"Most mysterious thing, this, Dr. Bryce," remarked Mrs. Folliot in her deepest tones, encountering Bryce, the day after the funeral, at the corner of a back street down which she was about to sail on one of her charitable missions, to the terror of any of the women who happened to be caught gossiping. "What, now, should make Dr. Ransford cause flowers to be laid on the grave of a total stranger? A sentimental feeling? Fiddle-de-dee! There must be some reason."

"I'm afraid I don't know what you're talking about, Mrs. Folliot," answered Bryce, whose ears had already lengthened. "Has Dr. Ransford been laying flowers on a grave?—I didn't know of it. My engagement with Dr. Ransford terminated two days ago—so I've seen nothing of him."

"My son, Mr. Sackville Bonham," said Mrs. Folliot, "tells me that yesterday Miss Bewery came into Gardales' and spent a sovereign—actually a sovereign!—on a wreath, which, she told Sackville, she was about to carry, at her guardian's desire, to this strange man's grave. Sackville, who is a warm-hearted boy, was touched—he, too, bought flowers and accompanied Miss Bewery. Most extraordinary! A perfect stranger! Dear me —why, nobody knows who the man was!"

"Except his bank-manager," remarked Bryce, "who says he's holding ten thousand pounds of his."

"That," admitted Mrs. Folliot gravely, "is certainly a consideration. But then, who knows?—the money may have been stolen. Now, really, did you ever hear of a quite respectable man who hadn't even a visiting–card or a letter upon him? And from Australia, too!—where all the people that are wanted run away to! I have actually been tempted to wonder, Dr. Bryce, if Dr. Ransford knew this man—in years gone by? He might have, you know, he might have—certainly! And that, of course, would explain the flowers."

"There is a great deal in the matter that requires explanation, Mrs. Folliot," said Bryce. He was wondering if it would be wise to instil some minute drop of poison into the lady's mind, there to increase in potency and in due course to spread. "I—of course, I may have been mistaken—I certainly thought Dr. Ransford seemed unusually agitated by this affair —it appeared to upset him greatly."

"So I have heard—from others who were at the inquest," responded Mrs. Folliot. "In my opinion our Coroner—a worthy man otherwise—is not sufficiently particular. I said to Mr. Folliot this morning, on reading the newspaper, that in my view that inquest should have been adjourned for further particulars. Now I know of one particular that was never mentioned at the inquest!"

"Oh?" said Bryce. "And what?"

"Mrs. Deramore, who lives, as you know, next to Dr. Ransford," replied Mrs. Folliot, "told me this morning that on the morning of the accident, happening to look out of one of her upper windows, she saw a man whom, from the description given in the newspapers, was, Mrs. Deramore feels assured, was the mysterious stranger, crossing the Close towards the Cathedral in, Mrs. Deramore is positive, a dead straight line from Dr. Ransford's garden—as if he had been there. Dr. Bryce!—a direct question should have been asked of Dr. Ransford—had he ever seen that man before?"

"Ah, but you see, Mrs. Folliot, the Coroner didn't know what Mrs. Deramore saw, so he couldn't ask such a question, nor could any one else," remarked Bryce, who was wondering how long Mrs. Deramore remained at her upper window and if she saw him follow Braden. "But there are circumstances, no doubt, which ought to be inquired into. And it's certainly very curious that Dr. Ransford should send a wreath to the grave of—a stranger."

The Paradise Mystery

He went away convinced that Mrs. Folliot's inquisitiveness had been aroused, and that her tongue would not be idle: Mrs. Folliot, left to herself, had the gift of creating an atmosphere, and if she once got it into her head that there was some mysterious connection between Dr. Ransford and the dead man, she would never rest until she had spread her suspicions. But as for Bryce himself, he wanted more than suspicions—he wanted facts, particulars, data. And once more he began to go over the sum of evidence which had accrued.

The question of the scrap of paper found in Braden's purse, and of the exact whereabouts of Richard Jenkins's grave in Paradise, be left for the time being. What was now interesting him chiefly was the advertisement in the Times to which the bank–manager from London had drawn attention. He had made haste to, buy a copy of the Times and to cut out the advertisement. There it was—old friend Marco was wanted by (presumably old friend) Sticker, and whoever Sticker might be he could certainly be found under care of J. Braden. It had never been in doubt a moment, in Bryce's mind, that Sticker was J. Braden himself. Who, now, was Marco? Who—a million to one on it!—but Ransford, whose Christian name was Mark?

He reckoned up his chances of getting at the truth of the affair anew that night. As things were, it seemed unlikely that any relations of Braden would now turn up. The Wrychester Paradise case, as the reporters had aptly named it, had figured largely in the newspapers, London and provincial; it could scarcely have had more publicity—yet no one, save this bank–manager, had come forward. If there had been any one to come forward the bank–manager's evidence would surely have proved an incentive to speed—for there was a sum of ten thousand pounds awaiting John Braden's next–of–kin. In Bryce's, opinion the chance of putting in a claim to ten thousand pounds is not left waiting forty–eight hours—whoever saw such a chance would make instant use of telegraph or telephone. But no message from anybody professing relationship with the dead man had so far reached the Wrychester police.

When everything had been taken into account, Bryce saw no better clue for the moment than that suggested by Ambrose Campany—Barthorpe. Ambrose Campany, bookworm though he was, was a shrewd, sharp fellow, said Bryce—a man of ideas. There was certainly much in his suggestion that a man wasn't likely to buy an old book about a little insignificant town like Barthorpe unless he had some interest in it—Barthorpe, if Campany's theory were true, was probably the place of John Braden's origin.

Therefore, information about Braden, leading to knowledge of his association or connection with Ransford, might be found at Bartborpe. True, the Barthorpe police had already reported that they could tell nothing about any Braden, but that, in Bryce's opinion, was neither here nor there—he had already come to the conclusion that Braden was an assumed name. And if he went to Barthorpe, he was not going to trouble the police—he knew better methods than that of finding things out. Was he going?—was it worth his while? A moment's reflection decided that matter—anything was worth his while which would help him to get a strong hold on Mark Ransford. And always practical in his doings, he walked round to the Free Library, obtained a gazeteer, and looked up particulars of Barthorpe. There he learnt that Barthorpe was an ancient market–town of two thousand inhabitants in the north of Leicestershire, famous for nothing except that it had been the scene of a battle at the time of the Wars of the Roses, and that its trade was mainly in agriculture and stocking–making —evidently a slow, sleepy old place.

That night Bryce packed a hand–bag with small necessaries for a few days' excursion, and next morning he took an early train to London; the end of that afternoon found him in a Midland northern–bound express, looking out on the undulating, green acres of Leicestershire. And while his train was making a three minutes' stop at Leicester itself, the purpose of his journey was suddenly recalled to him by hearing the strident voices of the porters on the platform.

"Barthorpe next stop!—next stop Barthorpe!"

One of two other men who shared a smoking compartment with Bryce turned to his companion as the train moved off again.

"Barthorpe?" he remarked. "That's the place that was mentioned in connection with that very queer affair at Wrychester, that's been reported in the papers so much these last few days. The mysterious stranger who kept ten thousand in a London bank, and of whom nobody seems to know anything, had nothing on him but a history of Barthorpe. Odd! And yet, though you'd think he'd some connection with the place, or had known it, they say nobody at Barthorpe knows anything about anybody of his name."

"Well, I don't know that there is anything so very odd about it, after all," replied the other man. "He may have picked up that old book for one of many reasons that could be suggested. No—I read all that case in the papers, and I wasn't so much impressed by the old book feature of it. But I'll tell you what—there was a thing struck me. I know this Barthorpe district—we shall be in it in a few minutes—I've been a good deal over it. This strange man's name was given in the papers as John Braden. Now close to Barthorpe—a mile or two outside it, there's a village of that name—Braden Medworth. That's a curious coincidence—and taken in conjunction with the man's possession of an old book about Barthorpe—why, perhaps there's something in it—possibly more than I thought for at first."

"Well—it's an odd case—a very odd case," said the first speaker. "And—as there's ten thousand pounds in question, more will be heard of it. Somebody'll be after that, you may be sure!"

Bryce left the train at Barthorpe thanking his good luck—the man in the far corner had unwittingly given him a hint. He would pay a visit to Braden Medworth—the coincidence was too striking to be neglected. But first Barthorpe itself—a quaint old-world little market-town, in which some of even the principal houses still wore roofs of thatch, and wherein the old custom of ringing the curfew bell was kept up. He found an old-fashioned hotel in the marketplace, under the shadow of the parish church, and in its oak-panelled dining-room, hung about with portraits of masters of foxhounds and queer old prints of sporting and coaching days, he dined comfortably and well.

It was too late to attempt any investigations that evening, and when Bryce had finished his leisurely dinner he strolled into the smoking-room—an even older and quainter apartment than that which he had just left. It was one of those rooms only found in very old houses—a room of nooks and corners, with a great open fireplace, and old furniture and old pictures and curiosities—the sort of place to which the old-fashioned tradesmen of the small provincial towns still resort of an evening rather than patronize the modern political clubs. There were several men of this sort in the room when Bryce entered, talking local politics amongst themselves, and he found a quiet corner and sat down in it to smoke, promising himself some amusement from the conversation around him it was his way to find interest and amusement in anything that offered. But he had scarcely settled down in a comfortably cushioned elbow chair when the door opened again and into the room walked old Simpson Harker.

CHAPTER VIII. THE BEST MAN

Old Harker's shrewd eyes, travelling round the room as if to inspect the company in which he found himself, fell almost immediately on Bryce—but not before Bryce had had time to assume an air and look of innocent and genuine surprise. Harker affected no surprise at all—he looked the astonishment he felt as the younger man rose and motioned him to the comfortable easy–chair which he himself had just previously taken.

"Dear me!" he exclaimed, nodding his thanks. "I'd no idea that I should meet you in these far–off parts, Dr. Bryce! This is a long way from Wrychester, sir, for Wrychester folk to meet in."

"I'd no idea of meeting you, Mr, Harker," responded Bryce. "But it's a small world, you know, and there are a good many coincidences in it. There's nothing very wonderful in my presence here, though—I ran down to see after a country practice—I've left Dr. Ransford."

He had the lie ready as soon as he set eyes on Harker, and whether the old man believed it or not, he showed no sign of either belief or disbelief. He took the chair which Bryce drew forward and pulled out an old–fashioned cigar–case, offering it to his companion.

"Will you try one, doctor?" he asked. "Genuine stuff that, sir—I've a friend in Cuba who remembers me now and then. No," he went on, as Bryce thanked him and took a cigar, "I didn't know you'd finished with the doctor. Quietish place this to practise in, I should think—much quieter even than our sleepy old city."

"You know it?" inquired Bryce.

"I've a friend lives here—old friend of mine," answered Harker. "I come down to see him now and then—I've been here since yesterday. He does a bit of business for me. Stopping long, doctor?"

"Only just to look round," answered Bryce.

"I'm off tomorrow morning—eleven o'clock," said Harker. "It's a longish journey to

Wrychester—for old bones like mine."

"Oh, you're all right!—worth half a dozen younger men," responded Bryce. "You'll see a lot of your contemporaries out, Mr. Harker. Well—as you've treated me to a very fine cigar, now you'll let me treat you to a drop of whisky?—they generally have something of pretty good quality in these old–fashioned establishments, I believe."

The two travellers sat talking until bedtime—but neither made any mention of the affair which had recently set all Wrychester agog with excitement. But Bryce was wondering all the time if his companion's story of having a friend at Barthorpe was no more than an excuse, and when he was alone in his own bedroom and reflecting more seriously he came to the conclusion that old Harker was up to some game of his own in connection with the Paradise mystery.

"The old chap was in the Library when Ambrose Campany said that there was a clue in that Barthorpe history," he mused. "I saw him myself examining the book after the inquest. No, no, Mr. Harker!—the facts are too plain—the evidences too obvious. And yet—what interest has a retired old tradesman of Wrychester got in this affair? I'd give a good deal to know what Harker really is doing here—and who his Barthorpe friend is."

If Bryce had risen earlier next morning, and had taken the trouble to track old Harker's movements, he would have learnt something that would have made him still more suspicious. But Bryce, seeing no reason for hurry, lay in bed till well past nine o'clock, and did not present himself in the coffee–room until nearly half–past ten. And at that hour Simpson Harker, who had breakfasted before nine, was in close consultation with his friend—that friend being none other than the local superintendent of police, who was confidentially closeted with the old man in his private house, whither Harker, by previous arrangement, had repaired as soon as his breakfast was over. Had Bryce been able to see through walls or hear through windows, he would have been surprised to find that the Harker of this consultation was not the quiet, easygoing, gossipy old gentleman of Wrychester, but an eminently practical and business–like man of affairs.

"And now as regards this young fellow who's staying across there at the Peacock," he was saying in conclusion, at the very time that Bryce was leisurely munching his second mutton chop in the Peacock coffee–room, "he's after something or other—his talk about coming here to see after a practice is all lies!—and you'll keep an eye on him while he's in your neighbourhood. Put your best plainclothes man on to him at once—he'll easily know him from the description I gave you —and let him shadow him wherever he goes. And then let me know of his movement—he's certainly on the track of something, and what he does may be useful to me—I can link it up with my own work. And as regards the other matter—keep me informed if you come on anything further. Now I'll go out by your garden and down the back of the town to the station. Let me know, by the by, when this young man at the Peacock leaves here, and, if possible—and you can find out—for where."

Bryce was all unconscious that any one was interested in his movements when he strolled out into Barthorpe market−place just after eleven. He had asked a casual question of the waiter and found that the old gentleman had departed—he accordingly believed himself free from observation. And forthwith he set about his work of inquiry in his own fashion. He was not going to draw any attention to himself by asking questions of present−day inhabitants, whose curiosity might then be aroused; he knew better methods than that. Every town, said Bryce to himself, possesses public records—parish registers, burgess rolls, lists of voters; even small towns have directories which are more or less complete—he could search these for any mention or record of anybody or any family of the name of Braden. And he spent all that day in that search, inspecting numerous documents and registers and books, and when evening came he had a very complete acquaintance with the family nomenclature of Barthorpe, and he was prepared to bet odds against any one of the name of Braden having lived there during the past half−century. In all his searching he had not once come across the name.

The man who had spent a very lazy day in keeping an eye on Bryce, as he visited the various public places whereat he made his researches, was also keeping an eye upon him next morning, when Bryce, breakfasting earlier than usual, prepared for a second day's labours. He followed his quarry away from the little town: Bryce was walking out to Braden Medworth. In Bryce's opinion, it was something of a wild−goose chase to go there, but the similarity in the name of the village and of the dead man at Wrychester might have its significance, and it was but a two miles' stroll from Barthorpe. He found Braden Medworth a very small, quiet, and picturesque place, with an old church on the banks of a river which promised good sport to anglers. And there he pursued his tactics of the day before and went straight to the vicarage and its vicar, with a request to be allowed to inspect the parish registers. The vicar, having no objection to earning the resultant fees, hastened to comply with Bryce's request, and inquired how far back he wanted to search and for what particular entry.

"No particular entry," answered Bryce, "and as to period —fairly recent. The fact is, I am interested in names. I am thinking"—here he used one more of his easily found inventions—"of writing a book on English surnames, and am just now inspecting parish registers in the 'Midlands for that purpose."

"Then I can considerably simplify your labours," said the vicar, taking down a book from one of his shelves. "Our parish registers have been copied and printed, and here is the volume—everything is in there from 1570 to ten years ago, and there is a very full index. Are you staying in the neighbourhood—or the village?"

"In the neighbourhood, yes; in the village, no longer than the time I shall spend in getting some lunch at the inn yonder," answered Bryce, nodding through an open window at an ancient tavern which stood in the valley beneath, close to an old stone bridge. "Perhaps you will kindly lend me this book for an hour?—then, if I see anything very noteworthy in the index, I can look at the actual registers when I bring it back."

The vicar replied that that was precisely what he had been about to suggest, and Bryce carried the book away. And while he sat in the inn parlour awaiting his lunch, he turned to the carefully–compiled index, glancing it through rapidly. On the third page he saw the name Bewery.

If the man who had followed Bryce from Barthorpe to Braden Medworth had been with him in the quiet inn parlour he would have seen his quarry start, and heard him let a stifled exclamation escape his lips. But the follower, knowing his man was safe for an hour, was in the bar outside eating bread and cheese and drinking ale, and Bryce's surprise was witnessed by no one. Yet he had been so much surprised that if all Wrychester had been there he could not, despite his self–training in watchfulness, have kept back either start or exclamation.

Bewery! A name so uncommon that here—here, in this out–of–the–way Midland village!—there must be some connection with the object of his search. There the name stood out before him, to the exclusion of all others—Bewery—with just one entry of figures against it. He turned to page 387 with a sense of sure discovery.

The Paradise Mystery

And there an entry caught his eye at once—and he knew that he had discovered more than he had ever hoped for. He read it again and again, gloating over his wonderful luck.

June 19th, 1891. John Brake, bachelor, of the parish of St. Pancras, London, to Mary Bewery, spinster, of this parish, by the Vicar. Witnesses, Charles Claybourne, Selina Womersley, Mark Ransford.

Twenty–two years ago! The Mary Bewery whom Bryce knew in Wrychester was just about twenty—this Mary Bewery, spinster, of Braden Medworth, was, then, in all probability, her mother. But John Brake who married that Mary Bewery—who was he? Who indeed, laughed Bryce, but John Braden, who had just come by his death in Wrychester Paradise? And there was the name of Mark Ransford as witness. What was the further probability? That Mark Ransford had been John Brake's best man; that he was the Marco of the recent Times advertisement; that John Braden, or Brake, was the Sticker of the same advertisement. Clear! —clear as noonday! And—what did it all mean, and imply, and what bearing had it on Braden or Brake's death?

Before he ate his cold beef, Bryce had copied the entry from the reprinted register, and had satisfied himself that Ransford was not a name known to that village—Mark Ransford was the only person of the name mentioned in the register. And his lunch done, he set off for the vicarage again, intent on getting further information, and before he reached the vicarage gates noticed, by accident, a place whereat he was more likely to get it than from the vicar—who was a youngish man. At the end of the few houses between the inn and the bridge he saw a little shop with the name Charles Claybourne painted roughly above its open window. In that open window sat an old, cheery–faced man, mending shoes, who blinked at the stranger through his big spectacles.

Bryce saw his chance and turned in—to open the book and point out the marriage entry.

"Are you the Charles Claybourne mentioned there?" he asked, without ceremony.

"That's me, sir!" replied the old shoemaker briskly, after a glance. "Yes—right enough!"

"How came you to witness that marriage?" inquired Bryce.

The old man nodded at the church across the way.

"I've been sexton and parish clerk two–and–thirty years, sir," he said. "And I took it on from my father—and he had the job from his father."

"Do you remember this marriage?" asked Bryce, perching himself on the bench at which the shoemaker was working. "Twenty–two years since, I see."

"Aye, as if it was yesterday!" answered the old man with a smile. "Miss Bewery's marriage?—why, of course!"

"Who was she?" demanded Bryce.

"Governess at the vicarage," replied Claybourne. "Nice, sweet young lady."

"And the man she married?—Mr. Brake," continued Bryce. "Who was he?"

"A young gentleman that used to come here for the fishing, now and then," answered Claybourne, pointing at the river. "Famous for our trout we are here, you know, sir. And Brake had come here for three years before they were married—him and his friend Mr. Ransford."

"You remember him, too?" asked Bryce.

"Remember both of 'em very well indeed," said Claybourne, "though I never set eyes on either after Miss Mary was wed to Mr. Brake. But I saw plenty of 'em both before that. They used to put up at the inn there—that I saw you come out of just now. They came two or three times a year—and they were a bit thick with our parson of that time—not this one: his predecessor—and they used to go up to the vicarage and smoke their pipes and cigars with him—and of course, Mr. Brake and the governess fixed it up. Though, you know, at one time it was considered it was going to be her and the other young gentleman, Mr. Ransford—yes! But, in the end, it was Brake —and Ransford stood best man for him."

Bruce assimilated all this information greedily—and asked for more.

"I'm interested in that entry," he said, tapping the open book. "I know some people of the name of Bewery—they may be relatives."

The Paradise Mystery

The shoemaker shook his head as if doubtful.

"I remember hearing it said," he remarked, "that Miss Mary had no relations. She'd been with the old vicar some time, and I don't remember any relations ever coming to see her, nor her going away to see any."

"Do you know what Brake was?" asked Bryce. "As you say he came here for a good many times before the marriage, I suppose you'd hear something about his profession, or trade, or whatever it was?"

"He was a banker, that one," replied Claybourne. "A banker —that was his trade, sir. T'other gentleman, Mr. Ransford, he was a doctor—I mind that well enough, because once when him and Mr. Brake were fishing here, Thomas Joynt's wife fell downstairs and broke her leg, and they fetched him to her —he'd got it set before they'd got the reg'lar doctor out from Barthorpe yonder."

Bryce had now got all the information he wanted, and he made the old parish clerk a small present and turned to go. But another question presented itself to his mind and he reentered the little shop.

"Your late vicar?" he said. "The one in whose family Miss Bewery was governess—where is he now t Dead?"

"Can't say whether he's dead or alive, sir," replied Claybourne. "He left this parish for another—a living in a different part of England—some years since, and I haven't heard much of him from that time to this—he never came back here once, not even to pay us a friendly visit he was a queerish sort. But I'll tell you what, sir," he added, evidently anxious to give his visitor good value for his half-crown, "our present vicar has one of those books with the names of all the clergymen in 'em, and he'd tell you where his predecessor is now, if he's alive—name of Reverend Thomas Gilwaters, M.A.—an Oxford college man he was, and very high learned."

Bryce went back to the vicarage, returned the borrowed book, and asked to look at the registers for the year 1891. He verified his copy and turned to the vicar.

"I accidentally came across the record of a marriage there in which I'm interested," he said as he paid the search fees. "Celebrated by your predecessor, Mr. Gilwaters. I should be glad to know where Mr. Gilwaters is to be found. Do you happen to possess a clerical directory?"

The vicar produced a "Crockford", and Bryce turned over its pages. Mr. Gilwaters, who from the account there given appeared to be an elderly man who had now retired, lived in London, in Bayswater, and Bryce made a note of his address and prepared to depart.

"Find any names that interested you?" asked the vicar as his caller left. "Anything noteworthy?"

"I found two or three names which interested me immensely," answered Bryce from the foot of the vicarage steps. "They were well worth searching for."

And without further explanation he marched off to Barthorpe duly followed by his shadow, who saw him safely into the Peacock an hour later—and, an hour after that, went to the police superintendent with his report.

"Gone, sir," he said. "Left by the five–thirty express for London."

CHAPTER IX. THE HOUSE OF HIS FRIEND

Bryce found himself at eleven o'clock next morning in a small book–lined parlour in a little house which stood in a quiet street in the neighbourhood of Westbourne Grove. Over the mantelpiece, amongst other odds and ends of pictures and photographs, hung a water–colour drawing of Braden Medworth —and to him presently entered an old, silver–haired clergyman whom he at once took to be Braden Medworth's former vicar, and who glanced inquisitively at his visitor and then at the card which Bryce had sent in with a request for an interview.

"Dr. Bryce?" he said inquiringly. "Dr. Pemberton Bryce?"

Bryce made his best bow and assumed his suavest and most ingratiating manner.

The Paradise Mystery

"I hope I am not intruding on your time, Mr. Gilwaters?" he said. "The fact is, I was referred to you, yesterday, by the present vicar of Braden Medworth—both he, and the sexton there, Claybourne, whom you, of course, remember, thought you would be able to give me some information on a subject which is of great importance—to me."

"I don't know the present vicar," remarked Mr. Gilwaters, motioning Bryce to a chair, and taking another close by. "Clayborne, of course, I remember very well indeed—he must be getting an old man now—like myself! What is it you want to know, now?"

"I shall have to take you into my confidence," replied Bryce, who had carefully laid his plans and prepared his story, "and you, I am sure, Mr. Gilwaters, will respect mine. I have for two years been in practice at Wry Wrychester, and have there made the acquaintance of a young lady whom I earnestly desire to marry. She is the ward of the man to whom I have been assistant. And I think you will begin to see why I have come to you when I say that this young lady's name is—Mary Bewery."

The old clergyman started, and looked at his visitor with unusual interest. He grasped the arm of his elbow chair and leaned forward.

"Mary Bewery!" he said in a low whisper. "What—what is the name of the man who is her—guardian?"

"Dr. Mark Ransford," answered Bryce promptly.

The old man sat upright again, with a little toss of his head.

"Bless my soul!" he exclaimed. "Mark Ransford! Then—it must have been as I feared—and suspected!"

Bryce made no remark. He knew at once that he had struck on something, and it was his method to let people take their own time. Mr. Gilwaters had already fallen into something closely resembling a reverie: Bryce sat silently waiting and expectant. And at last the old man leaned forward again, almost eagerly.

"What is it you want to know?" he asked, repeating his first question. "Is—is there some—some mystery?"

64

The Paradise Mystery

"Yes!" replied Bryce. "A mystery that I want to solve, sir. And I dare say that you can help me, if you'll be so good. I am convinced—in fact, I know!—that this young lady is in ignorance of her 'parentage, that Ransford is keeping some fact, some truth back from her—and I want to find things out. By the merest chance—accident, in fact—I discovered yesterday at Braden Medworth that some twenty–two years ago you married one Mary Bewery, who, I learnt there, was your governess, to a John Brake, and that Mark Ransford was John Brake's best man and a witness of the marriage. Now, Mr. Gilwaters, the similarity in names is too striking to be devoid of significance. So—it's of the utmost importance to me!—can or will you tell me—who was the Mary Bewery you married to John Brake? Who was John Brake? And what was Mark Ransford to either, or to both?"

He was wondering, all the time during which he reeled off these questions, if Mr. Gilwaters was wholly ignorant of the recent affair at Wrychester. He might be—a glance round his book–filled room had suggested to Bryce that he was much more likely to be a bookworm than a newspaper reader, and it was quite possible that the events of the day had small interest for him. And his first words in reply to Bryce's questions convinced Bryce that his surmise was correct and that the old man had read nothing of the Wrychester Paradise mystery, in which Ransford's name had, of course, figured as a witness at the inquest.

"It is nearly twenty years since I heard any of their names," remarked Mr. Gilwaters. "Nearly twenty years—a long time! But, of course, I can answer you. Mary Bewery was our governess at Braden Medworth. She came to us when she was nineteen—she was married four years later. She was a girl who had no friends or relatives—she had been educated at a school in the North—I engaged her from that school, where, I understood, she had lived since infancy. Now then, as to Brake and Ransford. They were two young men from London, who used to come fishing in Leicestershire. Ransford was a few years the younger—he was either a medical student in his last year, or he was an assistant somewhere in London. Brake—was a bank manager in London—of a branch of one of the big banks. They were pleasant young fellows, and I used to ask them to the vicarage. Eventually, Mary Bewery and John Brake became engaged to be married. My wife and I were a good deal surprised—we had believed, somehow, that the favoured man would be Ransford. However, it was Brake—and Brake she married, and, as you say, Ransford was best man. Of course, Brake took his wife off to London—and from the day of her wedding, I never saw her again."

"Did you ever see Brake again?" asked Bryce. The old clergyman shook his head.

"Yes!" he said sadly. "I did see Brake again—under grievous, grievous circumstances!"

"You won't mind telling me what circumstances?" suggested Bryce. "I will keep your confidence, Mr. Gilwaters."

"There is really no secret in it—if it comes to that," answered the old man. "I saw John Brake again just once. In a prison cell!"

"A prison cell!" exclaimed Bryce. "And he—a prisoner?"

"He had just been sentenced to ten years' penal servitude," replied Mr. Gilwaters. "I had heard the sentence—I was present. I got leave to see him. Ten years' penal servitude! —a terrible punishment. He must have been released long ago —but I never heard more."

Bryce reflected in silence for a moment—reckoning and calculating.

"When was this—the trial?" he asked.

"It was five years after the marriage—seventeen years ago," replied Mr. Gilwaters.

"And—what had he been doing?" inquired Bryce.

"Stealing the bank's money," answered the old man. "I forget what the technical offence was—embezzlement, or something of that sort. There was not much evidence came out, for it was impossible to offer any defence, and he pleaded guilty. But I gathered from what I heard that something of this sort occurred. Brake was a branch manager. He was, as it were, pounced upon one morning by an inspector, who found that his cash was short by two or three thousand pounds. The bank people seemed to have been unusually strict and even severe —Brake, it was said, had some explanation, but it was swept aside and he was given in charge. And the sentence was as I said just now—a very savage one, I thought. But there had recently been some bad cases of that sort in the banking world, and I suppose the judge felt that he must make an example. Yes—a most trying affair!—I have a report of the case somewhere, which I cut out of a London newspaper at the time."

The Paradise Mystery

Mr. Gilwaters rose and turned to an old desk in the corner of his room, and after some rummaging of papers in a drawer, produced a newspaper–cutting book and traced an insertion in its pages. He handed the book to his visitor.

"There is the account," he said. "You can read it for yourself. You will notice that in what Brake's counsel said on his behalf there are one or two curious and mysterious hints as to what might have been said if it had been of any use or advantage to say it. A strange case!"

Bryce turned eagerly to the faded scrap of newspaper.

BANK MANAGER'S DEFALCATION.

At the Central Criminal Court yesterday, John Brake, thirty–three, formerly manager of the Upper Tooting branch of the London Home Counties Bank, Ltd., pleaded guilty to embezzling certain sums, the property of his employers.

Mr. Walkinshaw, Q.C., addressing the court on behalf of the prisoner, said that while it was impossible for his client to offer any defence, there were circumstances in the case which, if it had been worth while to put them in evidence, would have shown that the prisoner was a wronged and deceived man. To use a Scriptural phrase, Brake had been wounded in the house of his friend. The man who was really guilty in this affair had cleverly escaped all consequences, nor would it be of the least use to enter into any details respecting him. Not one penny of the money in question had been used by the prisoner for his own purposes. It was doubtless a wrong and improper thing that his client had done, and he had pleaded guilty and would submit to the consequences. But if everything in connection with the case could have been told, if it would have served any useful purpose to tell it, it

would have been seen that what the prisoner really was
guilty of was a foolish and serious error of judgment.
He himself, concluded the learned counsel, would go so
far as to say that, knowing what he did, knowing what
had been told him by his client in strict confidence,
the prisoner, though technically guilty, was morally
innocent.

His Lordship, merely remarking that no excuse of any
sort could be offered in a case of this sort, sentenced
the prisoner to ten years' penal servitude.

Bryce read this over twice before handing back the book.

"Very strange and mysterious, Mr. Gilwaters," he remarked. "You say that you saw
Brake after the case was over. Did you learn anything?"

"Nothing whatever!" answered the old clergyman. "I got permission to see him before he
was taken away. He did not seem particularly pleased or disposed to see me. I begged
him to tell me what the real truth was. He was, I think, somewhat dazed by the
sentence—but he was also sullen and morose. I asked him where his wife and two
children—one, a mere infant —were. For I had already been to his private address and
had found that Mrs. Brake had sold all the furniture and disappeared—completely. No
one—thereabouts, at any rate —knew where she was, or would tell me anything. On my
asking this, he refused to answer. I pressed him—he said finally that he was only
speaking the truth when he replied that he did not know where his wife was. I said I must
find her. He forbade me to make any attempt. Then I begged him to tell me if she was
with friends. I remember very well what he replied.—'I'm not going to say one word
more to any man living, Mr. Gilwaters,' he answered determinedly. 'I shall be dead to the
world—only because I've been a trusting fool! —for ten years or thereabouts, but, when I
come back to it, I'll let the world see what revenge means! Go away!' he concluded. 'I
won't say one word more.' And—I left him."

"And—you made no more inquiries?—about the wife?" asked Bryce.

"I did what I could," replied Mr. Gilwaters. "I made some inquiry in the neighbourhood in which they had lived. All I could discover was that Mrs. Brake had disappeared under extraordinarily mysterious circumstances. There was no trace whatever of her. And I speedily found that things were being said—the usual cruel suspicions, you know."

"Such as—what?" asked Bryce.

"That the amount of the defalcations was much larger than had been allowed to appear," replied Mr. Gilwaters. "That Brake was a very clever rogue who had got the money safely planted somewhere abroad, and that his wife had gone off somewhere —Australia, or Canada, or some other far-off region—to await his release. Of course, I didn't believe one word of all that. But there was the fact—she had vanished! And eventually, I thought of Ransford, as having been Brake's great friend, so I tried to find him. And then I found that he, too, who up to that time had been practising in a London suburb—Streatham—had also disappeared. Just after Brake's arrest, Ransford had suddenly sold his practice and gone—no one knew where, but it was believed—abroad. I couldn't trace him, anyway. And soon after that I had a long illness, and for two or three years was an invalid, and—well, the thing was over and done with, and, as I said just now, I have never heard anything of any of them for all these years. And now! —now you tell me that there is a Mary Bewery who is a ward of a Dr. Mark Ransford at—where did you say?"

"At Wrychester," answered Bryce. "She is a young woman of twenty, and she has a brother, Richard, who is between seventeen and eighteen."

"Without a doubt those are Brake's children!" exclaimed the old man. "The infant I spoke of was a boy. Bless me!—how extraordinary. How long have they been at Wrychester?"

"Ransford has been in practice there some years—a few years," replied Bryce. "These two young people joined him there definitely two years ago. But from what I have learnt, he has acted as their guardian ever since they were mere children."

"And—their mother?" asked Mr. Gilwaters.

"Said to be dead—long since," answered Bryce. "And their father, too. They know nothing. Ransford won't tell them anything. But, as you say—I've no doubt of it myself now —they must be the children of John Brake."

"And have taken the name of their mother!" remarked the old man.

"Had it given to them," said Bryce. "They don't know that it isn't their real name. Of course, Ransford has given it to them! But now—the mother?"

"Ah, yes, the mother!" said Mr. Gilwaters. "Our old governess! Dear me!"

"I'm going to put a question to you," continued Bryce, leaning nearer and speaking in a low, confidential tone. "You must have seen much of the world, Mr. Gilwaters—men of your profession know the world, and human nature, too. Call to mind all the mysterious circumstances, the veiled hints, of that trial. Do you think—have you ever thought—that the false friend whom the counsel referred to was—Ransford? Come, now!"

The old clergyman lifted his hands and let them fall on his knees.

"I do not know what to say!" he exclaimed. "To tell you the truth, I have often wondered if—if that was what really did happen. There is the fact that Brake's wife disappeared mysteriously—that Ransford made a similar mysterious disappearance about the same time—that Brake was obviously suffering from intense and bitter hatred when I saw him after the trial—hatred of some person on whom he meant to be revenged—and that his counsel hinted that he had been deceived and betrayed by a friend. Now, to my knowledge, he and Ransford were the closest of friends—in the old days, before Brake married our governess. And I suppose the friendship continued—certainly Ransford acted as best man at the wedding! But how account for that strange double disappearance?"

Bryce had already accounted for that, in his own secret mind. And now, having got all that he wanted out of the old clergyman, he rose to take his leave.

"You will regard this interview as having been of a strictly private nature, Mr. Gilwaters?" he said.

"Certainly!" responded the old man. "But—you mentioned that you wished to marry the daughter? Now that you know about her father's past—for I am sure she must be John Brake's child —you won't allow that to—eh?"

"Not for a moment!" answered Bryce, with a fair show of magnanimity. "I am not a man of that complexion, sir. No!—I only wished to clear up certain things, you understand."

"And—since she is apparently—from what you say—in ignorance of her real father's past—what then?" asked Mr. Gilwaters anxiously. "Shall you—"

"I shall do nothing whatever in any haste," replied Bryce. "Rely upon me to consider her feelings in everything. As you have been so kind, I will let you know, later, how matters go."

This was one of Pemberton Bryce's ready inventions. He had not the least intention of ever seeing or communicating with the late vicar of Braden Medworth again; Mr. Gilwaters had served his purpose for the time being. He went away from Bayswater, and, an hour later, from London, highly satisfied. In his opinion, Mark Ransford, seventeen years before, had taken advantage of his friend's misfortunes to run away with his wife, and when Brake, alias Braden, had unexpectedly turned up at Wrychester, he had added to his former wrong by the commission of a far greater one.

CHAPTER X. DIPLOMACY

Bryce went back to Wrychester firmly convinced that Mark Ransford had killed John Braden. He reckoned things up in his own fashion. Some years must have elapsed since Braden, or rather Brake's release. He had probably heard, on his release, that Ransford and his, Brake's, wife had gone abroad —in that case he would certainly follow them. He might have lost all trace of them; he might have lost his original interest in his first schemes of revenge; he might have begun a new life for himself in Australia, whence he had undoubtedly come to England recently. But he had come, at last, and he had evidently tracked Ransford to Wrychester—why, otherwise, had he presented himself at Ransford's door on that eventful morning which was to witness his death? Nothing, in Bryce's opinion, could be clearer. Brake had turned up. He and Ransford had met—most likely in the precincts of the Cathedral. Ransford, who knew all the quiet corners of the old place, had in all probability induced Brake to walk up into the gallery with him, had noticed the open doorway, had thrown Brake through it. All the facts pointed to that conclusion—it was a theory which, so far as Bryce could see, was perfect. It ought to be enough—proved—to put Ransford in a criminal dock. Bryce resolved it in his own mind over and over again as he sped home to Wrychester—he pictured the police listening greedily to all that he could tell them if he liked. There was only one factor in the whole sum of the affair which seemed against him—the advertisement in the Times. If Brake desired to find Ransford in order to be revenged on him, why did he insert that advertisement, as if he were longing to meet a cherished friend again? But Bryce gaily surmounted that obstacle—full of shifts and subtleties himself, he was ever ready to credit others with trading in them, and he put the advertisement down as a clever ruse to attract, not Ransford, but some person who could give information about Ransford. Whatever its exact meaning might have been, its existence made no difference to Bryce's firm opinion that it was Mark Ransford who flung John Brake down St. Wrytha's Stair and killed him. He was as sure of that as he was certain that Braden was Brake. And he was not going to tell the police of his discoveries—he was not going to tell anybody. The one thing that concerned him was—how best to make use of his knowledge with a view to bringing about a marriage between himself and Mark Ransford's ward. He had set his mind on that for twelve months past, and he was not a man to be baulked of his purpose. By fair means, or foul—he himself ignored the last word and would have substituted the term skilful for it—Pemberton Bryce meant to have Mary Bewery.

Mary Bewery herself had no thought of Bryce in her head when, the morning after that worthy's return to Wrychester, she set out, alone, for the Wrychester Golf Club. It was her habit to go there almost every day, and Bryce was well acquainted with her movements and knew precisely where to waylay her. And empty of Bryce though her mind was, she was not surprised when, at a lonely place on Wrychester Common, Bryce turned the corner of a spinny and met her face to face.

Mary would have passed on with no more than a silent recognition—she had made up her mind to have no further speech with her guardian's dismissed assistant. But she had to pass through a wicket gate at that point, and Bryce barred the way, with unmistakable purpose. It was plain to the girl that he had laid in wait for her. She was not without a temper of her own, and she suddenly let it out on the offender.

"Do you call this manly conduct, Dr. Bryce?" she demanded, turning an indignant and flushed face on him. "To waylay me here, when you know that I don't want to have anything more to do with you. Let me through, please—and go away!"

But Bryce kept a hand on the little gate, and when he spoke there was that in his voice which made the girl listen in spite of herself.

"I'm not here on my own behalf," he said quickly. "I give you my word I won't say a thing that need offend you. It's true I waited here for you—it's the only place in which I thought I could meet you, alone. I want to speak to you. It's this—do you know your guardian is in danger?"

Bryce had the gift of plausibility—he could convince people, against their instincts, even against their wills, that he was telling the truth. And Mary, after a swift glance, believed him.

"What danger?" she asked. "And if he is, and if you know he is—why don't you go direct to him?"

"The most fatal thing in the world to do!" exclaimed Bryce. "You know him—he can be nasty. That would bring matters to a crisis. And that, in his interest, is just what mustn't happen."

"I don't understand you," said Mary.

Bryce leaned nearer to her—across the gate.

"You know what happened last week," he said in a low voice. "The strange death of that man—Braden."

"Well?" she asked, with a sudden look of uneasiness. "What of it?"

"It's being rumoured—whispered—in the town that Dr. Ransford had something to do with that affair," answered Bryce. "Unpleasant—unfortunate—but it's a fact."

"Impossible!" exclaimed Mary with a heightening colour. "What could he have to do with it? What could give rise to such foolish—wicked—rumours?"

"You know as well as I do how people talk, how they will talk," said Bryce. "You can't stop them, in a place like Wrychester, where everybody knows everybody. There's a mystery around Braden's death—it's no use denying it. Nobody knows who he was, where he came from, why he came. And it's being hinted—I'm only telling you what I've gathered—that Dr. Ransford knows more than he's ever told. There are, I'm afraid, grounds."

"What grounds?" demanded Mary. While Bryce had been speaking, in his usual slow, careful fashion, she had been reflecting —and remembering Ransford's evident agitation at the time of the Paradise affair—and his relief when the inquest was over —and his sending her with flowers to the dead man's grave and she began to experience a sense of uneasiness and even of fear. "What grounds can there be?" she added. "Dr. Ransford didn't know that man—had never seen him!"

"That's not certain," replied Bryce. "It's said—remember, I'm only repeating things—it's said that just before the body was discovered, Dr. Ransford was seen —seen, mind you! —leaving the west porch of the Cathedral, looking as if he had just been very, much upset. Two persons saw this."

"Who are they?" asked Mary.

"That I'm not allowed to tell you," said Bryce, who had no intention of informing her that one person was himself and the other imaginary. "But I can assure you that I am certain —absolutely certain!—that their story is true. The fact is —I can corroborate it."

"You!" she exclaimed.

"I!" replied Bryce. "I will tell you something that I have never told anybody—up to now. I shan't ask you to respect my confidence—I've sufficient trust in you to know that you will, without any asking. Listen!—on that morning, Dr. Ransford went out of the surgery in the direction of the Deanery, leaving me alone there. A few minutes later, a tap came at the door. I opened it—and found—a man standing outside!"

"Not—that man?" asked Mary fearfully.

"That man—Braden," replied Bryce. "He asked for Dr. Ransford. I said he was out—would the caller leave his name? He said no—he had called because he had once known a Dr. Ransford, years before. He added something about calling again, and he went away—across the Close towards the Cathedral. I saw him again—not very long afterwards—lying in the corner of Paradise—dead!"

Mary Bewery was by this time pale and trembling—and Bryce continued to watch her steadily. She stole a furtive look at him.

"Why didn't you tell all this at the inquest?" she asked in a whisper.

"Because I knew how damning it would be to—Ransford," replied Bryce promptly. "It would have excited suspicion. I was certain that no one but myself knew that Braden had been to the surgery door—therefore, I thought that if I kept silence, his calling there would never be known. But—I have since found that I was mistaken. Braden was seen—going away from Dr. Ransford's."

"By—whom?" asked Mary.

"Mrs. Deramore—at the next house," answered Bryce. "She happened to be looking out of an upstairs window. She saw him go away and cross the Close."

"Did she tell you that?" demanded Mary, who knew Mrs. Deramore for a gossip.

"Between ourselves," said Bryce, "she did not! She told Mrs. Folliot—Mrs. Folliot told me."

"So—it is talked about!" exclaimed Mary.

"I said so," assented Bryce. "You know what Mrs. Folliot's tongue is."

"Then Dr. Ransford will get to hear of it," said Mary.

"He will be the last person to get to hear of it," affirmed Bryce. "These things are talked of, hole–and–corner fashion, a long time before they reach the ears of the person chiefly concerned."

Mary hesitated a moment before she asked her next question.

"Why have you told me all this?" she demanded at last.

"Because I didn't want you to be suddenly surprised," answered Bryce. "This—whatever it is—may come to a sudden head—of an unpleasant sort. These rumours spread—and the police are still keen about finding out things concerning this dead man. If they once get it into their heads that Dr. Ransford knew him—"

Mary laid her hand on the gate between them—and Bryce, who had done all he wished to do at that time, instantly opened it, and she passed through.

"I am much obliged to you," she said. "I don't know what it all means—but it is Dr. Ransford's affair—if there is any affair, which I doubt. Will you let me go now, please?"

Bryce stood aside and lifted his hat, and Mary, with no more than a nod, walked on towards the golf club–house across the Common, while Bryce turned off to the town, highly elated with his morning's work. He had sown the seeds of uneasiness and suspicion broadcast—some of them, he knew, would mature.

Mary Bewery played no golf that morning. In fact, she only went on to the club–house to rid herself of Bryce, and presently she returned home, thinking. And indeed, she said to herself, she had abundant food for thought. Naturally candid and honest, she did not at that moment doubt Bryce's good faith; much as she disliked him in most ways she knew that he had certain commendable qualities, and she was inclined to believe him when he said that he had kept silence in order to ward off consequences which might indirectly be unpleasant for her. But of him and his news she thought little—what occupied her mind was the possible connection between the stranger who had come so suddenly and disappeared so suddenly—and for ever!—and Mark Ransford. Was it possible—really possible—that there had been some meeting between them in or about the Cathedral precincts that morning? She knew, after a moment's reflection, that it was very possible—why not? And from that her thoughts followed a natural trend—was the mystery surrounding this man connected in any way with the mystery about herself and her brother? —that mystery of which (as it seemed to her) Ransford was so shy of speaking. And again—and for the hundredth time—she asked herself why he was so reticent, so evidently full of dislike of the subject, why he could not tell her and Dick whatever there was to tell, once for all?

She had to pass the Folliots' house in the far corner of the Close on her way home—a fine old mansion set in well-wooded grounds, enclosed by a high wall of old red brick. A door in that wall stood open, and inside it, talking to one of his gardeners, was Mr. Folliot—the vistas behind him were gay with flowers and rich with the roses which he passed all his days in cultivating. He caught sight of Mary as she passed the open doorway and called her back.

"Come in and have a look at some new roses I've got," he said. "Beauties! I'll give you a handful to carry home."

Mary rather liked Mr. Folliot. He was a big, half-asleep sort of man, who had few words and could talk about little else than his hobby. But he was a passionate lover of flowers and plants, and had a positive genius for rose-culture, and was at all times highly delighted to take flower-lovers round his garden. She turned at once and walked in, and Folliot led her away down the scented paths.

"It's an experiment I've been trying," he said, leading her up to a cluster of blooms of a colour and size which she had never seen before. "What do you think of the results?"

"Magnificent!" exclaimed Mary. "I never saw Anything so fine!"

"No!" agreed Folliot, with a quiet chuckle. "Nor anybody else—because there's no such rose in England. I shall have to go to some of these learned parsons in the Close to invent me a Latin name for this—it's the result of careful experiments in grafting—took me three years to get at it. And see how it blooms,—scores on one standard."

He pulled out a knife and began to select a handful of the finest blooms, which he presently pressed into Mary's hand.

"By the by," he remarked as she thanked him and they turned away along the path, "I wanted to have a word with you—or with Ransford. Do you know—does he know—that that confounded silly woman who lives near to your house—Mrs. Deramore—has been saying some things—or a thing—which—to put it plainly—might make some unpleasantness for him?"

Mary kept a firm hand on her wits—and gave him an answer which was true enough, so far as she was aware.

"I'm sure he knows nothing," she said. "What is it, Mr. Folliot?"

"Why, you know what happened last week," continued Folliot, glancing knowingly at her. "The accident to that stranger. This Mrs. Deramore, who's nothing but an old chatterer, has been saying, here and there, that it's a very queer thing Dr. Ransford doesn't know anything about him, and can't say anything, for she herself, she says, saw the very man going away from Dr. Ransford's house not so long before the accident."

"I am not aware that he ever called at Dr. Ransford's," said Mary. "I never saw him—and I was in the garden, about that very time, with your stepson, Mr. Folliot."

"So Sackville told me," remarked Folliot. "He was present —and so was I—when Mrs. Deramore was tattling about it in our house yesterday. He said, then, that he'd never seen the man go to your house. You never heard your servants make any remark about it?"

"Never!" answered Mary.

"I told Mrs. Deramore she'd far better hold her tongue," continued Folliot. "Tittle–tattle of that sort is apt to lead to unpleasantness. And when it came to it, it turned out that all she had seen was this stranger strolling across the Close as if he'd just left your house. If—there's always some if! But I'll tell you why I mentioned it to you," he continued, nudging Mary's elbow and glancing covertly first at her and then at his house on the far side of the garden. "Ladies that are—getting on a bit in years, you know—like my wife, are apt to let their tongues wag, and between you and me, I shouldn't wonder if Mrs. Folliot has repeated what Mrs. Deramore said—eh? And I don't want the doctor to think that —if he hears anything, you know, which he may, and, again, he might—to think that it originated here. So, if he should ever mention it to you, you can say it sprang from his next–door neighbour. Bah!—they're a lot of old gossips, these Close ladies!"

"Thank you," said Mary. "But—supposing this man had been to our house—what difference would that make? He might have been for half a dozen reasons."

Folliot looked at her out of his half–shut eyes.

"Some people would want to know why Ransford didn't tell that —at the inquest," he answered. "That's all. When there's a bit of mystery, you know—eh?"

He nodded—as if reassuringly—and went off to rejoin his gardener, and Mary walked home with her roses, more thoughtful than ever. Mystery?—a bit of mystery? There was a vast and heavy cloud of mystery, and she knew she could have no peace until it was lifted.

CHAPTER XI. THE BACK BOOM

In the midst of all her perplexity at that moment, Mary Bewery was certain of one fact about which she had no perplexity nor any doubt—it would not be long before the rumours of which Bryce and Mr. Folliot had spoken. Although she had only lived in Wrychester a comparatively short time she had seen and learned enough of it to know that the place was a hotbed of gossip. Once gossip was started there, it spread, widening in circle after circle. And though Bryce was probably right when he said that the person chiefly concerned was usually the last person to hear what was being whispered, she knew well enough that sooner or later this talk about Ransford would come to Ransford's own ears. But she had no idea that it was to come so soon, nor from her own brother.

Lunch in the Ransford menage was an informal meal. At a quarter past one every day, it was on the table—a cold lunch to which the three members of the household helped themselves as they liked, independent of the services of servants. Sometimes all three were there at the same moment; sometimes Ransford was half an hour late; the one member who was always there to the moment was Dick Bewery, who fortified himself sedulously after his morning's school labours. On this particular day all three met in the dining–room at once, and sat down together. And before Dick had eaten many mouthfuls of a cold pie to which he had just liberally helped himself he bent confidentially across the table towards his guardian.

"There's something I think you ought to be told about, sir," he remarked with a side–glance at Mary. "Something I heard this morning at school. You know, we've a lot of fellows —town boys—who talk."

"I daresay," responded Ransford dryly. "Following the example of their mothers, no doubt. Well—what is it?"

He, too, glanced at Mary—and the girl had her work set to look unconscious.

"It's this," replied Dick, lowering his voice in spite of the fact that all three were alone. "They're saying in the town that you know something which you won't tell about that affair last week. It's being talked of."

Ransford laughed—a little cynically.

"Are you quite sure, my boy, that they aren't saying that I daren't tell?" he asked. "Daren't is a much more likely word than won't, I think."

"Well—about that, sir," acknowledged Dick. "Comes to that, anyhow."

"And what are their grounds?" inquired Ransford. "You've heard them, I'll be bound!"

"They say that man—Braden—had been here—here, to the house!—that morning, not long before he was found dead," answered Dick. "Of course, I said that was all bosh!—I said that if he'd been here and seen you, I'd have heard of it, dead certain."

"That's not quite so dead certain, Dick, as that I have no knowledge of his ever having been here," said Ransford. "But who says he came here?"

"Mrs. Deramore," replied Dick promptly. "She says she saw him go away from the house and across the Close, a little before ten. So Jim Deramore says, anyway—and he says his mother's eyes are as good as another's."

"Doubtless!" assented Ransford. He looked at Mary again, and saw that she was keeping hers fixed on her plate. "Well," he continued, "if it will give you any satisfaction, Dick, you can tell the gossips that Dr. Ransford never saw any man, Braden or anybody else, at his house that morning, and that he never exchanged a word with Braden. So much for that! But," he added, "you needn't expect them to believe you. I know these people—if they've got an idea into their heads they'll ride it to death. Nevertheless, what I say is a fact."

Dick presently went off—and once more Ransford looked at Mary. And this time, Mary had to meet her guardian's inquiring glance.

"Have you heard anything of this?" he asked.

"That there was a rumour—yes," she replied without hesitation. "But—not until just now—this morning."

"Who told you of it?" inquired Ransford.

Mary hesitated. Then she remembered that Mr. Folliot, at any rate, had not bound her to secrecy.

"Mr. Folliot," she replied. "He called me into his garden, to give me those roses, and he mentioned that Mrs. Deramore had said these things to Mrs. Folliot, and as he seemed to think it highly probable that Mrs. Folliot would repeat them, he told me because he didn't want you to think that the rumour had originally arisen at his house."

"Very good of him, I'm sure," remarked Ransford dryly. "They all like to shift the blame from one to another! But," he added, looking searchingly at her, "you don't know anything about Braden's having come here?"

He saw at once that she did, and Mary saw a slight shade of anxiety come over his face.

"Yes, I do!" she replied. "That morning. But—it was told to me, only today, in strict confidence."

"In strict confidence!" he repeated. "May I know—by whom?"

"Dr. Bryce," she answered. "I met him this morning. And I think you ought to know. Only—it was in confidence." She paused for a moment, looking at him, and her face grew troubled. "I hate to suggest it," she continued, "but—will you come with me to see him, and I'll ask him—things being as they are—to tell you what he told me. I can't—without his permission."

Ransford shook his head and frowned.

"I dislike it!" he said. "It's—it's putting ourselves in his power, as it were. But—I'm not going to be left in the dark. Put on your hat, then."

Bryce, ever since his coming to Wrychester, had occupied rooms in an old house in Friary Lane, at the back of the Close. He was comfortably lodged. Downstairs he had a double sitting—room, extending from the front to the back of the house; his front window looked out on one garden, his back window on another. He had just finished lunch in the front part of his room, and was looking out of his window, wondering what to do with himself that afternoon, when he saw Ransford and Mary Bewery approaching. He guessed the reason of their visit at once, and went straight to the front door to meet them, and without a word motioned them to follow him into his own quarters. It was characteristic of him that he took the first word—before either of his visitors could speak.

"I know why you've come," he said, as he closed the door and glanced at Mary "You either want my permission that you should tell Dr. Ransford what I told you this morning, or, you want me to tell him myself. Am I right?"

"I should be glad if you would tell him," replied Mary. "The rumour you spoke of has reached him—he ought to know what you can tell. I have respected your confidence, so far."

The two men looked at each other. And this time it was Ransford who spoke first.

"It seems to me," he said, "that there is no great reason for privacy. If rumours are flying about in Wrychester, there is an end of privacy. Dick tells me they are saying at the school that it is known that Braden called on me at my house shortly before he was found dead. I know nothing whatever of any such call! But—I left you in my surgery that morning. Do you know if he came there?"

"Yes!" answered Bryce. "He did come. Soon after you'd gone out."

"Why did you keep that secret?" demanded Ransford. "You could have told it to the police—or to the Coroner—or to me. Why didn't you?"

Before Bryce could answer, all three heard a sharp click of the front garden gate, and looking round, saw Mitchington coming up the walk.

"Here's one of the police, now," said Bryce calmly. "Probably come to extract information. I would much rather he didn't see you here—but I'd also like you to hear what I shall say to him. Step inside there," he continued, drawing aside the curtains which shut off the back room. "Don't stick at trifles!—you don't know what may be afoot."

He almost forced them away, drew the curtains again, and hurrying to the front door, returned almost immediately with Mitchington.

"Hope I'm not disturbing you, doctor," said the inspector, as Bryce brought him in and again closed the door. "Not? All right, then—I came round to ask you a question. There's a queer rumour getting out in the town, about that affair last week. Seems to have sprung from some of those old dowagers in the Close."

"Of course!" said Bryce. He was mixing a whisky–and–soda for his caller, and his laugh mingled with the splash of the siphon. "Of course! I've heard it."

"You've heard?" remarked Mitchington. "Um! Good health, sir!—heard, of course, that—"

"That Braden called on Dr. Ransford not long before the accident, or murder, or whatever it was, happened," said Bryce. "That's it—eh?"

"Something of that sort," agreed Mitchington. "It's being said, anyway, that Braden was at Ransford's house, and presumably saw him, and that Ransford, accordingly, knows something about him which he hasn't told. Now—what do you know? Do you know if Ransford and Braden did meet that morning.

"Not at Ransford's house, anyway," answered Bryce promptly. "I can prove that. But since this rumour has got out, I'll tell you what I do know, and what the truth is. Braden did come to Ransford's—not to the house, but to the surgery. He didn't see Ransford—Ransford had gone out, across the Close. Braden saw—me!"

"Bless me!—I didn't know that," remarked Mitchington. "You never mentioned it."

"You'll not wonder that I didn't," said Bryce, laughing lightly, "when I tell you what the man wanted."

"What did he want, then?" asked Mitchington.

"Merely to be told where the Cathedral Library was," answered Bryce.

Ransford, watching Mary Bewery, saw her cheeks flush, and knew that Bryce was cheerfully telling lies. But Mitchington evidently had no suspicion.

"That all?" he asked. "Just a question?"

"Just a question—that question," replied Bryce. "I pointed out the Library—and he walked away. I never saw him again until I was fetched to him—dead. And I thought so little of the matter that—well, it never even occurred to me to mention it."

"Then—though he did call—he never saw Ransford?" asked the inspector.

"I tell you Ransford was already gone out," answered Bryce. "He saw no one but myself. Where Mrs. Deramore made her mistake—I happen to know, Mitchington, that she started this rumour—was in trying to make two and two into five. She saw this man crossing the Close, as if from Ransford's house and she at once imagined he'd seen and been talking with Ransford."

"Old fool!" said Mitchington. "Of course, that's how these tales get about. However, there's more than that in the air."

The two listeners behind the curtains glanced at each other. Ransford's glance showed that he was already chafing at the unpleasantness of his position—but Mary's only betokened apprehension. And suddenly, as if she feared that Ransford would throw the curtains aside and walk into the front room, she laid a hand on his arm and motioned him to be patient—and silent.

"Oh?" said Bryce. "More in the air? About that business?"

"Just so," assented Mitchington. "To start with, that man Varner, the mason, has never ceased talking. They say he's always at it—to the effect that the verdict of the jury at the inquest was all wrong, and that his evidence was put clean aside. He persists that he did see—what he swore he saw."

The Paradise Mystery

"He'll persist in that to his dying day," said Bryce carelessly. "If that's all there is—"

"It isn't," interrupted the inspector. "Not by a long chalk! But Varner's is a direct affirmation—the other matter's a sort of ugly hint. There's a man named Collishaw, a townsman, who's been employed as a mason's labourer about the Cathedral of late. This Collishaw, it seems, was at work somewhere up in the galleries, ambulatories, or whatever they call those upper regions, on the very morning of the affair. And the other night, being somewhat under the influence of drink, and talking the matter over with his mates at a tavern, he let out some dark hints that he could tell something if he liked. Of course, he was pressed to tell them—and wouldn't. Then—so my informant tells me—he was dared to tell, and became surlily silent. That, of course, spread, and got to my ears. I've seen Collishaw."

"Well?" asked Bryce.

"I believe the man does know something," answered Mitchington. "That's the impression I carried away, anyhow. But—he won't speak. I charged him straight out with knowing something—but it was no good. I told him of what I'd heard. All he would say was that whatever he might have said when he'd got a glass of beer or so too much, he wasn't going to say anything now neither for me nor for anybody!"

"Just so!" remarked Bryce. "But—he'll be getting a glass too much again, some day, and then—then, perhaps he'll add to what he said before. And—you'll be sure to hear of it."

"I'm not certain of that," answered Mitchington. "I made some inquiry and I find that Collishaw is usually a very sober and retiring sort of chap—he'd been lured on to drink when he let out what he did. Besides, whether I'm right or wrong, I got the idea into my head that he'd already been—squared!"

"Squared!" exclaimed Bryce. "Why, then, if that affair was really murder, he'd be liable to being charged as an accessory after the fact!"

"I warned him of that," replied Mitchington. "Yes, I warned him solemnly."

"With no effect?" asked Bryce.

"He's a surly sort of man," said Mitchington. "The sort that takes refuge in silence. He made no answer beyond a growl."

"You really think he knows something?" suggested Bryce. "Well—if there is anything, it'll come out—in time."

"Oh, it'll come out!" assented Mitchington. "I'm ay no means satisfied with that verdict of the coroner's inquiry. I believe there was foul play—of some sort. I'm still following things up—quietly. And—I'll tell you something —between ourselves—I've made an important discovery. It's this. On the evening of Braden's arrival at the Mitre he was out, somewhere, for a whole two hours—by himself."

"I thought we learned from Mrs. Partingley that he and the other man, Dellingham, spent the evening together?" said Bryce.

"So we did—but that was not quite so," replied Mitchington. "Braden went out of the Mitre just before nine o'clock and he didn't return until a few minutes after eleven. Now, then, where did he go?"

"I suppose you're trying to find that out?" asked Bryce, after a pause, during which the listeners heard the caller rise and make for the door.

"Of course!" replied Mitchington, with a confident laugh. "And—I shall! Keep it to yourself, doctor."

When Bryce had let the inspector out and returned to his sitting–room, Ransford and Mary had come from behind the curtains. He looked at them and shook his head.

"You heard—a good deal, you see," he observed.

"Look here!" said Ransford peremptorily. "You put that man off about the call at my surgery. You didn't tell him the truth."

"Quite right," assented Bryce. "I didn't. Why should I?"

"What did Braden ask you?" demanded Ransford. "Come, now?"

"Merely if Dr. Ransford was in," answered Bryce, "remarking that he had once known a Dr. Ransford. That was—literally —all. I replied that you were not in."

Ransford stood silently thinking for a moment or two. Then he moved towards the door.

"I don't see that any good will come of more talk about this," he said. "We three, at any rate, know this—I never saw Braden when he came to my house."

Then he motioned Mary to follow him, and they went away, and Bryce, having watched them out of sight, smiled at himself in his mirror—with full satisfaction.

CHAPTER XII. MURDER OF THE MASON'S LABOURER

It was towards noon of the very neat day that Bryce made a forward step in the matter of solving the problem of Richard Jenkins and his tomb in Paradise. Ever since his return from Barthorpe he had been making attempts to get at the true meaning of this mystery. He had paid so many visits to the Cathedral Library that Ambrose Campany had asked him jestingly if he was going in for archaeology; Bryce had replied that having nothing to do just then he saw no reason why he shouldn't improve his knowledge of the antiquities of Wrychester. But he was scrupulously careful not to let the librarian know the real object of his prying and peeping into the old books and documents. Campany, as Bryce was very well aware, was a walking encyclopaedia of information about Wrychester Cathedral: he was, in fact, at that time, engaged in completing a history of it. And it was through that history that Bryce accidentally got his precious information. For on the day following the interview with Mary Bewery and Ransford, Bryce being in the library was treated by Campany to an inspection of certain drawings which the librarian had made for illustrating his work–drawings, most of them, of old brasses, coats of arms, and the like,—And at the foot of one of these, a drawing of a shield on which was sculptured three crows, Bryce saw the name Richard Jenkins, armiger. It was all, he could do to repress a start and to check his tongue. But Campany, knowing nothing, quickly gave him the information he wanted.

"All these drawings," he said, "are of old things in and about the Cathedral. Some of them, like that, for instance, that Jenkins shield, are of ornamentations on tombs which are so old that the inscriptions have completely disappeared—tombs in the Cloisters, and in Paradise. Some of those tombs can only be identified by these sculptures and ornaments."

"How do you know, for instance, that any particular tomb or monument is, we'll say, Jerkins's?" asked Bryce, feeling that he was on safe ground. "Must be a matter of doubt if there's no inscription left, isn't it?"

"No!" replied Campany. "No doubt at all. In that particular case, there's no doubt that a certain tomb out there in the corner of Paradise, near the east wall of the south porch, is that of one Richard Jenkins, because it bears his coat-of-arms, which, as you see, bore these birds—intended either as crows or ravens. The inscription's clean gone from that tomb—which is why it isn't particularized in that chart of burials in Paradise—the man who prepared that chart didn't know how to trace things as we do nowadays. Richard Jenkins was, as you may guess, a Welshman, who settled here in Wrychester in the seventeenth century: he left some money to St. Hedwige's Church, outside the walls, but he was buried here. There are more instances—look at this, now—this coat-of-arms-that's the only means there is of identifying another tomb in Paradise—that of Gervase Tyrrwhit. You see his armorial bearings in this drawing? Now those—"

Bryce let the librarian go on talking and explaining, and heard all he had to say as a man hears things in a dream—what was really active in his own mind was joy at this unexpected stroke of luck: he himself might have searched for many a year and never found the last resting-place of Richard Jenkins. And when, soon after the great clock of the Cathedral had struck the hour of noon, he left Campany and quitted the Library, he walked over to Paradise and plunged in amongst its yews and cypresses, intent on seeing the Jenkins tomb for himself. No one could suspect anything from merely seeing him there, and all he wanted was one glance at the ancient monument.

But Bryce was not to give even one look at Richard Jenkins's tomb that day, nor the next, nor for many days—death met him in another form before he had taken many steps in the quiet enclosure where so much of Wrychester mortality lay sleeping.

From over the topmost branches of the old yew trees a great shaft of noontide sunlight fell full on a patch of the grey walls of the high-roofed nave. At the foot of it, his back comfortably planted against the angle of a projecting buttress, sat a man, evidently fast asleep in the warmth of those powerful rays. His head leaned down and forward over his chest, his hands were folded across his waist, his whole attitude was that of a man who, having eaten and drunken in the open air, has dropped off to sleep. That he had so dropped off while in the very act of smoking was evident from the presence of a short, well-blackened clay pipe which had fallen from his lips and lay in the grass beside him. Near the pipe, spread on a coloured handkerchief, were the remains of his dinner—Bryce's quick eye noticed fragments of bread, cheese, onions. And close by stood one of those tin bottles in which labouring men carry their drink; its cork, tied to the neck by a piece of string, dangled against the side. A few yards away, a mass of fallen rubbish and a shovel and wheelbarrow showed at what the sleeper had been working when his dinner–hour and time for rest had arrived.

Something unusual, something curiously noticeable—yet he could not exactly tell what—made Bryce go closer to the sleeping man. There was a strange stillness about him—a rigidity which seemed to suggest something more than sleep. And suddenly, with a stifled exclamation, he bent forward and lifted one of the folded hands. It dropped like a leaden weight when Bryce released it, and he pushed back the man's face and looked searchingly into it. And in that instant he knew that for the second time within a fortnight he had found a dead man in Wrychester Paradise.

There was no doubt whatever that the man was dead. His hands and body were warm enough—but there was not a flicker of breath; he was as dead as any of the folk who lay six feet beneath the old gravestones around him. And Bryce's practised touch and eye knew that he was only just dead—and that he had died in his sleep. Everything there pointed unmistakably to what had happened. The man had eaten his frugal dinner, washed it down from his tin bottle, lighted his pipe, leaned back in the warm sunlight, dropped asleep—and died as quietly as a child taken from its play to its slumbers.

After one more careful look, Bryce turned and made through the trees to the path which crossed the old graveyard. And there, going leisurely home to lunch, was Dick Bewery, who glanced at the young doctor inquisitively.

"Hullo!" he exclaimed with the freedom of youth towards something not much older. "You there? Anything on?"

Then he looked more clearly, seeing Bryce to be pale and excited. Bryce laid a hand on the lad's arm.

"Look here!" he said. "There's something wrong—again!—in here. Run down to the police-station—get hold of Mitchington—quietly, you understand!—bring him here at once. If he's not there, bring somebody else—any of the police. But—say nothing to anybody but them."

Dick gave him another swift look, turned, and ran. And Bryce went back to the dead man—and picked up the tin bottle, and making a cup of his left hand poured out a trickle of the contents. Cold tea!—and, as far as he could judge, nothing else. He put the tip of his little finger into the weak-looking stuff, and tasted—it tasted of nothing but a super-abundance of sugar.

He stood there, watching the dead man until the sound of footsteps behind him gave warning of the return of Dick Bewery, who, in another minute, hurried through the bushes, followed by Mitchington. The boy stared in silence at the still figure, but the inspector, after a hasty glance, turned a horrified face on Bryce.

"Good Lord!" he gasped. "It's Collishawl"

Bryce for the moment failed to comprehend this, and Mitchington shook his head.

"Collishaw!" he repeated. "Collishaw, you know! The man I told you about yesterday afternoon. The man that said—"

Mitchington suddenly checked himself, with a glance at Dick Bewery.

"I remember—now," said Bryce. "The mason's labourer! So —this is the man, eh? Well, Mitchington, he's dead!—I found him dead, just now. I should say he'd been dead five to ten minutes—not more. You'd better get help—and I'd like another medical man to see him before he's removed."

Mitchington looked again at Dick.

"Perhaps you'd fetch Dr. Ransford, Mr—Richard?" he asked. "He's nearest."

"Dr. Ransford's not at home," said Dick. "He went to Highminster—some County Council business or other—at ten this morning, and he won't be back until four—I happen to know that. Shall I run for Dr. Coates?"

"If you wouldn't mind," said Mitchington, "and as it's close by, drop in at the station again and tell the sergeant to come here with a couple of men. I say!" he went on, when the boy had hurried off, "this is a queer business, Dr. Bryce! What do you think?"

"I think this," answered Bryce. "That man!—look at him!—a strong, healthy-looking fellow, in the very prime of life—that man has met his death by foul means. You take particular care of those dinner things of his—the remains of his dinner, every scrap—and of that tin bottle. That, especially. Take all these things yourself, Mitchington, and lock them up —they'll be wanted for examination."

Mitchington glanced at the simple matters which Bryce indicated. And suddenly he turned a half-frightened glance on his companion.

"You don't mean to say that—that you suspect he's been poisoned?" he asked. "Good Lord, if that is so—"

"I don't think you'll find that there's much doubt about it," answered Bryce. "But that's a point that will soon be settled. You'd better tell the Coroner at once, Mitchington, and he'll issue a formal order to Dr. Coates to make a post-mortem. And," he added significantly, "I shall be surprised if it isn't as I say—poison!"

"If that's so," observed Mitchington, with a grim shake of his head, "if that really is so, then I know what I shall think! This!" he went on, pointing to the dead man, "this is—a sort of sequel to the other affair. There's been something in what the poor chap said—he did know something against somebody, and that somebody's got to hear of it—and silenced him. But, Lord, doctor, how can it have been done?"

"I can see how it can have been done, easy enough," said Bryce. "This man has evidently been at work here, by himself, all the morning. He of course brought his dinner with him. He no doubt put his basket and his bottle down somewhere, while he did his work. What easier than for some one to approach through these trees and shrubs while the man's back was turned, or he was busy round one of these corners, and put some deadly poison into that bottle? Nothing!"

"Well," remarked Mitchington, "if that's so, it proves something else—to my mind."

"What!" asked Bryce.

"Why, that whoever it was who did it was somebody who had a knowledge of poison!" answered Mitchington. "And I should say there aren't many people in Wrychester who have such knowledge outside yourselves and the chemists. It's a black business, this!"

Bryce nodded silently. He waited until Dr. Coates, an elderly man who was the leading practitioner in the town, arrived, and to him he gave a careful account of his discovery. And after the police had taken the body away, and he had accompanied Mitchington to the police–station and seen the tin bottle and the remains of Collishaw's dinner safely locked up, he went home to lunch, and to wonder at this strange development. The inspector was doubtless right in saying that Collishaw had been done to death by somebody who wanted to silence him—but who could that somebody be? Bryce's thoughts immediately turned to the fact that Ransford had overheard all that Mitchington had said, in that very room in which he, Bryce, was then lunching—Ransford! Was it possible that Ransford had realized a danger in Collishaw's knowledge, and had—

He was interrupted at this stage by Mitchington, who came hurriedly in with a scared face.

"I say, I say!" he whispered as soon as Bryce's landlady had shut the door on them. "Here's a fine business! I've heard something—something I can hardly credit—but it's true. I've been to tell Collishaw's family what's happened. And—I'm fairly dazed by it—yet it's there—it is so!"

"What's so?" demanded Bryce. "What is it that's true?"

Mitchington bent closer over the table.

"Dr. Ransford was fetched to Collishaw's cottage at six o'clock this morning!" he said. "It seems that Collishaw's wife has been in a poor way about her health of late, and Dr. Ransford has attended her, off and on. She had some sort of a seizure this morning—early—and Ransford was sent for. He was there some little time—and I've heard some queer things."

"What sort of queer things?" demanded Bryce. "Don't be afraid of speaking out, man!—there's no one to hear but myself."

"Well, things that look suspicious, on the face of it," continued Mitchington, who was obviously much upset. "As you'll acknowledge when you hear them. I got my information from the next-door neighbour, Mrs. Batts. Mrs. Batts says that when Ransford—who'd been fetched by Mrs. Batts's eldest lad—came to Collishaw's house, Collishaw was putting up his dinner to take to his work—"

"What on earth made Mrs. Batts tell you that?" interrupted Bryce.

"Oh, well, to tell you the truth, I put a few questions to her as to what went on while Ransford was in the house," answered Mitchington. "When I'd once found that he had been there, you know, I naturally wanted to know all I could."

"Well?" asked Bryce.

"Collishaw, I say, was putting up his dinner to take to his work," continued Mitchington. "Mrs. Batts was doing a thing or two about the house. Ransford went upstairs to see Mrs. Collishaw. After a while he came down and said he would have to remain a little. Collishaw went up to speak to his wife before going out. And then Ransford asked Mrs. Batts for something—I forget what—some small matter which the Collishaw's hadn't got and she had, and she went next door to fetch it. Therefore—do you see?—Ransford was left alone with—Collishaw's tin bottle!"

Bryce, who had been listening attentively, looked steadily at the inspector.

"You're suspecting Ransford already!" he said.

Mitchington shook his head.

"What's it look like?" he answered, almost appealingly. "I put it to you, now!—what does it look like? Here's this man been poisoned without a doubt—I'm certain of it.

And—there were those rumours—it's idle to deny that they centred in Ransford. And—this morning Ransford had the chance!"

"That's arguing that Ransford purposely carried a dose of poison to put into Collishaw's tin bottle!" said Bryce half-sneeringly. "Not very probable, you know, Mitchington."

Mitchington spread out his hands.

"Well, there it is!" he said. "As I say, there's no denying the suspicious look of it. If I were only certain that those rumours about what Collishaw hinted he could say had got to Ransford's ears!—why, then—"

"What's being done about that post-mortem?" asked Bryce.

"Dr. Coates and Dr. Everest are going to do it this afternoon," replied Mitchington. "The Coroner went to them at once, as soon as I told him."

"They'll probably have to call in an expert from London," said Bryce. "However, you can't do anything definite, you know, until the result's known. Don't say anything of this to anybody. I'll drop in at your place later and hear if Coates can say anything really certain."

Mitchington went away, and Bryce spent the rest of the afternoon wondering, speculating and scheming. If Ransford had really got rid of this man who knew something—why, then, it was certainly Ransford who killed Braden.

He went round to the police-station at five o'clock. Mitchington drew him aside.

"Coates says there's no doubt about it!" he whispered. "Poisoned! Hydrocyanic acid!"

CHAPTER XIII. BRYCE IS ASKED A QUESTION

Mitchington stepped aside into a private room, motioning Bryce to follow him. He carefully closed the door, and looking significantly at his companion, repeated his last words, with a shake of the head.

"Poisoned!—without the very least doubt," he whispered. "Hydrocyanic acid—which, I understand, is the same thing as what's commonly called prussic acid. They say then hadn't the least difficulty in finding that out! so there you are."

"That's what Coates has told you, of course?" asked Bryce. "After the autopsy?"

"Both of 'em told me—Coates, and Everest, who helped him," replied Mitchington. "They said it was obvious from the very start. And—I say!"

"Well?" said Bryce.

"It wasn't in that tin bottle, anyway," remarked Mitchington, who was evidently greatly weighted with mystery.

"No!—of course it wasn't!" affirmed Bryce. "Good Heavens, man—I know that!"

"How do you know?" asked Mitchington.

"Because I poured a few drops from that bottle into my hand when I first found Collishaw and tasted the stuff," answered Bryce readily. "Cold tea! with too much sugar in it. There was no H.C.N. in that besides, wherever it is, there's always a smell stronger or fainter—of bitter almonds. There was none about that bottle."

"Yet you were very anxious that we should take care of the bottle?" observed Mitchington.

"Of course!—because I suspected the use of some much rarer poison than that," retorted Bryce. "Pooh!—it's a clumsy way of poisoning anybody!—quick though it is."

"Well, there's where it is!" said Mitchington. "That'll be the medical evidence at the inquest, anyway. That's how it was done. And the question now is—"

"Who did it?" interrupted Bryce. "Precisely! Well—I'll say this much at once, Mitchington. Whoever did it was either a big bungler—or damned clever! That's what I say!"

The Paradise Mystery

"I don't understand you," said Mitchington.

"Plain enough—my meaning," replied Bryce, smiling. "To finish anybody with that stuff is easy enough—but no poison is more easily detected. It's an amateurish way of poisoning anybody—unless you can do it in such a fashion that no suspicion can attach you to. And in this case it's here —whoever administered that poison to Collishaw must have been certain—absolutely certain, mind you!—that it was impossible for any one to find out that he'd done so. Therefore, I say what I said—the man must be damned clever. Otherwise, he'd be found out pretty quick. And all that puzzles me is—how was it administered?"

"How much would kill anybody—pretty quick?" asked Mitchington.

"How much? One drop would cause instantaneous death!" answered Bryce. "Cause paralysis of the heart, there and then, instantly!"

Mitchington remained silent awhile, looking meditatively at Bryce. Then he turned to a locked drawer, produced a key, and took something out of the drawer—a small object, wrapped in paper.

"I'm telling you a good deal, doctor," he said. "But as you know so much already, I'll tell you a bit more. Look at this!"

He opened his hand and showed Bryce a small cardboard pill-box, across the face of which a few words were written —One after meals—Mr. Collishaw.

"Whose handwriting's that?" demanded Mitchington.

Bryce looked closer, and started.

"Ransford's!" he muttered. Ransford—of course!"

"That box was in Collishaw's waistcoat pocket," said Mitchington. "There are pills inside it, now. See!" He took off the lid of the box and revealed four sugar-coated pills. "It wouldn't hold more than six, this," he observed.

96

Bryce extracted a pill and put his nose to it, after scratching a little of the sugar coating away.

"Mere digestive pills," he announced.

"Could—it!—have been given in one of these?" asked Mitchington.

"Possible," replied Bryce. He stood thinking for a moment. "Have you shown those things to Coates and Everest?" he asked at last.

"Not yet," replied Mitchington. "I wanted to find out, first, if Ransford gave this box to Collishaw, and when. I'm going to Collishaw's house presently—I've certain inquiries to make. His widow'll know about these pills."

"You're suspecting Ransford," said Bryce. "That's certain!"

Mitchington carefully put away the pill–box and relocked the drawer.

"I've got some decidedly uncomfortable ideas—which I'd much rather not have—about Dr. Ransford," he said. "When one thing seems to fit into another, what is one to think. If I were certain that that rumour which spread, about Collishaw's knowledge of something—you know, had got to Ransford's ears —why, I should say it looked very much as if Ransford wanted to stop Collishaw's tongue for good before it could say more —and next time, perhaps, something definite. If men once begin to hint that they know something, they don't stop at hinting. Collishaw might have spoken plainly before long—to us!"

Bryce asked a question about the holding of the inquest and went away. And after thinking things over, he turned in the direction of the Cathedral, and made his way through the Cloisters to the Close. He was going to make another move in his own game, while there was a good chance. Everything at this juncture was throwing excellent cards into his hand—he would be foolish, he thought, not to play them to advantage. And so he made straight for Ransford's house, and before he reached it, met Ransford and Mary Bewery, who were crossing the Close from another point, on their way from the railway station, whither Mary had gone especially to meet her guardian. They were in such deep conversation that Bryce was close upon them before they observed his presence. When

The Paradise Mystery

Ransford saw his late assistant, he scowled unconsciously —Bryce, and the interview of the previous afternoon, had been much in his thoughts all day, and he had an uneasy feeling that Bryce was playing some game. Bryce was quick to see that scowl—and to observe the sudden start which Mary could not repress—and he was just as quick to speak.

"I was going to your house, Dr. Ransford," he remarked quietly. "I don't want to force my presence on you, now or at any time—but I think you'd better give me a few minutes."

They were at Ransford's garden gate by that time, and Ransford flung it open and motioned Bryce to follow. He led the way into the dining–room, closed the door on the three, and looked at Bryce. Bryce took the glance as a question, and put another, in words.

"You've heard of what's happened during the day?" he said.

"About Collishaw—yes," answered Ransford. "Miss Bewery has just told me—what her brother told her. What of it?"

"I have just come from the police–station," said Bryce. "Coates and Everest have carried out an autopsy this afternoon. Mitchington told me the result."

"Well?" demanded Ransford, with no attempt to conceal his impatience. "And what then?"

"Collishaw was poisoned," replied Bryce, watching Ransford with a closeness which Mary did not fail to observe. "H.C.N. No doubt at all about it."

"Well–and what then?" asked Ransford, still more impatiently. "To be explicit—what's all this to do with me?"

"I came here to do you a service," answered Bryce. "Whether you like to take it or not is your look–out. You may as well know it you're in danger. Collishaw is the man who hinted—as you heard yesterday in my rooms—that he could say something definite about the Braden affair—if he liked."

"Well?" said Ransford.

"It's known—to the police—that you were at Collishaw's house early this morning," said Bryce. "Mitchington knows it."

Ransford laughed.

"Does Mitchington know that I overheard what he said to you, yesterday afternoon?" he inquired.

"No, he doesn't," answered Bryce. "He couldn't possibly know unless I told him. I haven't told him—I'm not going to tell him. But—he's suspicious already."

"Of me, of course," suggested Ransford, with another laugh. He took a turn across the room and suddenly faced round on Bryce, who had remained standing near the door. "Do you really mean to tell me that Mitchington is such a fool as to believe that I would poison a poor working man—and in that clumsy fashion?" he burst out. "Of course you don't."

"I never said I did," answered Bryce. "I'm only telling you what Mitchington thinks his grounds for suspecting. He confided in me because—well, it was I who found Collishaw. Mitchington is in possession of a box of digestive pills which you evidently gave Collishaw."

"Bah!" exclaimed Ransford. "The man's a fool! Let him come and talk to me."

"He won't do that—yet," said Bryce. "But—I'm afraid he'll bring all this out at the inquest. The fact is—he's suspicious—what with one thing or another—about the former affair. He thinks you concealed the truth—whatever it may be—as regards any knowledge of Braden which you may or mayn't have."

"I'll tell you what it is!" said Ransford suddenly. "It just comes to this—I'm suspected of having had a hand—the hand, if you like!—in Braden's death, and now of getting rid of Collishaw because Collishaw could prove that I had that hand. That's about it!"

"A clear way of putting it, certainly," assented Bryce. "But —there's a very clear way, too, of dissipating any such ideas."

"What way?" demanded Ransford.

"If you do know anything about the Braden affair—why not reveal it, and be done with the whole thing," suggested Bryce. "That would finish matters."

Ransford took a long, silent look at his questioner. And Bryce looked steadily back—and Mary Bewery anxiously watched both men.

"That's my business," said Ransford at last. "I'm neither to be coerced, bullied, or cajoled. I'm obliged to you for giving me a hint of my—danger, I suppose! And—I don't propose to say any more."

"Neither do I," said Bryce. "I only came to tell you."

And therewith, having successfully done all that he wanted to do, he walked out of the room and the house, and Ransford, standing in the window, his hands thrust in his pockets, watched him go away across the Close.

"Guardian!" said Mary softly.

Ransford turned sharply.

"Wouldn't it be best," she continued, speaking nervously, "if —if you do know anything about that unfortunate man—if you told it? Why have this suspicion fastening itself on you? You!"

Ransford made an effort to calm himself. He was furiously angry—angry with Bryce, angry with Mitchington, angry with the cloud of foolishness and stupidity that seemed to be gathering.

"Why should I—supposing that I do know something, which I don't admit—why should I allow myself to be coerced and frightened by these fools?" he asked. "No man can prevent suspicion falling on him—it's my bad luck in this instance. Why should I rush to

100

the police–station and say, 'Here—I'll blurt out all I know—everything!' Why?"

"Wouldn't that be better than knowing that people are saying things?" she asked.

"As to that," replied Ransford, "you can't prevent people saying things—especially in a town like this. If it hadn't been for the unfortunate fact that Braden came to the surgery door, nothing would have been said. But what of that?—I have known hundreds of men in my time—aye, and forgotten them! No!—I am not going to fall a victim to this device—it all springs out of curiosity. As to this last affair—it's all nonsense!"

"But—if the man was really poisoned?" suggested Mary.

"Let the police find the poisoner!" said Ransford, with a grim smile. "That's their job."

Mary said nothing for a moment, and Ransford moved restlessly about the room.

"I don't trust that fellow Bryce," he said suddenly. "He's up to something. I don't forget what he said when I bundled him out that morning."

"What?" she asked.

"That he would be a bad enemy," answered Ransford. "He's posing now as a friend—but a man's never to be so much suspected as when he comes doing what you may call unnecessary acts of friendship. I'd rather that anybody was mixed up in my affairs—your affairs—than Pemberton Bryce!"

"So would I!" she said. "But—"

She paused there a moment and then looked appealingly at Ransford.

"I do wish you'd tell me—what you promised to tell me," she said. "You know what I mean—about me and Dick. Somehow—I don't quite know how or why—I've an uneasy feeling that Bryce knows something, and that he's mixing it all up with—this! Why not tell me—please!"

Ransford, who was still marching about the room, came to a halt, and leaning his hands on the table between them, looked earnestly at her.

"Don't ask that—now!" he said. "I can't—yet. The fact is, I'm waiting for something—some particulars. As soon as I get them, I'll speak to you—and to Dick. In the meantime—don't ask me again—and don't be afraid. And as to this affair, leave it to me—and if you meet Bryce again, refuse to discuss any thing with him. Look here!—there's only one reason why he professes friendliness and a desire to save me annoyance. He thinks he can ingratiate himself with—you!"

"Mistaken!" murmured Mary, shaking her head. "I don't trust him. And—less than ever because of yesterday. Would an honest man have done what he did? Let that police inspector talk freely, as he did, with people concealed behind a curtain? And—he laughed about it! I hated myself for being there—yet could we help it?"

"I'm not going to hate myself on Pemberton Bryce's account," said Ransford. "Let him play his game—that he has one, I'm certain."

Bryce had gone away to continue his game—or another line of it. The Collishaw matter had not made him forget the Richard Jenkins tomb, and now, after leaving Ransford's house, he crossed the Close to Paradise with the object of doing a little more investigation. But at the archway of the ancient enclosure he met old Simpson Harker, pottering about in his usual apparently aimless fashion. Harker smiled at sight of Bryce.

"Ah, I was wanting to have a word with you, doctor!" he said. "Something important. Have you got a minute or two to spare, sir? Come round to my little place, then—we shall be quiet there."

Bryce had any amount of time to spare for an interesting person like Harker, and he followed the old man to his house —a tiny place set in a nest of similar old–world buildings behind the Close. Harker led him into a little parlour, comfortable and snug, wherein were several shelves of books of a curiously legal and professional–looking aspect, some old pictures, and a cabinet of odds and ends, stowed away in of dark corner. The old man motioned him to an easy chair, and going over to a cupboard, produced a decanter of whisky and a box of cigars.

"We can have a peaceful and comfortable talk here, doctor," he remarked, as he sat down near Bryce, after fetching glasses and soda–water. "I live all alone, like a hermit—my bit of work's done by a woman who only looks in of a morning. So we're all by ourselves. Light your cigar!—same as that I gave you at Barthorpe. Um—well, now," he continued, as Bryce settled down to listen. "There's a question I want to put to you—strictly between ourselves—strictest of confidence, you know. It was you who was called to Braden by Varner, and you were left alone with Braden's body?"

"Well?" admitted Bryce, suddenly growing suspicious. "What of it?"

Harker edged his chair a little closer to his guest's, and leaned towards him.

"What," he asked in a whisper, "what have you done with that scrap of paper that you took out of Braden's purse?"

CHAPTER XIV. FROM THE PAST

If any remarkably keen and able observer of the odd characteristics of humanity had been present in Harker's little parlour at that moment, watching him and his visitor, he would have been struck by what happened when the old man put this sudden and point–blank question to the young one. For Harker put the question, though in a whisper, in no more than a casual, almost friendlily–confidential way, and Bryce never showed by the start of a finger or the flicker of an eyelash that he felt it to be what he really knew it to be —the most surprising and startling question he had ever had put to him. Instead, he looked his questioner calmly in the eyes, and put a question in his turn.

"Who are you, Mr. Harker?" asked Bryce quietly.

Harker laughed—almost gleefully.

"Yes, you've a right to ask that!" he said. "Of course!—glad you take it that way. You'll do!"

"I'll qualify it, then," added Bryce. "It's not who—it's what are you!"

103

The Paradise Mystery

Harker waved his cigar at the book–shelves in front of which his visitor sat.

"Take a look at my collection of literature, doctor," he said. "What d'ye think of it?"

Bryce turned and leisurely inspected one shelf after another.

"Seems to consist of little else but criminal cases and legal handbooks," he remarked quietly. "I begin to suspect you, Mr. Harker. They say here in Wrychester that you're a retired tradesman. I think you're a retired policeman—of the detective branch."

Harker laughed again.

"No Wrychester man has ever crossed my threshold since I came to settle down here," he said. "You're the first person I've ever asked in—with one notable exception. I've never even had Campany, the librarian, here. I'm a hermit."

"But—you were a detective?" suggested Bryce.

"Aye, for a good five–and–twenty years!" replied Harker. "And pretty well known, too, sir. But—my question, doctor. All between ourselves!"

"I'll ask you one, then," said Bryce. "How do you know I took a scrap of paper from Braden's purse?"

"Because I know that he had such a paper in his purse the night he came to the Mitre," answered Harker, "and was certain to have it there next morning, and because I also know that you were left alone with the body for some minutes after Varner fetched you to it, and that when Braden's clothing and effects were searched by Mitchington, the paper wasn't there. So, of course, you took it! Doesn't matter to me that ye did —except that I know, from knowing that, that you're on a similar game to my own—which is why you went down to Leicestershire."

"You knew Braden?" asked Bryce.

"I knew him!" answered Harker.

The Paradise Mystery

"You saw him—spoke with him—here in Wrychester?" suggested Bryce.

"He was here—in this room—in that chair—from five minutes past nine to close on ten o'clock the night before his death," replied Harker.

Bryce, who was quietly appreciating the Havana cigar which the old man had given him, picked up his glass, took a drink, and settled himself in his easy chair as if he meant to stay there awhile.

"I think we'd better talk confidentially, Mr. Harker," he said.

"Precisely what we are doing, Dr. Bryce," replied Harker.

"All right, my friend," said Bryce, laconically. "Now we understand each other. So—do you know who John Braden really was?"

"Yes!" replied Harker, promptly. "He was in reality John Brake, ex–bank manager, ex–convict."

"Do you know if he's any relatives here in Wrychester?" inquired Bryce.

"Yes," said Harker. "The boy and girl who live with Ransford —they're Brake's son and daughter."

"Did Brake know that—when he came here?" continued Bryce.

"No, he didn't—he hadn't the least idea of it," responded Harker.

"Had you—then?" asked Bryce.

"No—not until later—a little later," replied Harker.

"You found it out at Barthorpe?" suggested Bryce.

"Not a bit of it; I worked it out here—after Brake was dead," said Harker. "I went to Barthorpe on quite different business—Brake's business."

"Ah!" said Bryce. He looked the old detective quietly in the eyes. "You'd better tell me all about it," he added.

"If we're both going to tell each other—all about it," stipulated Harker.

"That's settled," assented Bryce.

Harker smoked thoughtfully for a moment and seemed to be thinking.

"I'd better go back to the beginning," he said. "But, first —what do you know about Brake? I know you went down to Barthorpe to find out what you could—how far did your searches take you?"

"I know that Brake married a girl from Braden Medworth, that he took her to London, where he was manager of a branch bank, that he got into trouble, and was sentenced to ten years' penal servitude," answered Bryce, "together with some small details into which we needn't go at present."

"Well, as long as you know all that, there's a common basis and a common starting–point," remarked Harker, "so I'll begin at Brake's trial. It was I who arrested Brake. There was no trouble, no bother. He'd been taken unawares, by an inspector of the bank. He'd a considerable deficiency—couldn't make it good—couldn't or wouldn't explain except by half–sullen hints that he'd been cruelly deceived. There was no defence —couldn't be. His counsel said that he could—"

"I've read the account of the trial," interrupted Bryce.

"All right—then you know as much as I can tell you on that point," said Harker. "He got, as you say, ten years. I saw him just before he was removed and asked him if there was anything I could do for him about his wife and children. I'd never seen them—I arrested him at the bank, and, of course, he was never out of custody after that. He answered in a queer, curt way that his wife and children were being looked after. I heard, incidentally, that his wife had left home, or was from home—there was something mysterious about it—either as soon as he was arrested or before. Anyway, he said nothing, and from that moment I never set eyes on him again until I met him in the street here in Wrychester, the other night, when he came to the Mitre. I knew him at once—and he knew me. We met under one of those big standard lamps in the Market Place—I was following my usual practice of having an evening walk, last thing before going to bed. And we stopped and stared at each other. Then he came forward with his hand out, and we shook hands. 'This is an odd thing!' he said. 'You're the very man I wanted to find! Come somewhere, where it's quiet, and let me have a word with you.' So—I brought him here."

Bryce was all attention now—for once he was devoting all his faculties to tense and absorbed concentration on what another man could tell, leaving reflections and conclusions on what he heard until all had been told.

"I brought him here," repeated Harker. "I told him I'd been retired and was living here, as he saw, alone. I asked him no questions about himself—I could see he was a well-dressed, apparently well-to-do man. And presently he began to tell me about himself. He said that after he'd finished his term he left England and for some time travelled in Canada and the United States, and had gone then—on to New Zealand and afterwards to Australia, where he'd settled down and begun speculating in wool. I said I hoped he'd done well. Yes, he said, he'd done very nicely—and then he gave me a quiet dig in the ribs. 'I'll tell you one thing I've done, Harker,' he said. 'You were very polite and considerate to me when I'd my trouble, so I don't mind telling you. I paid the bank every penny of that money they lost through my foolishness at that time—every penny, four years ago, with interest, and I've got their receipt.' 'Delighted to hear it, Mr.—Is it the same name still?' I said. 'My name ever since I left England,' he said, giving me a look, 'is Braden—John Braden.' 'Yes,' he went on, 'I paid 'em—though I never had one penny of the money I was fool enough to take for the time being—not one halfpenny!' 'Who had it, Mr. Braden?' I asked him, thinking that he'd perhaps tell after all that time. 'Never mind, my lad!' he answered. 'It'll come out—yet. Never mind that, now. I'll tell you why I wanted to see you. The fact is, I've only been a few hours in England, so to speak, but I'd thought of you, and wondered where I could get hold of you —you're the only man of your profession I ever met, you see,' he added, with a laugh. 'And I want a bit of help in that way.' 'Well, Mr. Braden,' I said, 'I've retired, but if it's an easy job—' 'It's one you can do, easy enough,' he said. 'It's just this—I met a man in Australia who's extremely anxious to get some news of another man, named Falkiner Wraye, who hails from Barthorpe, in Leicestershire. I promised to make inquiries for him. Now, I have strong reasons why I don't want to go near Barthorpe—Barthorpe has unpleasant memories and associations for me, and I don't want to be seen there. But this thing's got to be personal investigation —will you go here, for me? I'll make it worth your while. All you've got to do,' he went on, 'is to go there—see the police authorities, town officials, anybody that knows the place, and ask them if they can tell you anything of one Falkiner Wraye, who was at one time a small estate agent in Barthorpe, left the place about seventeen years ago—maybe eighteen—and is believed to have recently gone back to the neighbourhood. That's all. Get what information you can, and write it to me, care of my bankers in London. Give me a sheet of paper and I'll put down particulars for you.'"

Harker paused at this point and nodded his head at an old bureau which stood in a corner of his room.

"The sheet of paper's there," he said. "It's got on it, in his writing, a brief memorandum of what he wanted and the address of his bankers. When he'd given it to me, he put his hand in his pocket and pulled out a purse in which I could see he was carrying plenty of money. He took out some notes. 'Here's five–and–twenty pounds on account, Harker,' he said. 'You might have to spend a bit. Don't be afraid—plenty more where that comes from. You'll do it soon?' he asked. 'Yes, I'll do it, Mr. Braden,' I answered. 'It'll be a bit of a holiday for me.' 'That's all right,' he said. 'I'm delighted I came across you.' 'Well, you couldn't be more delighted than I was surprised,' I said. 'I never thought to see you in Wrychester. What brought you here, if one may ask —sight–seeing?' He laughed at that, and he pulled out his purse again. 'I'll show you something—a secret,' he said, and he took a bit of folded paper out of his purse. 'What do you make of that?' he asked. 'Can you read Latin?' 'No —except a word or two,' I said, 'but I know a man who can.' 'Ah, never mind,' said he. 'I know enough Latin for this—and it's a secret. However, it won't be a secret long, and you'll hear all about it.' And with that he put the bit of paper in his purse again, and we began talking about other matters, and before long he said he'd promised to have a chat with a gentleman at the Mitre whom he'd come along with in the train, and away he went, saying he'd see me before be left the town."

"Did he say how long he was going to stop here?" asked Bryce.

"Two or three days," replied Harker.

"Did he mention Ransford?" inquired Bryce.

"Never!" said Harker.

"Did he make any reference to his wife and children?"

"Not the slightest!"

"Nor to the hint that his counsel threw out at the trial?"

"Never referred to that time except in the way I told you —that he hadn't a penny of the money, himself and that he'd himself refunded it."

Bryce meditated awhile. He was somewhat puzzled by certain points in the old detective's story, and he saw now that there was much more mystery in the Braden affair than he had at first believed.

"Well," he asked, after a while, "did you see him again ?"

"Not alive!" replied Harker. "I saw him dead—and I held my tongue, and have held it. But—something happened that day. After I heard of the accident, I went into the Crown and Cushion tavern—the fact was, I went to get a taste of whisky, for the news had upset me. And in that long bar of theirs, I saw a man whom I knew—a man whom I knew, for a fact, to have been a fellow convict of Brake's. Name of Glassdale—forgery. He got the same sentence that Brake got, about the same time, was in the same convict prison with Brake, and he and Brake would be released about the same date. There was no doubt about his identity—I never forget a face, even after thirty years I'd tell one. I saw him in that bar before he saw me, and I took a careful look at him. He, too, like Brake, was very well dressed, and very prosperous looking. He turned as he set down his glass, and caught sight of me—and he knew me. Mind you, he'd been through my hands in times past! And he instantly moved to a side–door and—vanished. I went out and looked up and down—he'd gone. I found out afterwards, by a little quiet inquiry, that he'd gone straight to the station, boarded the first train—there was one just giving out, to the junction—and left the city. But I can lay hands on him!"

"You've kept this quiet, too?" asked Bryce.

"Just so—I've my own game to play," replied darker. "This talk with you is part of it—you come in, now—I'll tell you why, presently. But first, as you know, I went to Barthorpe. For, though Brake was dead, I felt I must go—for this reason. I was certain

109

that he wanted that information for himself—the man in Australia was a fiction. I went, then—and learned nothing. Except that this Falkiner Wraye had been, as Brake said, a Barthorpe man, years ago. He'd left the town eighteen years since, and nobody knew anything about him. So I came home. And now then, doctor—your turn! What were you after, down there at Barthorpe?"

Bryce meditated his answer for a good five minutes. He had always intended to play the game off his own bat, but he had heard and seen enough since entering Harker's little room to know that he was in company with an intellect which was keener and more subtle than his, and that it would be all to his advantage to go in with the man who had vast and deep experience. And so he made a clean breast of all he had done in the way of investigation, leaving his motive completely aside.

"You've got a theory, of course?" observed Harker, after listening quietly to all that Bryce could tell. "Naturally, you have! You couldn't accumulate all that without getting one."

"Well," admitted Bryce, "honestly, I can't say that I have. But I can see what theory there might be. This—that Ransford was the man who deceived Brake, that he ran away with Brake's wife, that she's dead, and that he's brought up the children in ignorance of all that—and therefore—"

"And therefore," interrupted Harker with a smile, "that when he and Brake met—as you seem to think they did—Ransford flung Brake through that open doorway; that Collishaw witnessed it, that Ransford's found out about Collishaw, and that Collishaw has been poisoned by Ransford. Eh?"

"That's a theory that seems to be supported by facts," said Bryce.

"It's a theory that would doubtless suit men like Mitchington," said the old detective, with another smile. "But—not me, sir! Mind you, I don't say there isn't something in it—there's doubtless a lot. But—the mystery's a lot thicker than just that. And Brake didn't come here to find Ransford. He came because of the secret in that scrap of paper. And as you've got it, doctor—out with it!"

Bryce saw no reason for concealment and producing the scrap of paper laid it on the table between himself and his host. Harker peered inquisitively at it.

"Latin!" he said. "You can read it, of course. What does it say?"

Bryce repeated a literal translation.

"I've found the place," he added. "I found it this morning. Now, what do you suppose this means?"

Harker was looking hard at the two lines of writing.

"That's a big question, doctor," he answered. "But I'll go so far as to say this—when we've found out what it does mean, we shall know a lot more than we know now!"

CHAPTER XV. THE DOUBLE OFFER

Bryce, who was deriving a considerable and peculiar pleasure from his secret interview with the old detective, smiled at Harker's last remark.

"That's a bit of a platitude, isn't it?" he suggested. "Of course we shall know a lot more—when we do know a lot more!"

"I set store by platitudes, sir," retorted Harker. "You can't repeat an established platitude too often—it's got the hallmark of good use on it. But now, till we do know more —you've no doubt been thinking a lot about this matter, Dr. Bryce—hasn't it struck you that there's one feature in connection with Brake, or Braden's visit to Wrychester to which nobody's given any particular attention up to now—so far as we know, at any rate?"

"What?" demanded Bryce.

"This," replied Harker. "Why did he wish to see the Duke of Saxonsteade? He certainly did want to see him—and as soon as possible. You'll remember that his Grace was questioned about that at the inquest and could give no explanation—he knew nothing of Brake, and couldn't suggest any reason why Brake should wish to have an interview with him. But—I can!"

"You?" exclaimed Bryce.

"I," answered Harker. "And it's this—I spoke just now of that man Glassdale. Now you, of course; have no knowledge of him, and as you don't keep yourself posted in criminal history, you don't know what his offence was?"

"You said—forgery?" replied Bryce.

"Just so—forgery," assented Harker. "And the signature that he forged was—the Duke of Saxonsteade's! As a matter of fact, he was the Duke's London estate agent. He got wrong, somehow, and he forged the Duke's name to a cheque. Now, then, considering who Glassdale is, and that he was certainly a fellow–convict of Brake's, and that I myself saw him here in Wrychester on the day of Brake's death—what's the conclusion to be drawn? That Brake wanted to see the Duke on some business of Glassdale's! Without a doubt! It may have been that he and Glassdale wanted to visit the Duke, together."

Bryce silently considered this suggestion for awhile.

"You said, just now, that Glassdale could be traced?" he remarked at last.

"Traced—yes," replied Harker. "So long as he's in England."

"Why not set about it?" suggested Bryce.

"Not yet," said Harker. "There's things to do before that. And the first thing is—let's get to know what the mystery of that scrap of paper is. You say you've found Richard Jenkins's tomb? Very well—then the thing to do is to find out if anything is hidden there. Try it tomorrow night. Better go by yourself—after dark. If you find anything, let me know. And then—then we can decide on a next step. But between now and then, there'll be the inquest on this man Collishaw. And, about that—a word in your ear! Say as little as ever you can!—after all, you know nothing beyond what you saw. And—we mustn't meet and talk in public—after you've done that bit of exploring in Paradise tomorrow night, come round here and we'll consider matters."

There was little that Bryce could say or could be asked to say at the inquest on the mason's labourer next morning. Public interest and excitement was as keen about Collishaw's mysterious death as about. Braden's, for it was already rumoured through the town that if Braden had not met with his death when he came to Wrychester, Collishaw would still be alive. The Coroner's court was once more packed; once more there was the same atmosphere of mystery. But the proceedings were of a very different nature to those which had attended the inquest on Braden. The foreman under whose orders Collishaw had been working gave particulars of the dead man's work on the morning of his death. He had been instructed to clear away an accumulation of rubbish which had gathered at the foot of the south wall of the nave in consequence of some recent repairs to the masonry—there was a full day's work before him. All day he would be in and out of Paradise with his barrow, wheeling away the rubbish he gathered up. The foreman had looked in on him once or twice; he had seen him just before noon, when he appeared to be in his usual health —he had made no complaint, at any rate. Asked if he had happened to notice where Collishaw had set down his dinner basket and his tin bottle while he worked, he replied that it so happened that he had—he remembered seeing both bottle and basket and the man's jacket deposited on one of the box–tombs under a certain yew–tree—which he could point out, if necessary.

Bryce's account of his finding of Collishaw amounted to no more than a bare recital of facts. Nor was much time spent in questioning the two doctors who had conducted the post–mortem examination. Their evidence, terse and particular, referred solely to the cause of death. The man had been poisoned by a dose of hydrocyanic acid, which, in their opinion, had been taken only a few minutes before his body was discovered by Dr. Bryce. It had probably been a dose which would cause instantaneous death. There were no traces of the poison in the remains of his dinner, nor in the liquid in his tin bottle, which was old tea. But of the cause of his sudden death there was no more doubt than of the effects. Ransford had been in the court from the outset of the proceedings, and when the medical evidence had been given he was called. Bryce, watching him narrowly, saw that he was suffering from repressed excitement—and that that excitement was as much due to anger as to anything else. His face was set and stern, and he looked at the Coroner with an expression which portended something not precisely clear at that moment. Bryce, trying to analyse it, said to himself that he shouldn't be surprised if a scene followed—Ransford looked like a man who is bursting to say something in no unmistakable fashion. But at first he answered the questions put to him calmly and decisively.

"When this man's clothing was searched," observed the Coroner, "a box of pills was found, Dr. Ransford, on which your writing appears. Had you been attending him—professionally?"

"Yes," replied Ransford. "Both Collishaw and his wife. Or, rather, to be exact, I had been in attendance on the wife, for some weeks. A day or two before his death, Collishaw complained to me of indigestion, following on his meals. I gave him some digestive pills—the pills you speak of, no doubt."

"These?" asked the Coroner, passing over the box which Mitchington had found.

"Precisely!" agreed Ransford. "That, at any rate, is the box, and I suppose those to be the pills."

"You made them up yourself?" inquired the Coroner.

"I did—I dispense all my own medicines."

"Is it possible that the poison we have beard of, just now, could get into one of those pills—by accident?"

"Utterly impossible!—under my hands, at any rate," answered Ransford.

"Still, I suppose, it could have been administered in a pill?" suggested the Coroner.

"It might," agreed Ransford. "But," he added, with a significant glance at the medical men who had just given evidence. "It was not so administered in this case, as the previous witnesses very well know!"

The Coroner looked round him, and waited a moment.

"You are at liberty to explain—that last remark," he said at last. "That is—if you wish to do so." "Certainly!" answered Ransford, with alacrity. "Those pills are, as you will observe, coated, and the man would swallow them whole—immediately after his food. Now, it would take some little time for a pill to dissolve, to disintegrate, to be digested. If Collishaw took one of my pills as soon as he had eaten his dinner, according to instructions, and if poison had been in that pill, he would not have died at once—as he evidently did. Death would probably have been delayed some little time until the pill had dissolved. But, according to the evidence you have had before you, he died quite suddenly while eating his dinner—or immediately after it. I am not legally represented here—I don't consider it at all necessary —but I ask you to recall Dr. Coates and to put this question to him: Did he find one of those digestive pills in this man's stomach?"

The Coroner turned, somewhat dubiously, to the two doctors who had performed the autopsy. But before he could speak, the superintendent of police rose and began to whisper to him, and after a conversation between them, he looked round at the jury, every member of which had evidently been much struck by Ransford's suggestion.

"At this stage," he said, "it will be necessary to adjourn. I shall adjourn the inquiry for a week, gentlemen. You will—" Ransford, still standing in the witness–box, suddenly lost control of himself. He uttered a sharp exclamation and smote the ledge before him smartly with his open hand.

"I protest against that!" he said vehemently. "Emphatically, I protest! You first of all make a suggestion which tells against me—then, when I demand that a question shall be put which is of immense importance to my interests, you close down the inquiry—even if only for the moment. That is grossly unfair and unjust!"

"You are mistaken," said the Coroner. "At the adjourned inquiry, the two medical men can be recalled, and you will have the opportunity—or your solicitor will have—of asking any questions you like for the present—"

"For the present you have me under suspicion!" interrupted Ransford hotly. "You know it—I say this with due respect to your office—as well as I do. Suspicion is rife in the city against me. Rumour is being spread—secretly—and, I am certain—from the police, who ought to know better. And—I will not be silenced, Mr. Coroner!—I take this public opportunity, as I am on oath, of saying that I know nothing whatever of the causes of the deaths of either Collishaw or of Braden—upon my solemn oath!"

"The inquest is adjourned to this day week," said the Coroner quietly.

Ransford suddenly stepped down from the witness–box and without word or glance at any one there, walked with set face and determined look out of the court, and the excited spectators, gathering into groups, immediately began to discuss his vigorous outburst and to take sides for and against him.

Bryce, judging it advisable to keep away from Mitchington just then, and, for similar reasons, keeping away from Harker also, went out of the crowded building alone—to be joined in the street outside by Sackville Bonham, whom he had noticed in court, in company with his stepfather, Mr. Folliot.

Folliot, Bryce had observed, had stopped behind, exchanging some conversation with the Coroner. Sackville came up to Bryce with a knowing shake of the hand. He was one of those very young men who have a habit of suggesting that their fund of knowledge is extensive and peculiar, and Bryce waited for a manifestation.

"Queer business, all that, Bryce!" observed Sackville confidentially. "Of course, Ransford is a perfect ass!"

"Think so?" remarked Bryce, with an inflection which suggested that Sackville's opinion on anything was as valuable as the Attorney–General's. "That's how it strikes you, is it?"

"Impossible that it could strike one in any other way, you know," answered Sackville with fine and lofty superiority. "Ransford should have taken immediate steps to clear himself of any suspicion. It's ridiculous, considering his position —guardian to—to Miss Bewery, for instance—that he should allow such rumours to circulate. By God, sir, if it had been me, I'd have stopped 'em!—before they left the parish pump!"

"Ah?" said Bryce. "And—how?"

"Made an example of somebody," replied Sackville, with emphasis. "I believe there's law in this country, isn't there?—law against libel and slander, and that sort of thing, eh? Oh, yes!"

"Not been much time for that—yet," remarked Bryce.

"Piles of time," retorted Sackville, swinging his stick vigorously. "No, sir, Ransford is an ass! However, if a man won't do things for himself, well, his friends must do something for him. Ransford, of course, must be pulled—dragged!—out of this infernal hole. Of course he's suspected! But my stepfather—he's going to take a hand. And my stepfather, Bryce, is a devilish cute old hand at a game of this sort!"

"Nobody doubts Mr. Folliot's abilities, I'm sure," said Bryce. "But—you don't mind saying—how is he going to take a hand?"

"Stir things towards a clearing–up," announced Sackville promptly. "Have the whole thing gone into—thoroughly. There are matters that haven't been touched on, yet. You'll see, my boy!"

"Glad to hear it," said Bryce. "But—why should Mr. Folliot be so particular about clearing Ransford?"

Sackville swung his stick, and pulled up his collar, and jerked his nose a trifle higher.

"Oh, well," he said. "Of course, it's—it's a pretty well understood thing, don't you know—between myself and Miss Bewery, you know—and of course, we couldn't have any suspicions attaching to her guardian, could we, now? Family interest, don't you know—Caesar's wife, and all that sort of thing, eh?"

"I see," answered Bryce, quietly—sort of family arrangement. With Ransford's consent and knowledge, of course?"

"Ransford won't even be consulted," said Sackville, airily. "My stepfather—sharp man, that, Bryce!—he'll do things in his own fashion. You look out for sudden revelations!"

"I will," replied Bryce. "By–bye!"

He turned off to his rooms, wondering how much of truth there was in the fatuous Sackville's remarks. And—was there some mystery still undreamt of by himself and Harker? There might be—he was still under the influence of Ransford's indignant and dramatic assertion of his innocence. Would Ransford have allowed himself an outburst of that sort if he had not been, as he said, utterly ignorant of the immediate cause of Braden's death? Now Bryce, all through, was calculating, for his own purposes, on Ransford's share, full or partial, in that death—if Ransford really knew nothing whatever about it, where did his, Bryce's theory, come in—and how would his present machinations result? And, more—if Ransford's assertion were true, and if Varner's story of the hand, seen for an instant in the archway, were also true—and Varner was persisting in it—then, who was the man who flung Braden to his death that morning? He realized

117

that, instead of straightening out, things were becoming more and more complicated.

But he realized something else. On the surface, there was a strong case of suspicion against Ransford. It had been suggested that very morning before a coroner and his jury; it would grow; the police were already permeated with suspicion and distrust. Would it not pay him, Bryce, to encourage, to help it? He had his own score to pay off against Ransford; he had his own schemes as regards Mary Bewery. Anyway, he was not going to share in any attempts to clear the man who had bundled him out of his house unceremoniously—he would bide his time. And in the meantime there were other things to be done—one of them that very night.

But before Bryce could engage in his secret task of excavating a small portion of Paradise in the rear of Richard Jenkins's tomb, another strange development came. As the dark fell over the old city that night and he was thinking of setting out on his mission, Mitchington came in, carrying two sheets of paper, obviously damp from the press, in his hand. He looked at Bryce with an expression of wonder.

"Here's a queer go!" he said. "I can't make this out at all! Look at these big handbills—but perhaps you've seen 'em? They're being posted all over tho city—we've had a bundle of 'em thrown in on us."

"I haven't been out since lunch," remarked Bryce. "What are they?"

Mitchington spread out the two papers on the table, pointing from one to the other.

"You see?" he said. "Five Hundred Pounds Reward!—One Thousand Pounds Reward! And—both out at the same time, from different sources!"

"What sources?" asked Bryce, bending over the bills. "Ah—I see. One signed by Phipps Maynard, the other by Beachcroft. Odd, certainly!"

"Odd?" exclaimed Mitchington. "I should think so! But, do you see, doctor? that one—five hundred reward—is offered for information of any nature relative to the deaths of John Braden and James Collishaw, both or either. That amount will be paid for satisfactory information by Phipps Maynard. And Phipps Maynard are Ransford's solicitors! That bill, sir, comes from him! And now the other, the thousand pound one, that offers the reward to any one who can give definite information as to the circumstances attending the death of John Braden—to be paid by Mr. Beachcroft. And he's Mr. Folliot's solicitor! So—that comcs from Mr. Folliot. What has he to do with it? And are these two putting their heads together—or are these bills quite independent of each other? Hang me if I understand it!"

Bryce read and re-read the contents of the two bills. And then he thought for awhile before speaking.

"Well," he said at last, "there's probably this in it—the Folliots are very wealthy people. Mrs. Folliot, it's pretty well known, wants her son to marry Miss Bewery—Dr. Ransford's ward. Probably she doesn't wish any suspicion to hang over the family. That's all I can suggest. In the other case, Ransford wants to clear himself. For don't forget this, Mitchington!—somewhere, somebody may know something! Only something. But that something might clear Ransford of the suspicion that's undoubtedly been cast upon him. If you're thinking to get a strong case against Ransford, you've got your work set. He gave your theory a nasty knock this morning by his few words about that pill. Did Coates and Everest find a pill, now?"

"Not at liberty to say, sir," answered Mitchington. "At present, anyway. Um! I dislike these private offers of reward—it means that those who make 'em get hold of information which is kept back from us, d'you see! They're inconvenient."

Then he went away, and Bryce, after waiting awhile, until night had settled down, slipped quietly out of the house and set off for the gloom of Paradise.

CHAPTER XVI. BEFOREHAND

In accordance with his undeniable capacity for contriving and scheming, Bryce had made due and careful preparations for his visit to the tomb of Richard Jenkins. Even in the momentary confusion following upon his discovery of Collishaw's dead body, he had been sufficiently alive to his own immediate purposes to notice that the tomb—a very ancient and dilapidated structure—stood in the midst of a small expanse of stone pavement between the yew-trees and the wall of the nave; he had noticed also that the pavement consisted of small squares of stone, some of which bore initials and dates. A sharp glance at the presumed whereabouts of the particular spot which he wanted, as indicated in the scrap of paper taken from Braden's purse, showed him that he would have to raise one of those small squares—possibly two or three of them. And so he had furnished himself with a short crowbar of tempered steel, specially purchased at the iron-monger's, and with a small bull's-eye lantern. Had he been arrested and searched as he made his way towards the cathedral precincts he might reasonably have been suspected of a design to break into the treasury and appropriate the various ornaments for which Wrychester was famous. But Bryce feared neither arrest nor observation. During his residence in Wrychester he had done a good deal of prowling about the old city at night, and he knew that Paradise, at any time after dark, was a deserted place. Folk might cross from the close archway to the wicket-gate by the outer path, but no one would penetrate within the thick screen of yew and cypress when night had fallen. And now, in early summer, the screen of trees and bushes was so thick in leaf, that once within it, foliage on one side, the great walls of the nave on the other, there was little likelihood of any person overlooking his doings while he made his investigation. He anticipated a swift and quiet job, to be done in a few minutes.

But there was another individual in Wrychester who knew just as much of the geography of Paradise as Pemberton Bryce knew. Dick Bewery and Betty Campany had of late progressed out of the schoolboy and schoolgirl hail-fellow-well-met stage to the first, dawnings of love, and in spite of their frequent meetings had begun a romantic correspondence between each other, the joy and mystery of which was increased a hundredfold by a secret method of exchange of these missives. Just within the wicket-gate entrance of Paradise there was an old monument wherein was a convenient cavity—Dick Bewery's ready wits transformed this into love's post-office. In it he regularly placed letters for Betty: Betty stuffed into it letters for him. And on this particular evening Dick had gone to Paradise to collect a possible mail, and as Bryce walked leisurely up the narrow path, enclosed by trees and old masonry which led from Friary Lane to the ancient enclosure, Dick turned a corner and ran full into him. In the light of the single lamp which illumined the path, the two recovered themselves and looked at each other.

"Hullo!" said Bryce. "What's your hurry, young Bewery?"

Dick, who was panting for breath, more from excitement than haste, drew back and looked at Bryce. Up to then he knew nothing much against Bryce, whom he had rather liked in the fashion in which boys sometimes like their seniors, and he was not indisposed to confide in him.

"Hullo!" he replied. "I say! Where are you off to?"

"Nowhere!—strolling round," answered Bryce. "No particular purpose, why?"

"You weren't going in—there?" asked Dick, jerking a thumb towards Paradise.

"In—there!" exclaimed Bryce. "Good Lord, no!—dreary enough in the daytime! What should I be going in there for?"

Dick seized Bryce's coat–sleeve and dragged him aside.

"I say!" he whispered. "There's something up in there—a search of some sort!"

Bryce started in spite of an effort to keep unconcerned.

"A search? In there?" he said. "What do you mean?"

Dick pointed amongst the trees, and Bryce saw the faint glimmer of a light.

"I was in there—just now," said Dick. "And some men—three or four—came along. They're in there, close up by the nave, just where you found that chap Collishaw. They're—digging —or something of that sort!"

"Digging!" muttered Bryce. "Digging?"'

"Something like it, anyhow," replied Dick. "Listen."

Bryce heard the ring of metal on stone. And an unpleasant conviction stole over him that he was being forestalled, that somebody was beforehand with him, and he cursed himself for not having done the previous night what he had left undone till this night.

"Who are they?" he asked. "Did you see them—their faces?"

"Not their faces," answered Dick. "Only their figures in the gloom. But I heard Mitchington's voice."

"Police, then!" said Bryce. "What on earth are they after?"

"Look here!" whispered Dick, pulling at Bryce's arm again. "Come on! I know how to get in there without their seeing us. You follow me."

Bryce followed readily, and Dick stepping through the wicket–gate, seized his companion's wrist and led him amongst the bushes in the direction of the spot from whence came the metallic sounds. He walked with the step of a cat, and Bryce took pains to follow his example. And presently from behind a screen of cypresses they looked out on the expanse of flagging in the midst of which stood the tomb of Richard Jenkins.

Round about that tomb were five men whose faces were visible enough in the light thrown by a couple of strong lamps, one of which stood on the tomb itself, while the other was set on the ground. Four out of the five the two watchers recognized at once. One, kneeling on the flags, and busy with a small crowbar similar to that which Bryce carried inside his overcoat, was the master–mason of the cathedral. Another, standing near him, was Mitchington. A third was a clergyman —one of the lesser dignitaries of the Chapter. A fourth —whose presence made Bryce start for the second time that. evening—was the Duke of Saxonsteade. But the fifth was a stranger—a tall man who stood between Mitchington and the Duke, evidently paying anxious attention to the master–mason's proceedings. He was no Wrychester man–Bryce was convinced of that.

And a moment later he was convinced of another equally certain fact. Whatever these five men were searching for, they had no clear or accurate idea of its exact whereabouts. The master–mason was taking up the small squares of flagstone with his crowbar one by one, from the outer edge of the foot of the old box–tomb; as he removed each, he probed the earth beneath it. And Bryce, who had instinctively realized what was happening, and knew that somebody else than himself was in possession of the secret of the scrap of paper, saw that it would be some time before they arrived at the precise spot indicated in the Latin directions. He quietly drew back and tugged at Dick Dewery.

"Stop here, and keep quiet!" he whispered when they had retreated out of all danger of being overheard. "Watch 'em! I want to fetch somebody—want to know who that stranger is. You don't know him?"

"Never seen him before," replied Dick. "I say! come quietly back—don't give it away. I want to know what it's all about."

Bryce squeezed the lad's arm by way of assurance and made his way back through the bushes. He wanted to get hold of Harker, and at once, and he hurried round to the old man's house and without ceremony walked into his parlour. Harker, evidently expecting him, and meanwhile amusing himself with his pipe and book, rose from his chair as the younger man entered.

"Found anything?" he asked.

"We're done!" answered Bryce. "I was a fool not to go last night! We're forestalled, my friend!—that's about it!"

"By—whom?" inquired Harker.

"There are five of them at it, now," replied Bryce. "Mitchington, a mason, one of the cathedral clergy, a stranger, and the Duke of Saxonsteade! What do you think of that?"

Harker suddenly started as if a new light had dawned on him.

"The Duke!" he exclaimed. "You don't say so! My conscience! —now, I wonder if that can really be? Upon my word, I'd never thought of it!"

"Thought of what?" demanded Bryce.

"Never mind! tell you later," said Harker. "At present, is there any chance of getting a look at them?"

"That's what I came for," retorted Bryce. "I've been watching them, with young Bewery. He put me up to it. Come on! I want to see if you know the man who's a stranger."

Harker crossed the room to a chest of drawers, and after some rummaging pulled something out.

"Here!" he said, handing some articles to Bryce. "Put those on over your boots. Thick felt overshoes—you could walk round your own mother's bedroom in those and she'd never hear you. I'll do the same. A stranger, you say? Well, this is a proof that somebody knows the secret of that scrap of paper besides us, doctor!"

"They don't know the exact spot," growled Bryce, who was chafing at having been done out of his discovery. "But, they'll find it, whatever may be there."

He led Harker back to Paradise and to the place where he had left Dick Bewery, whom they approached so quietly that Bryce was by the lad's side before Dick knew he was there. And Harker, after one glance at the ring of faces, drew Bryce back and put his lips close to his ear and breathed a name in an almost imperceptible yet clear whisper.

"Glassdale!"

Bryce started for the third time. Glassdale!—the man whom Harker had seen in Wrychester within an hour or so of Braden's death: the ex−convict, the forger, who had forged the Duke of Saxonsteade's name! And there! standing, apparently quite at his ease, by the Duke's side. What did it all mean?

There was no explanation of what it meant to be had from the man whom Bryce and Harker and Dick Bewery secretly watched from behind the screen of cypress trees. Four of them watched in silence, or with no more than a whispered word now and then while the fifth worked. This man worked methodically, replacing each stone as he took it up and examined the soil beneath it. So far nothing had resulted, but he was by that time working at some distance from the tomb, and Bryce, who had an exceedingly accurate idea of where the spot might be, as indicated in the measurements on the scrap of paper, nudged Harker as the master−mason began to take up the last of the small flags. And suddenly there was a movement amongst the watchers, and the master−mason looked up from his job and motioned Mitchington to pass him a trowel which lay at a little distance.

"Something here!" he said, loudly enough to reach the ears of Bryce and his companions. "Not so deep down, neither, gentlemen!"

A few vigorous applications of the trowel, a few lumps of earth cast out of the cavity, and the master−mason put in his hand and drew forth a small parcel, which in the light of the lamp held close to it by Mitchington looked to be done up in coarse sacking, secured by great blotches of black sealing wag. And now it was Harker who nudged Bryce, drawing his attention to the fact that the parcel, handed by the master-mason to Mitchington was at once passed on by Mitchington to the Duke of Saxonsteade, who, it was very plain to see, appeared to be as much delighted as surprised at receiving it.

"Let us go to your office, inspector," he said. "We'll examine the contents there. Let us all go at once!"

The three figures behind the cypress trees remained immovable and silent until the five searchers had gone away with their lamps and tools and the sound of their retreating footsteps in Friary Lane had died out. Then Dick Bewery moved and began to slip off, and Bryce reached out a hand and took him by the shoulder.

"I say, Bewery!" he said. "Going to tell all that?"

Harker got in a word before Dick could answer.

"No matter if he does, doctor," he remarked quietly. "Whatever it is, the whole town'll know of it by tomorrow. They'll not keep it back."

Bryce let Dick go, and the boy immediately darted off in the direction of the close, while the two men went towards Harker's house. Neither spoke until they were safe in the old detective's little parlour, then Harker, turning up his lamp, looked at Bryce and shook his head.

"It's a good job I've retired!" he said, almost sadly. "I'm getting too old for my trade, doctor. Once upon a time I should have been fit to kick myself for not having twigged the meaning of this business sooner than I have done!"

"Have you twigged it?" demanded Bryce, almost scornfully. "You're a good deal cleverer than I am if you have. For hang me if I know what it means!"

"I do!" answered Harker. He opened a drawer in his desk and drew out a scrap-book, filled, as Bryce saw a moment later, with cuttings from newspapers, all duly arranged and indexed. The old man glanced at the index, turned to a certain page, and put his finger on an entry. "There you are!" he said. "And that's only one—there are several more. They'll tell you in detail what I can tell you in a few words and what I ought to have remembered. It's fifteen years since the famous robbery at Saxonsteade which has never been accounted for—robbery of the Duchess's diamonds—one of the cleverest burglaries ever known, doctor. They were got one night after a grand ball there; no arrest was ever made, they were never traced. And I'll lay all I'm worth to a penny–piece that the Duke and those men are gladding their eyes with the sight of them just now!—in Mitchington's office—and that the information that they were where they've just been found was given to the Duke by—Glassdale!"

"Glassdale! That man!" exclaimed Bryce, who was puzzling his brain over possible developments.

"That man, sir!" repeated Harker. "That's why Glassdale was in Wrychester the day of Braden's death. And that's why Braden, or Brake, came to Wrychester at all. He and Glassdale, of course, had somehow come into possession of the secret, and no doubt meant to tell the Duke together, and get the reward—there was £5,000 offered! And as Brake's dead, Glassdale's spoken, but"—here the old man paused and gave his companion a shrewd look—"the question still remains: How did Brake come to his end?"

CHAPTER XVII. TO BE SHADOWED

Dick Bewery burst in upon his sister and Ransford with a budget of news such as it rarely fell to the lot of romance–loving seventeen to tell. Secret and mysterious digging up of grave–yards by night–discovery of sealed packets, the contents of which might only be guessed at—the whole thing observed by hidden spectators—these were things he had read of in fiction, but had never expected to have the luck to see in real life. And being gifted with some powers of imagination and of narrative, he made the most of his story to a pair of highly attentive listeners, each of whom had his, and her, own reasons for particular attention.

"More mystery!" remarked Mary when Dick's story had come to an end. "What a pity they didn't open the parcel!" She looked at Ransford, who was evidently in deep thought. "I suppose it will all come out?" she suggested.

"Sure to!" he answered, and turned to Dick. "You say Bryce fetched old Harker—after you and Bryce had watched these operations a bit? Did he say why he fetched him?"

"Never said anything as to his reasons," answered Dick. "But, I rather guessed, at the end, that Bryce wanted me to keep quiet about it, only old Harker said there was no need."

Ransford made no comment on this, and Dick, having exhausted his stock of news, presently went off to bed.

"Master Bryce," observed Ransford, after a period of silence, "is playing a game! What it is, I don't know—but I'm certain of it. Well, we shall see! You've been much upset by all this," he went on, after another pause, "and the knowledge that you have has distressed me beyond measure! But just have a little—a very little—more patience, and things will be cleared—I can't tell all that's in my mind, even to you."

Mary, who had been sewing while Ransford, as was customary with him in an evening, read the Times to her, looked down at her work.

"I shouldn't care, if only these rumours in the town—about you—could be crushed!" she said. "It's so cruel, so vile, that such things—"

Ransford snapped his fingers.

"I don't care that about the rumours!" he answered, contemptuously. "They'll be crushed out just as suddenly as they arose—and then, perhaps, I'll let certain folk in Wrychester know what I think of them. And as regards the suspicion against me, I know already that the only people in the town for whose opinion I care fully accept what I said before the Coroner. As to the others, let them talk! If the thing comes to a head before its due time—"

"You make me think that you know more—much more!—than you've ever told me!" interrupted Mary.

"So I do!" he replied. "And you'll see in the end why I've kept silence. Of course, if people who don't know as much will interfere—"

He was interrupted there by the ringing of the front door bell, at the sound of which he and Mary looked at each other.

"Who can that be?" said Mary. "It's past ten o'clock."

Ransford offered no suggestion. He sat silently waiting, until the parlourmaid entered.

"Inspector Mitchington would be much obliged if you could give him a few minutes, sir," she said.

Ransford got up from his chair.

"Take Inspector Mitchington into the study," he said. "Is he alone?"

"No, sir—there's a gentleman with him," replied the girl.

"All right—I'll be with them presently," answered Ransford. "Take them both in there and light the gas. Police!" he went on, when the parlourmaid had gone. "They get hold of the first idea that strikes them, and never even look round for another, You're not frightened?"

"Frightened—no! Uneasy—yes!" replied Mary. "What can they want, this time of night"

"Probably to tell me something about this romantic tale of Dick's," answered Ransford, as he left the room. "It'll be nothing more serious, I assure you."

But he was not so sure of that. He was very well aware that the Wrychester police authorities had a definite suspicion of his guilt in the Braden and Collishaw matters, and he knew from experience that police suspicion is a difficult matter to dissipate. And before he opened the door of the little room which he used as a study he warned himself to be careful—and silent.

The two visitors stood near the hearth—Ransford took a good look at them as he closed the door behind him. Mitchington he knew well enough; he was more interested in the other man, a stranger. A quiet-looking, very ordinary individual, who might have been half a dozen things—but Ransford instantly set him down as a detective. He turned from this man to the inspector.

"Well?" he said, a little brusquely. "What is it?"

"Sorry to intrude so late, Dr. Ransford," answered Mitchington, "but I should be much obliged if you would give us a bit of information—badly wanted, doctor, in view of recent events," he added, with a smile which was meant to be reassuring. "I'm sure you can—if you will."

"Sit down," said Ransford, pointing to chairs. He took one himself and again glanced at the stranger. "To whom am I speaking, in addition to yourself, Inspector?" he asked. "I'm not going to talk to strangers."

"Oh, well!" said Mitchington, a little awkwardly. "Of course, doctor, we've had to get a bit of professional help in these unpleasant matters. This gentleman's Detective–Sergeant Jettison, from the Yard."

"What information do you want?" asked Ransford.

Mitchington glanced at the door and lowered his voice. "I may as well tell you, doctor," he said confidentially, "there's been a most extraordinary discovery made tonight, which has a bearing on the Braden case. I dare say you've heard of the great jewel robbery which took place at the Duke of Saxonsteade's some years ago, which has been a mystery to this very day?"

"I have heard of it," answered Ransford.

"Very well—tonight those jewels—the whole lot!—have been discovered in Paradise yonder, where they'd been buried, at the time of the robbery, by the thief," continued Mitchington. "They've just been examined, and they're now in the Duke's own hands again—after all these years! And—I may as well tell you—we now know that the object of Braden's visit to Wrychester was to tell the Duke where those jewels were hidden. Braden—and another man—had learned the secret, from the real thief, who's dead in Australia. All that I may tell you, doctor—for it'll be public property tomorrow."

"Well?" said Ransford.

Mitchington hesitated a moment, as if searching for his next words. He glanced at the detective; the detective remained immobile; he glanced at Ransford; Ransford gave him no encouragement.

"Now look here, doctor!" he exclaimed, suddenly. "Why not tell us something? We know now who Braden really was! That's settled. Do you understand?"

"Who was he, then?" asked Ransford, quietly.

"He was one John Brake, some time manager of a branch of a London bank, who, seventeen years ago, got ten years' penal servitude for embezzlement," answered Mitchington, watching Ransford steadily. "That's dead certain—we know it! The man who shared this secret with him about the Saxonsteade jewels has told us that much, today. John Brake!"

"What have you come here for?" asked Ransford.

"To ask you—between ourselves—if you can tell us anything about Brake's earlier days—antecedents—that'll help us," replied Mitchington. "It may be—Jettison here—a man of experience—thinks it'll be found to be—that Brake, or Braden as we call him—was murdered because of his possession of that secret about the jewels. Our informant tells us that Braden certainly had on him, when he came to Wrychester, a sort of diagram showing the exact location of the spot where the jewels were hidden—that diagram was most assuredly not found on Braden when we examined his clothing and effects. It may be that it was wrested from him in the gallery of the clerestory that morning, and that his assailant, or assailants—for there may have been two men at the job—afterwards pitched him through that open doorway, after half–stifling him. And if that theory's correct—and I, personally, am now quite inclined to it—it'll help a lot if you'll tell us what you know of Braden's—Brake's —antecedents. Come now, doctor!—you know very well that Braden, or Brake, did come to your surgery that morning and said to your assistant that he'd known a Dr. Ransford in times past! Why not speak?"

Ransford, instead of answering Mitchington's evidently genuine appeal, looked at the New Scotland Yard man.

"Is that your theory?" he asked.

Jettison nodded his head, with a movement indicative of conviction.

"Yes, sir!" he replied. "Having regard to all the circumstances of the case, as they've been put before me since I came here, and with special regard to the revelations which have resulted in the discovery of these jewels, it is! Of course, today's events have altered everything. If it hadn't been for our informant—"

"Who is your informant?" inquired Ransford.

The two callers looked at each other—the detective nodded at the inspector.

"Oh, well!" said Mitchington. "No harm in telling you, doctor. A man named Glassdale—once a fellow-convict with Brake. It seems they left England together after their time was up, emigrated together, prospered, even went so far—both of 'em!—as to make good the money they'd appropriated, and eventually came back together—in possession of this secret. Brake came specially to Wrychester to tell the Duke—Glassdale was to join him on the very morning Brake met his death. Glassdale did come to the town that morning—and as soon as he got here, heard of Brake's strange death. That upset him—and he went away—only to come back today, go to Saxonsteade, and tell everything to the Duke—with the result we've told you of."

"Which result," remarked Ransford, steadily regarding Mitchington, "has apparently altered all your ideas about —me!"

Mitchington laughed a little awkwardly.

"Oh, well, come, now, doctor!" he said. "Why, yes—frankly, I'm inclined to Jettison's theory—in fact, I'm certain that's the truth."

"And your theory," inquired Ransford, turning to the detective, "is—put it in a few words."

"My theory–and I'll lay anything it's the correct one!—is this," replied Jettison. "Brake came to Wrychester with his secret. That secret wasn't confined to him and Glassdale —either he let it out to somebody, or it was known to somebody. I understand from Inspector Mitchington here that on the evening of his arrival Brake was away from the

Mitre Hotel for two hours. During that time, he was somewhere—with whom? Probably with somebody who got the secret out of him, or to whom he communicated it. For, think!—according to Glassdale, who, we are quite sure, has told the exact truth about everything, Brake had on him a scrap of paper, on which were instructions, in Latin, for finding the exact spot whereat the missing Saxonsteade jewels had been hidden, years before, by the actual thief—who, I may tell you, sir, never had the opportunity of returning to re–possess himself of them. Now, after Brake's death, the police examined his clothes and effects—they never found that scrap of paper! And I work things out this way. Brake was followed into that gallery—a lonely, quiet place—by the man or men who had got possession of the secret; he was, I'm told, a slightly–built, not over–strong man—he was seized and robbed of that paper and flung to his death. And all that fits in with the second mystery of Collishaw—who probably knew, if not everything, then something, of the exact circumstances of Brake's death, and let his knowledge get to the ears of—Brake's assailant! —who cleverly got rid of him. That's my notion," concluded the detective. "And—I shall be surprised if it isn't a correct one!"

"And, as I've said, doctor," chimed in Mitchington, "can't you give us a bit of information, now? You see the line we're on? Now, as it's evident you once knew Braden, or Brake—"

"I have never said so!" interrupted Ransford sharply.

"Well—we infer it, from the undoubted fact that he called here," remarked Mitchington. "And if—"

"Wait!" said Ransford. He had been listening with absorbed attention to Jettison's theory, and he now rose from his chair and began to pace the room, hands in pockets, as if in deep thought. Suddenly he paused and looked at Mitchington. "This needs some reflection," he said. "Are you pressed for time?"

"Not in the least," answered Mitchington, readily. "Our time's yours, sir. Take as long as you like."

Ransford touched a bell and summoning the parlourmaid told her to fetch whisky, soda, and cigars. He pressed these things on the two men, lighted a cigar himself, and for a long time continued to walk up and down his end of the room, smoking and evidently in very deep thought. The visitors left him alone, watching him curiously now and then—until, when quite ten minutes had gone by, he suddenly drew a chair close to them and sat down again.

"Now, listen to me!" he said. "If I give my confidence to you, as police officials, will you give me your word that you won't make use of my information until I give you leave—or until you have consulted me further? I shall rely on your word, mind!"

"I say yes to that, doctor," answered Mitchington.

"The same here, sir," said the detective.

"Very well," continued Ransford. "Then—this is between ourselves, until such time as I say something more about it. First of all, I am not going to tell you anything whatever about Braden's antecedents—at present! Secondly—I am not sure that your theory, Mr. Jettison, is entirely correct, though I think it is by way of coming very near to the right one—which is sure to be worked out before long. But—on the understanding of secrecy for the present I can tell you something which I should not have been able to tell you but for the events of tonight, which have made me put together certain facts. Now attention! To begin with, I know where Braden was for at any rate some time on the evening of the day on which he came to Wrychester. He was with the old man whom we all know as Simpson Harker."

Mitchington whistled; the detective, who knew nothing of Simpson Harker, glanced at him as if for information. But Mitchington nodded at Ransford, and Ransford went on.

"I know this for this reason," he continued. "You know where Harker lives. I was in attendance for nearly two hours that evening on a patient in a house opposite—I spent a good deal of time in looking out of the window. I saw Harker take a man into his house: I saw the man leave the house nearly an hour later: I recognized that man next day as the man who met his death at the Cathedral. So much for that."

"Good!" muttered Mitchington. "Good! Explains a lot."

"But," continued Ransford, "what I have to tell you now is of a much more serious—and confidential—nature. Now, do you know—but, of course, you don't!—that your proceedings tonight were watched?"

"Watched" exclaimed Mitchington. "Who watched us?"

"Harker, for one," answered Ransford. "And—for another—my late assistant, Mr. Pemberton Bryce."

Mitchington's jaw dropped.

"God bless my soul!" he said. "You don't mean it, doctor! Why, how did you—"

"Wait a minute," interrupted Ransford. He left the room, and the two callers looked at each other.

"This chap knows more than you think," observed Jettison in a whisper. "More than he's telling now!"

"Let's get all we can, then," said Mitchington, who was obviously much surprised by Ransford's last information. "Get it while he's in the mood."

"Let him take his own time," advised Jettison. "But—you mark me!—he knows a lot! This is only an instalment."

Ransford came back—with Dick Bewery, clad in a loud patterned and gaily coloured suit of pyjamas.

"Now, Dick," said Ransford. "Tell Inspector Mitchington precisely what happened this evening, within your own knowledge."

Dick was nothing loth to tell his story for the second time —especially to a couple of professional listeners. And he told it in full detail, from the moment of his sudden encounter with Bryce to that in which he parted with Bryce and Harker. Ransford, watching the official faces, saw what it was in the story that caught the official attention and excited the official mind.

"Dr: Bryce went off at once to fetch Harker, did he?" asked Mitchington, when Dick had made a end.

"At once," answered Dick. "And was jolly quick back with him!"

"And Harker said it didn't matter about your telling as it would be public news soon enough?" continued Mitchington.

"Just that," said Dick.

Mitchington looked at Ransford, and Ransford nodded to his ward.

"All right, Dick," he said, "That'll do,"

The boy went off again, and Mitchington shook his head.

"Queer!" he said. "Now what have those two been up to? —something, that's certain. Can you tell us more, doctor?"

"Under the same conditions—yes," answered Ransford, taking his seat again. "The fact is, affairs have got to a stage where I consider it my duty to tell you more. Some of what I shall tell you is hearsay—but it's hearsay that you can easily verify for yourselves when the right moment comes. Mr. Campany, the librarian, lately remarked to me that my old assistant, Mr. Bryce, seemed to be taking an extraordinary interest in archaeological matters since he left me—he was now, said Campany, always examining documents about the old tombs and monuments of the Cathedral and its precincts."

"Ah—just so!" exclaimed Mitchington. "To be sure!—I'm beginning to see!"

"And," continued Ransford, "Campany further remarked, as a matter for humorous comment, that Bryce was also spending much time looking round our old tombs. Now you made this discovery near an old tomb, I understand?"

"Close by one—yes," assented the inspector.

"Then let me draw your attention to one or two strange facts —which are undoubted facts," continued Ransford. "Bryce was left alone with the dead body of Braden for some minutes, while Varner went to fetch the police. That's one."

"That's true," muttered Mitchington. "He was—several minutes!"

"Bryce it was who discovered Collishaw—in Paradise," said Ransford. "That's fact two. And fact three—Bryce evidently had a motive in fetching Harker tonight—to overlook your operations. What was his motive? And taking things altogether; what are, or have been, these secret affairs which Bryce and Harker have evidently been engaged in?"

Jettison suddenly rose, buttoning his light overcoat. The action seemed to indicate a newly–formed idea, a definite conclusion. He turned sharply to Mitchington.

"There's one thing certain, inspector," he said. "You'll keep an eye on those two from this out! From—just now!"

"I shall!" assented Mitchington. "I'll have both of 'em shadowed wherever they go or are, day or night. Harker, now, has always been a bit of a mystery, but Bryce—hang me if I don't believe he's been having me! Double game!—but, never mind. There's no more, doctor?"

"Not yet," replied Ransford. "And I don't know the real meaning or value of what I have told you. But—in two days from now, I can tell you more. In the meantime—remember your promise!"

He let his visitors out then, and went back to Mary.

"You'll not have to wait long for things to clear," he said. "The mystery's nearly over!"

CHAPTER XVIII. SURPRISE

Mitchington and the man from New Scotland Yard walked away in silence from Ransford's house and kept the silence up until they were in the middle of the Close and accordingly in solitude. Then Mitchington turned to his companion.

"What d'ye think of that?" he asked, with a half laugh. "Different complexion it puts on things, eh?"

"I think just what I said before—in there," replied the detective. "That man knows more than he's told, even now!"

"Why hasn't he spoken sooner, then?" demanded Mitchington. "He's had two good chance—at the inquests."

"From what I saw of him, just now," said Jettison, "I should say he's the sort of man who can keep his own counsel till he considers the right time has come for speaking. Not the sort of man who'll care twopence whatever's said about him, you understand? I should say he's known a good lot all along, and is just keeping it back till he can put a finishing touch to it. Two days, didn't he say? Aye, well, a lot can happen in two days!"

"But about your theory?" questioned Mitchington. "What do you think of it now—in relation to what we've just heard?"

"I'll tell you what I can see," answered Jettison. "I can see how one bit of this puzzle fits into another—in view of what Ransford has just told us. Of course, one's got to do a good deal of supposing it's unavoidable in these cases. Now supposing Braden let this man Harker into the secret of the hidden jewels that night, and supposing that Harker and Bryce are in collusion—as they evidently are, from what that boy told us—and supposing they between them, together or separately, had to do with Braden's death, and supposing that man Collishaw saw some thing that would incriminate one or both—eh?"

"Well?" asked Mitchington.

"Bryce is a medical man," observed Jettison. "It would be an easy thing for a medical man to get rid of Collishaw as he undoubtedly was got rid of. Do you see my point?"

"Aye—and I can see that Bryce is a clever hand at throwing dust in anybody's eyes!" muttered Mitchington. "I've had some dealings with him over this affair and I'm beginning to think —only now!—that he's been having me for the mug! He's evidently a deep 'un—and so's the other man."

"I wanted to ask you that," said Jettison. "Now, exactly who are these two?—tell me about them—both."

"Not so much to tell," answered Mitchington. "Harker's a quiet old chap who lives in a little house over there—just off that far corner of this Close. Said to be a retired tradesman, from London. Came here a few years ago, to settle down. Inoffensive, pleasant old chap. Potters about the town—puts in his time as such old chaps do—bit of reading at the libraries—bit of gossip here and—there you know the sort. Last man in the world I should have thought would have been mixed up in an affair of this sort!"

"And therefore all the more likely to be!" said Jettison. "Well—the other?"

"Bryce was until the very day of Braden's appearance, Ransford's assistant," continued Mitchington. "Been with Ransford about two years. Clever chap, undoubtedly, but certainly deep and, in a way, reserved, though he can talk plenty if he's so minded and it's to his own advantage. He left Ransford suddenly—that very morning. I don't know why. Since then he's remained in the town. I've heard that he's pretty keen on Ransford's ward—sister of that lad we saw tonight. I don't know myself, if it's true—but I've wondered if that had anything to do with his leaving Ransford so suddenly."

"Very likely," said Jettison. They had crossed the Close by that time and come to a gas–lamp which stood at the entrance, and the detective pulled out his watch and glanced at it. "Ten past eleven," he said. "You say you know this Bryce pretty well? Now, would it be too late—if he's up still—to take a look at him! If you and he are on good terms, you could make an excuse. After what I've heard, I'd like to get at close quarters with this gentleman."

"Easy enough," assented Mitchington. "I've been there as late as this—he's one of the sort that never goes to bed before midnight. Come on!—it's close by. But—not a word of where we've been. I'll say I've dropped in to give him a bit of news. We'll tell him about the jewel business—and see how he takes it. And while we're there—size him up!"

Mitchington was right in his description of Bryce's habits —Bryce rarely went to bed before one o'clock in the morning. He liked to sit up, reading. His. favourite mental food was found in the lives of statesmen and diplomatists, most of them of the sort famous for trickery and chicanery—he not only made a close study of the ways of these gentry but wrote down notes and abstracts of passages which particularly appealed to him. His lamp was burning when Mitchington and Jettison came in view of his windows—but that night Bryce was doing no thinking about statecraft: his mind was fixed on his own affairs. He had lighted his fire on going home and for an hour had sat with his legs stretched out on the fender, carefully weighing things up. The event of the night had convinced him that he was at a critical phase of his present adventure, and it behoved him, as a good general, to review his forces.

The forestalling of his plans about the hiding–place in Paradise had upset Bryce's schemes—he had figured on being able to turn that secret, whatever it was, to his own advantage. It struck him now, as he meditated, that he had never known exactly what he expected to get out of that secret—but he had hoped that it would have been something which would make a few more considerable and tightly—strung meshes in the net which he was endeavouring to weave around Ransford. Now he was faced by the fact that it was not going to yield anything in the way of help—it was a secret no longer, and it had yielded nothing beyond the mere knowledge that John Braden, who was in reality John Brake, had carried the secret to Warchester—to reveal it in the proper quarter. That helped Bryce in no way—so far as he could see. And therefore it was necessary to re–state his case to himself; to take stock; to see where he stood—and more than all, to put plainly before his own mind exactly what he wanted.

And just before Mitchington and the detective came up the path to his door, Bryce had put his notions into clear phraseology. His aim was definite—he wanted to get Ransford completely into his power, through suspicion of Ransford's guilt in the affairs of Braden and Collishaw. He wanted, at the same time, to have the means of exonerating him—whether by fact or by craft—so that, as an ultimate method of success for his own projects he would be able to go to Mary Bewery and say "Ransford's very life is at my mercy: if I keep silence, he's lost: if I speak, he's saved: it's now for you to say whether I'm to speak or hold my tongue—and you're the price I want for my speaking to save him!" It was in accordance with his views of human nature that Mary Bewery would accede to his terms: he had not known her and Ransford for nothing, and he was aware that she had a profound gratitude for her guardian, which might even be akin to a yet unawakened warmer feeling. The probability was that she would willingly sacrifice herself to save Ransford—and Bryce cared little by what means he won her, fair or foul, so long as he was successful. So now, he said to himself, he must make a still more definite move against Ransford. He must strengthen and deepen the suspicions which the

139

police already had: he must give them chapter and verse and supply them with information, and get Ransford into the tightest of corners, solely that, in order to win Mary Bewery, he might have the credit of pulling him out again. That, he felt certain, he could do—if he could make a net in which to enclose Ransford he could also invent a two–edged sword which would cut every mesh of that net into fragments. That would be—child's play—mere statecraft —elementary diplomacy. But first—to get Ransford fairly bottled up—that was the thing! He determined to lose no more time—and he was thinking of visiting Mitchington immediately after breakfast neat morning when Mitchington knocked at his door.

Bryce was rarely taken back, and on seeing Mitchington and a companion, he forthwith invited them into his parlour, put out his whisky and cigars, and pressed both on them as if their late call were a matter of usual occurrence. And when he had helped both to a drink, he took one himself, and tumbler in hand, dropped into his easy chair again.

"We saw your light, doctor—so I took the liberty of dropping into tell you a bit of news," observed the inspector. "But I haven't introduced my friend—this is Detective–Sergeant Jettison, of the Yard—we've got him down about this business —must have help, you know."

Bryce gave the detective a half–sharp, half–careless look and nodded.

"Mr. Jettison will have abundant opportunities for the exercise of his talents!" he observed in his best cynical manner. "I dare say he's found that out already."

"Not an easy affair, sir, to be sure," assented Jettison. "Complicated!"

"Highly so!" agreed Bryce. He yawned, ands glanced at the inspector. "What's your news, Mitchington?" he asked, almost indifferently.

"Oh, well!" answered Mitchington. "As the Herald's published tomorrow you'll see it in there, doctor—I've supplied an account for this week's issue; just a short one—but I thought you'd like to know. You've heard of the famous jewel robbery at the Duke's, some years ago? Yes?—well, we've found all the whole bundle tonight—buried in Paradise! And how do you think the secret came out?"

The Paradise Mystery

"No good at guessing," said Bryce.

"It came out," continued Mitchington, "through a man who, with Braden—Braden, mark you!—got in possession of it—it's a long story—and, with Braden, was going to reveal it to the Duke that very day Braden was killed. This man waited until this very morning and then told his Grace—his Grace came with him to us this afternoon, and tonight we made a search and found—everything! Buried—there in Paradise! Dug 'em up, doctor!"

Bryce showed no great interest. He took a leisurely sip at his liquor and set down the glass and pulled out his cigarette case. The two men, watching him narrowly, saw that his fingers were steady as rocks as he struck the match.

"Yes," he said as he threw the match away. "I saw you busy."

In spite of himself Mitchington could not repress a start nor a glance at Jettison. But Jettison was as imperturbable as Bryce himself, and Mitchington raised a forced laugh.

"You did!" he said, incredulously. "And we thought we had it all to ourselves! How did you come to know, doctor?"

"Young Bewery told me what was going on," replied Bryce, "so I took a look at you. And I fetched old Harker to take a look, too. We all watched you—the boy, Harker, and I—out of sheer curiosity, of course. We saw you get up the parcel. But, naturally, I didn't know what was in it—till now."

Mitchington, thoroughly taken aback by this candid statement, was at a loss for words, and again he glanced at Jettison. But Jettison gave no help, and Mitchington fell back on himself.

"So you fetched old Harker?" he said. "What—what for, doctor? If one may ask, you know."

Bryce made a careless gesture with his cigarette.

"Oh—old Harker's deeply interested in what's going on," he answered. "And as young Bewery drew my attention to your proceedings, why, I thought I'd draw Harker's. And

141

Harker was—interested."

Mitchington hesitated before saying more. But eventually he risked a leading question.

"Any special reason why he should be, doctor?" he asked.

Bryce put his thumbs in the armholes of his waistcoat and looked half–lazily at his questioner.

"Do you know who old Harker really is?" he inquired.

"No!" answered Mitchington. "I know nothing about him—except that he's said to be a retired tradesman, from London, who settled down here some time ago."

Bryce suddenly turned on Jettison.

"Do you?" he asked.

"I, sir!" exclaimed Jettison. "I don't know this gentleman —at all!"

Bryce laughed—with his usual touch of cynical sneering.

"I'll tell you—now—who old Harker is, Mitchington," he said. "You may as well know. I thought Mr. Jettison might recognize the name. Harker is no retired London tradesman—he's a retired member of your profession, Mr. Jettison. He was in his day one of the smartest men in the service of your department. Only he's transposed his name—ask them at the Yard if they remember Harker Simpson? That seems to startle you, Mitchington! Well, as you're here, perhaps I'd better startle you a bit more."

CHAPTER XIX. THE SUBTILTY OF THE DEVIL

There was a sudden determination and alertness in Bryce's last words which contrasted strongly, and even strangely, with the almost cynical indifference's that had characterized him since his visitors came in, and the two men recognized it and glanced questioningly at each other. There was an alteration, too, in his manner; instead of lounging lazily in his chair, as if he had no other thought than of personal ease, he was now sitting erect, looking sharply from one man to the other; his whole attitude, bearing, speech seemed to indicate that he had suddenly made up his mind to adopt some definite course of action.

"I'll tell you more!" he repeated. "And, since you're here —now!"

Mitchington, who felt a curious uneasiness, gave Jettison another glance. And this time it was Jettison who spoke.

"I should say," he remarked quietly, "knowing what I've gathered of the matter, that we ought to be glad of any information Dr. Bryce can give us."

"Oh, to be sure!" assented Mitchington. "You know more, then, doctor?"

Bryce motioned his visitors to draw their chairs nearer to his, and when he spoke it was in the low, concentrated tones of a man who means business—and confidential business.

"Now look here, Mitchington," he said, "and you, too, Mr. Jettison, as you're on this job—I'm going to talk straight to both of you. And to begin with, I'll make a bold assertion—I know more of this Wrychester Paradise mystery—involving the deaths of both Braden and Collishaw, than any man living —because, though you don't know it, Mitchington, I've gone right into it. And I'll tell you in confidence why I went into it—I want to marry Dr. Ransford's ward, Miss Bewery!"

Bryce accompanied this candid admission with a look which seemed to say: Here we are, three men of the world, who know what things are—we understand each other! And while Jettison merely nodded comprehendingly, Mitchington put his thoughts into words.

"To be sure, doctor, to be sure!" he said. "And accordingly —what's their affair, is yours! Of course!"

"Something like that," assented Bryce. "Naturally no man wishes to marry unless he knows as much as he can get to know about the woman he wants, her family, her antecedents—and all that. Now, pretty nearly everybody in Wrychester who knows them, knows that there's a mystery about Dr. Ransford and his two wards—it's been talked of, no end, amongst the old dowagers and gossips of the Close, particularly—you know what they are! Miss Bewery herself, and her brother, young Dick, in a lesser degree, know there's a mystery. And if there's one man in the world who knows the secret, it's Ransford. And, up to now, Ransford won't tell—he won't even tell Miss Bewery. I know that she's asked him—he keeps up an obstinate silence. And so—I determined to find things out for myself."

"Aye—and when did you start on that little game, now, doctor?" asked Mitchington. "Was it before, or since, this affair developed?"

"In a really serious way—since," replied Bryce. "What happened on the day of Braden's death made me go thoroughly into the whole matter. Now, what did happen? I'll tell you frankly, now, Mitchington, that when we talked once before about this affair, I didn't tell you all I might have told. I'd my reasons for reticence. But now I'll give you full particulars of what happened that morning within my knowledge—pay attention, both of you, and you'll see how one thing fits into another. That morning, about half-past nine, Ransford left his surgery and went across the Close. Not long after he'd gone, this man Braden came to the door, and asked me if Dr. Ransford was in? I said he wasn't—he'd just gone out, and I showed the man in which direction. He said he'd once known a Dr. Ransford, and went away. A little later, I followed. Near the entrance of Paradise, I saw Ransford leaving the west porch of the Cathedral. He was undeniably in a state of agitation—pale, nervous. He didn't see me. I went on and met Varner, who told me of the accident. I went with him to the foot of St. Wrytha's Stair and found the man who had recently called at the surgery. He died just as I reached him. I sent for you. When you came, I went back to the surgery—I found Ransford there in a state of most unusual agitation—he looked like a man who has had a terrible shock. So much for these events. Put them together."

Bryce paused awhile, as if marshalling his facts.

"Now, after that," he continued presently, "I began to investigate matters myself—for my own satisfaction. And very soon I found out certain things—which I'll summarize, briefly, because some of my facts are doubtless known to you already. First of all—the man who came here as John Braden was, in reality, one John Brake. He was at one time manager of a branch of a well-known London banking company. He appropriated money from them under apparently mysterious circumstances of which I, as yet, knew nothing; he was prosecuted, convicted, and sentenced to ten years' penal servitude. And those two wards of Ransford's, Mary and Richard Bewery, as they are called, are, in reality, Mary and Richard Brake—his children."

"You've established that as a fact?" asked Jettison, who was listening with close attention. "It's not a surmise on your part?"

Bryce hesitated before replying to this question. After all, he reflected, it was a surmise. He could not positively prove his assertion.

"Well," he answered after a moment's thought, "I'll qualify that by saying that from the evidence I have, and from what I know, I believe it to be an indisputable fact. What I do know of fact, hard, positive fact, is this:—John Brake married a Mary Bewery at the parish church of Braden Medworth, near Barthorpe, in Leicestershire: I've seen the entry in the register with my own eyes. His best man, who signed the register as a witness, was Mark Ransford. Brake and Ransford, as young men, had been in the habit of going to Braden Medworth to fish; Mary Bewery was governess at the vicarage there. It was always supposed she would marry Ransford; instead, she married Brake, who, of course, took her off to London. Of their married life, I know nothing. But within a few years, Brake was in trouble, for the reason I have told you. He was arrested—and Harker was the man who arrested him."

"Dear me!" exclaimed Mitchington. "Now, if I'd only known—"

"You'll know a lot before I'm through," said Bryce. "Now, Harker, of course, can tell a lot—yet it's unsatisfying. Brake could make no defence—but his counsel threw out strange hints and suggestions—all to the effect that Brake had been cruelly and wickedly deceived—in fact, as it were, trapped into doing what he did. And—by a man whom he'd trusted as a close friend. So much came to Harker's ears—but no more, and on that particular point I've no light. Go on from that to Brake's private affairs. At the time of his arrest he had a wife and two very young children. Either just before, or at, or immediately after his arrest they completely disappeared—and Brake himself utterly refused to say one single word about them. Harker asked if he could do anything —Brake's answer was that no one was to concern himself. He preserved an obstinate silence on that point. The clergyman in whose family Mrs. Brake had been governess saw Brake, after his conviction—Brake would say nothing to him. Of Mrs. Brake, nothing more is known—to me at any rate. What was known at the time is this—Brake communicated to all who came in contact with him, just then, the idea of a man who has been cruelly wronged and deceived, who takes refuge in sullen silence, and who is already planning and cherishing—revenge!"

"Aye, aye!" muttered Mitchington. "Revenge?—just Sol"

"Brake, then," continued Bryce, "goes off to his term of penal servitude, and so disappears—until he reappears here in Wrychester. Leave him for a moment, and go back. And—it's a going back, no doubt, to supposition and to theory—but there's reason in what I shall advance. We know—beyond doubt—that Brake had been tricked and deceived, in some money matter, by some man—some mysterious man—whom he referred to as having been his closest friend. We know, too, that there was extraordinary mystery in the disappearance of his wife and children. Now, from all that has been found out, who was Brake's closest friend? Ransford! And of Ransford, at that time, there's no trace. He, too, disappeared—that's a fact which I've established. Years later, he reappears—here at Wrychester, where he's bought a practice. Eventually he has two young people, who are represented as his wards, come to live with him. Their name is Bewery. The name of the young woman whom John Brake married was Bewery. What's the inference? That their mother's dead—that they're known under her maiden name: that they, without a shadow of doubt, are John Brake's children. And that leads up to my theory—which I'll now tell you in confidence—if you wish for it."

"It's what I particularly wish for," observed Jettison quietly. "The very thing!"

"Then, it's this," said Bryce. "Ransford was the close friend who tricked and deceived Brake:

"He probably tricked him in some money affair, and deceived him in his domestic affairs. I take it that Ransford ran away with Brake's wife, and that Brake, sooner than air all his grievance to the world, took it silently and began to concoct his ideas of revenge. I put the whole thing this way. Ransford ran away with Mrs. Brake and the two children—mere infants—and disappeared. Brake, when he came out of prison, went abroad—possibly with the idea of tracking them. Meanwhile, as is quite evident, he engaged in business and did well. He came back to England as John Braden, and, for the reason of which you're aware, he paid a visit to Wrychester, utterly unaware that any one known to him lived here. Now, try to reconstruct what happened. He looks round the

The Paradise Mystery

Close that morning. He sees the name of Dr. Mark Ransford on the brass plate of a surgery door. He goes to the surgery, asks a question, makes a remark, goes away. What is the probable sequence of events? He meets Ransford near the Cathedral —where Ransford certainly was. They recognize each other —most likely they turn aside, go up to that gallery as a quiet place, to talk—there is an altercation—blows—somehow or other, probably from accident, Braden is thrown through that open doorway, to his death. And—Collishaw saw what happened!"

Bryce was watching his listeners, turning alternately from one to the other. But it needed little attention on his part to see that theirs was already closely strained; each man was eagerly taking in all that he said and suggested. And he went on emphasizing every point as he made it.

"Collishaw saw what happened?" he repeated. "That, of course, is theory—supposition. But now we pass from theory back to actual fact. I'll tell you something now, Mitchington, which you've never heard of, I'm certain. I made it in my way, after Collishaw's death, to get some information, secretly, from his widow, who's a fairly shrewd, intelligent woman for her class. Now, the widow, in looking over her husband's effects, in a certain drawer in which he kept various personal matters, came across the deposit book of a Friendly Society of which Collishaw had been a member for some years. It appears that he, Collishaw, was something of a saving man, and every year he managed to put by a bit of money out of his wages, and twice or thrice in the year he took these savings—never very much; merely a pound or two—to this Friendly Society, which, it seems, takes deposits in that way from its members. Now, in this book is an entry—I saw it—which shows that only two days before his death, Collishaw paid fifty pounds—fifty pounds, mark you!—into the Friendly Society. Where should Collishaw get fifty pounds, all of a sudden! He was a mason's labourer, earning at the very outside twenty–six or eight shillings a week. According to his wife, there was no one to leave him a legacy. She never heard of his receipt of this money from any source. But—there's the fact! What explains it? My theory—that the rumour that Collishaw, with a pint too much ale in him, had hinted that he could say something about Braden's death if he chose, had reached Braden's assailant; that he had made it his business to see Collishaw and had paid him that fifty pounds as hush–money—and, later, had decided to rid himself of Collishaw altogether, as he undoubtedly did, by poison."

Once more Bryce paused—and once more the two listeners showed their attention by complete silence.

"Now we come to the question—how was Collishaw poisoned?" continued Bryce. "For poisoned he was, without doubt. Here we go back to theory and supposition once more. I haven't the least doubt that the hydrocyanic acid which caused his death was taken by him in a pill—a pill that was in that box which they found on him, Mitchington, and showed me. But that particular pill, though precisely similar in appearance, could not be made up of the same ingredients which were in the other pills. It was probably a thickly coated bill which contained the poison;—in solution of course. The coating would melt almost as soon as the man had swallowed it—and death would result instantaneously. Collishaw, you may say, was condemned to death when he put that box of pills in his waistcoat pocket. It was mere chance, mere luck, as to when the exact moment of death came to him. There had been six pills in that box—there were five left. So Collishaw picked out the poisoned pill–first! It might have been delayed till the sixth dose, you see—but he was doomed."

Mitchington showed a desire to speak, and Bryce paused.

"What about what Ransford said before the Coroner?" asked Mitchington. "He demanded certain information about the post–mortem, you know, which, he said, ought to have shown that there was nothing poisonous in those pills."

"Pooh!" exclaimed Bryce contemptuously. "Mere bluff! Of such a pill as that I've described there'd be no trace but the sugar coating—and the poison. I tell you, I haven't the least doubt that that was how the poison was administered. It was easy. And—who is there that would know how easily it could be administered but—a medical man?"

Mitchington and Jettison exchanged glances. Then Jettison leaned nearer to Bryce.

"So your theory is that Ransford got rid of both Braden and Collishaw—murdered both of them, in fact?" he suggested. "Do I understand that's what it really comes to—in plain words?"

"Not quite," replied Bryce. "I don't say that Ransford meant to kill Braden—my notion is that they met, had an altercation, probably a struggle, and that Braden lost his life in it.

148

But as regards Collishaw—"

"Don't forget!" interrupted Mitchington. "Varner swore that he saw Braden flung through that doorway! Flung out! He saw a hand."

"For everything that Varner could prove to the contrary," answered Bryce, "the hand might have been stretched out to pull Braden back. No—I think there may have been accident in that affair. But, as regards Collishaw—murder, without doubt—deliberate!"

He lighted another cigarette, with the air of a man who had spoken his mind, and Mitchington, realizing that he had said all he had to say, got up from his seat.

"Well—it's all very interesting and very clever, doctor," he said, glancing at Jettison. "And we shall keep it all in mind. Of course, you've talked all this over with Harker? I should like to know what he has to say. Now that you've told us who he is, I suppose we can talk to him?"

"You'll have to wait a few days, then," said Bryce. "He's gone to town—by the last train tonight—on this business. I've sent him. I had some information today about Ransford's whereabouts during the time of disappearance, and I've commissioned Harker to examine into it. When I hear what he's found out, I'll let you know."

"You're taking some trouble," remarked Mitchington.

"I've told you the reason," answered Bryce.

Mitchington hesitated a little; then, with a motion of his head towards the door, beckoned Jettison to follow him.

"All right," he said. "There's plenty for us to see into, I'm thinking!"

Bryce laughed and pointed to a shelf of books near the fireplace.

"Do you know what Napoleon Bonaparte once gave as sound advice to police?" he asked. "No! Then I'll tell you. 'The art of the police,' he said, 'is not to see that which it is useless for it to see.' Good counsel, Mitchington!"

The two men went away through the midnight streets, and kept silence until they were near the door of Jettison's hotel. Then Mitchington spoke.

"Well!" he said. "We've had a couple of tales, anyhow! What do you think of things, now?"

Jettison threw back his head with a dry laugh.

"Never been better puzzled in all my time!" he said. "Never! But—if that young doctor's playing a game—then, by the Lord Harry, inspector, it's a damned deep 'un! And my advice is —watch the lot!"

CHAPTER XX. JETTISON TAKES A HAND

By breakfast time next morning the man from New Scotland Yard had accomplished a series of meditations on the confidences made to him and Mitchington the night before and had determined on at least one course of action. But before entering upon it he had one or two important letters to write, the composition of which required much thought and trouble, and by the time he had finished them, and deposited them by his own hand in the General Post Office, it was drawing near to noon—the great bell of the Cathedral, indeed, was proclaiming noontide to Wrychester as Jettison turned into the police–station and sought Mitchington in his office.

"I was just coming round to see if you'd overslept yourself," said Mitchington good–humouredly. "We were up pretty late last night, or, rather, this morning."

"I've had letters to write," said Jettison. He sat down and picked up a newspaper and cast a casual glance over it. "Got anything fresh?"

"Well, this much," answered Mitchington. "The two gentlemen who told us so much last night are both out of town. I made an excuse to call on them both early this morning—just on nine o'clock. Dr. Ransford went up to London by the eight–fifteen.

"Dr. Bryce, says his landlady, went out on his bicycle at half–past eight—where, she didn't know, but, she fancied, into the country. However, I ascertained that Ransford is expected back this evening, and Bryce gave orders for his usual dinner to be ready at seven o'clock, and so—"

Jettison flung away the newspaper and pulled out his pipe.

"Oh, I don't think they'll run away—either of 'em," he remarked indifferently. "They're both too cock–sure of their own ways of looking at things."

"You looked at 'em any more?" asked Mitchington.

"Done a bit of reflecting—yes," replied the detective. "Complicated affair, my lad! More in it than one would think at first sight. I'm certain of this quite apart from whatever mystery there is about the Braden affair and the Collishaw murder, there's a lot of scheming and contriving been going on—and is going on!—somewhere, by somebody. Underhand work, you understand? However, my particular job is the Collishaw business—and there's a bit of information I'd like to get hold of at once. Where's the office of that Friendly Society we heard about last night?"

"That'll be the Wrychester Second Friendly," answered Mitchington. "There are two such societies in the town—the first's patronized by small tradesmen and the like; the second by workingmen. The second does take deposits from its members. The office is in Fladgate—secretary's name outside —Mr. Stebbing. What are you after?"

"Tell you later," said Jettison. "Just an idea."

He went leisurely out and across the market square and into the narrow, old–world street called Fladgate, along which he strolled as if doing no more than looking about him until he came to an ancient shop which had been converted into an office, and had a wire blind over the lower half of its front window, wherein was woven in conspicuous gilt letters Wrychester Second Friendly Society—George Stebbing, Secretary. Nothing betokened romance or mystery in that essentially humble place, but it was in Jettison's mind that when he crossed its threshold he was on his way to discovering something that would possibly clear up the problem on which he was engaged.

The staff of the Second Friendly was inconsiderable in numbers—an outer office harboured a small boy and a tall young man; an inner one accommodated Mr. Stebbing, also a young man, sandy—haired and freckled, who, having inspected Detective—Sergeant Jettison's professional card, gave him the best chair in the room and stared at him with a mingling of awe and curiosity which plainly showed that he had never entertained a detective before. And as if to show his visitor that he realized the seriousness of the occasion, he nodded meaningly at his door.

"All safe, here, sir!" he whispered. "Well fitting doors in these old houses—knew how to make 'em in those days. No chance of being overheard here—what can I do for you, sir?"

"Thank you—much obliged to you," said Jettison. "No objection to my pipe, I suppose? Just so. Ah!—well, between you and me, Mr. Stebbing, I'm down here in connection with that Collishaw case—you know."

"I know, sir—poor fellow!" said the secretary. "Cruel thing, sir, if the man was put an end to. One of our members, was Collishaw, sir."

"So I understand," remarked Jettison. "That's what I've come about. Bit of information, on the quiet, eh? Strictly between our two selves—for the present."

Stebbing nodded and winked, as if he had been doing business with detectives all his life. "To be sure, sir, to be sure!" he responded with alacrity. "Just between you and me and the door post!—all right. Anything I can do, Mr. Jettison, shall be done. But it's more in the way of what I can tell, I suppose?"

"Something of that sort," replied Jettison in his slow, easy—going fashion. "I want to know a thing or two. Yours is a working—man's society, I think? Aye—and I understand you've a system whereby such a man can put his bits of savings by in your hands?"

"A capital system, too!" answered the secretary, seizing on a pamphlet and pushing it into his visitor's hand. "I don't believe there's better in England! If you read that—"

"I'll take a look at it some time," said Jettison, putting the pamphlet in his pocket. "Well, now, I also understand that Collishaw was in the habit of bringing you a bit of saved money now and then a sort of saving fellow, wasn't he?" Stebbing nodded assent and reached for a ledger which lay on the farther side of his desk.

"Collishaw," he answered, "had been a member of our society ever since it started—fourteen years ago. And he'd been putting in savings for some eight or nine years. Not much, you'll understand. Say, as an average, two to three pounds every half-year—never more. But, just before his death, or murder, or whatever you like to call it, he came in here one day with fifty pounds! Fairly astounded me, sir! Fifty pounds—all in a lump!"

"It's about that fifty pounds I want to know something," said Jettison. "He didn't tell you how he'd come by it? Wasn't a legacy, for instance?"

"He didn't say anything but that he'd had a bit of luck," answered Stebbing. "I asked no questions. Legacy, now?—no, he didn't mention that. Here it is," he continued, turning over the pages of the ledger. "There! 50 pounds. You see the date—that 'ud be two days before his death."

Jettison glanced at the ledger and resumed his seat.

"Now, then, Mr. Stebbing, I want you to tell me something very definite," he said. "It's not so long since this happened, so you'll not have to tag your memory to any great extent. In what form did Collishaw pay that fifty pounds to you?"

"That's easy answered, sir," said the secretary. "It was in gold. Fifty sovereigns—he had 'em in a bit of a bag." Jettison reflected on this information for a moment or two. Then he rose.

"Much obliged to you, Mr. Stebbing," he said. "That's something worth knowing. Now there's something else you can tell me as long as I'm here—though, to be sure, I could save you the trouble by using my own eyes. How many banks are there in this little city of yours?"

"Three," answered Stebbing promptly. "Old Bank, in Monday Market; Popham Hargreaves, in the Square; Wrychester Bank, in Spurriergate. That's the lot."

"Much obliged," said Jettison. "And—for the present—not a word of what we've talked about. You'll be hearing more —later."

He went away, memorizing the names of the three banking establishments—ten minutes later he was in the private parlour of the first, in serious conversation with its manager. Here it was necessary to be more secret, and to insist on more secrecy than with the secretary of the Second Friendly, and to produce all his credentials and give all his reasons. But Jettison drew that covert blank, and the next, too, and it was not until he had been closeted for some time with the authorities of the third bank that he got, the information he wanted. And when he had got it, he impressed secrecy and silence on his informants in a fashion which showed them that however easy–going his manner might be, he knew his business as thoroughly as they knew theirs.

It was by that time past one o'clock, and Jettison turned into the small hotel at which he had lodged himself. He thought much and gravely while he ate his dinner; he thought still more while he smoked his after–dinner pipe. And his face was still heavy with thought when, at three o'clock, he walked into Mitchington's office and finding the Inspector alone shut the door and drew a chair to Mitchington's desk.

"Now then," he said. "I've had a rare morning's work, and made a discovery, and you and me, my lad, have got to have about as serious a bit of talk as we've had since I came here."

Mitchington pushed his papers aside and showed his keen attention.

"You remember what that young fellow told us last night about that man Collishaw paying in fifty pounds to the Second Friendly two days before his death," said Jettison. "Well, I thought over that business a lot, early this morning, and I fancied I saw how I could find something out about it. So I have—on the strict quiet. That's why I went to the Friendly Society. The fact was—I wanted to know in what form Collishaw handed in that fifty pounds. I got to know. Gold!"

Mitchington, whose work hitherto had not led him into the mysteries of detective enterprise, nodded delightedly.

"Good!" he said. "Rare idea! I should never have thought of it! And—what do you make out of that, now?"

"Nothing," replied Jettison. "But—a good deal out of what I've learned since that bit of a discovery. Now, put it to yourself—whoever it was that paid Collishaw that fifty pounds in gold did it with a motive. More than one motive, to be exact—but we'll stick to one, to begin with. The motive for paying in gold was—avoidance of discovery. A cheque can be readily traced. So can bank–notes. But gold is not easily traced. Therefore the man who paid Collishaw fifty pounds took care to provide himself with gold. Now then—how many men are there in a small place like this who are likely to carry fifty pounds in gold in their pockets, or to have it at hand?"

"Not many, "'agreed Mitchington.

"Just so—and therefore I've been doing a bit of secret inquiry amongst the bankers, as to who supplied himself with gold about that date," continued Jettison. "I'd to convince 'em of the absolute necessity of information, too, before I got any! But I got some—at the third attempt. On the day previous to that on which Collishaw handed that fifty pounds to Stebbing, a certain Wrychester man drew fifty pounds in gold at his bank. Who do you think he was?"

"Who—who?" demanded Mitchington.

Jettison leaned half–across the desk.

"Bryce!" he said in a whisper. "Bryce!"

Mitchington sat up in his chair and opened his mouth in sheer astonishment.

"Good heavens!" he muttered after a moment's silence. "You don't mean it?"

"Fact!" answered Jettison. "Plain, incontestable fact, my lad. Dr. Bryce keeps an account at the Wrychester bank. On the day I'm speaking of he cashed a cheque to self for fifty pounds and took it all in gold."

The two men looked at each other as if each were asking his companion a question.

"Well?" said Mitchington at last. "You're a cut above me, Jettison. What do you make of it?"

The Paradise Mystery

"I said last night that the young man was playing a deep game," replied Jettison. "But—what game? What's he building up? For mark you, Mitchington, if—I say if, mind!—if that fifty pounds which he drew in gold is the identical fifty paid to Collishaw, Bryce didn't pay it as hush—money!"

"Think not?" said Mitchington, evidently surprised. "Now, that was my first impression. If it wasn't hush—money—"

"It wasn't hush—money, for this reason," interrupted Jettison. "We know that whatever else he knew, Bryce didn't know of the accident to Braden until Varner fetched him to Braden. That's established—on what you've put before me. Therefore, whatever Collishaw saw, before or at the time that accident happened, it wasn't Bryce who was mixed up in it. Therefore, why should Bryce pay Collishaw hush—money?"

Mitchington, who had evidently been thinking, suddenly pulled out a drawer in his desk and took some papers from it which he began to turn over.

"Wait a minute," he said. "I've an abstract here—of what the foreman at the Cathedral mason's yard told me of what he knew as to where Collishaw was working that morning when the accident happened—I made a note of it when I questioned him after Collishaw's death. Here you are:

'Foreman says that on morning of Braden's accident,
Collishaw was at work in the north gallery of the
clerestory, clearing away some timber which the
carpenters had left there. Collishaw was certainly
thus engaged from nine o'clock until past eleven
that morning. Mem. Have investigated this myself.
From the exact spot where C. was clearing the timber,
there is an uninterrupted view of the gallery on the
south side of the nave, and of the arched doorway at
the head of St. Wrytha's Stair.'"

"'Well," observed Jettison, "that proves what I'm saying. It wasn't hush—money. For whoever it was that Collishaw saw lay hands on Braden, it wasn't Bryce—Bryce, we know, was at that time coming across the Close or crossing that path through the part you

156

call Paradise: Varner's evidence proves that. So—if the fifty pounds wasn't paid for hush—money, what was it paid for?"

"Do you suggest anything?" asked Mitchington.

"I've thought of two or three things," answered the detective. "One's this—was the fifty pounds paid for information? If so, and Bryce has that information, why doesn't he show his hand more plainly? If he bribed Collishaw with fifty pounds: to tell him who Braden's assailant was, he now knows!—so why doesn't he let it out, and have done with it?"

"Part of his game—if that theory's right," murmured Mitchington.

"It mayn't be right," said Jettison. "But it's one. And there's another—supposing he paid Collishaw that money on behalf of somebody else? I've thought this business out right and left, top—side and bottom—side, and hang me if I don't feel certain there is somebody else! What did Ransford tell us about Bryce and this old Harker—think of that! And yet, according to Bryce, Harker is one of our old Yard men!—and therefore ought to be above suspicion."

Mitchington suddenly started as if an idea had occurred to him.

"I say, you know!" he exclaimed. "We've only Bryce's word for it that Harker is an ex—detective. I never heard that he was —if he is, he's kept it strangely quiet. You'd have thought that he'd have let us know, here, of his previous calling—I never heard of a policeman of any rank who didn't like to have a bit of talk with his own sort about professional matters."

"Nor me," assented Jettison. "And as you say, we've only Bryce's word. And, the more I think of it, the more I'm convinced there's somebody—some man of whom you don't seem to have the least idea—who's in this. And it may be that Bryce is in with him. However—here's one thing I'm going to do at once. Bryce gave us that information about the fifty pounds. Now I'm going to tell Bryce straight out that I've gone into that matter in my own fashion—a fashion he evidently never thought of—and ask him to explain why he drew a similar amount in gold. Come on round to his rooms."

But Bryce was not to be found at his rooms—had not been back to his rooms, said his landlady, since he had ridden away early in the morning: all she knew was that he had ordered his dinner to be ready at his usual time that evening. With that the two men had to be content, and they went back to the police–station still discussing the situation. And they were still discussing it an hour later when a telegram was handed to Mitchington, who tore it open, glanced over its contents and passed it to his companion who read it aloud.

"Meet me with Jettison Wrychester Station on arrival of five–twenty express from London mystery cleared up guilty men known—Ransford."

Jettison handed the telegram back.

"A man of his word!" he said. "He mentioned two days—he's done it in one! And now, my lad—do you notice?—he says men, not man! It's as I said—there's been more than one of 'em in this affair. Now then—who are they?"

CHAPTER XXI. THE SAXONSTEADE ARMS

Bryce had ridden away on his bicycle from Wrychester that morning intent on a new piece of diplomacy. He had sat up thinking for some time after the two police officials had left him at midnight, and it had occurred to him that there was a man from whom information could be had of whose services he had as yet made no use but who must be somewhere in the neighbourhood—the man Glassdale. Glassdale had been in Wrychester the previous evening; he could scarcely be far away now; there was certainly one person who would know where he could be found, and that person was the Duke of Saxonsteade. Bryce knew the Duke to be an extremely approachable man, a talkative, even a garrulous man, given to holding converse with anybody about anything, and he speedily made up his mind to ride over to Saxonsteade, invent a plausible excuse for his call, and get some news out of his Grace. Even if Glassdale had left the neighbourhood, there might be fragments of evidence to pick up from the Duke, for Glassdale, he knew, had given his former employer the information about the stolen jewels and would, no doubt, have added more about his acquaintance with Braden. And before Bryce came to his dreamed–of master–stroke in that matter, there were one or two things he wanted to clear up, to complete his double net, and he had an idea that an hour's chat with Glassdale

158

would yield all that he desired.

The active brain that had stood Bryce in good stead while he spun his meshes and devised his schemes was more active than ever that early summer morning. It was a ten–mile ride through woods and valleys to Saxonsteade, and there were sights and beauties of nature on either side of him which any other man would have lingered to admire and most men would have been influenced by. But Bryce had no eyes for the clouds over the copper–crowned hills or the mystic shadows in the deep valleys or the new buds in the hedgerows, and no thought for the rustic folk whose cottages he passed here and there in a sparsely populated country. All his thoughts were fixed on his schemes, almost as mechanically as his eyes followed the white road in front of his wheel. Ever since he had set out on his campaign he had regularly taken stock of his position; he was for ever reckoning it up. And now, in his opinion, everything looked very promising. He had—so far as he was aware—created a definite atmosphere of suspicion around and against Ransford—it needed only a little more suggestion, perhaps a little more evidence to bring about Ransford's arrest. And the only question which at all troubled Bryce was—should he let matters go to that length before putting his ultimatum before Mary Bewery, or should he show her his hand first? For Bryce had so worked matters that a word from him to the police would damn Ransford or save him—and now it all depended, so far as Bryce himself was concerned, on Mary Bewery as to which word should be said. Elaborate as the toils were which he had laid out for Ransford to the police, he could sweep them up and tear them away with a sentence of added knowledge—if Mary Bewery made it worth his while. But first—before coming to the critical point—there was yet certain information which he desired to get, and he felt sure of getting it if he could find Glassdale. For Glassdale, according to all accounts, had known Braden intimately of late years, and was most likely in possession of facts about him—and Bryce had full confidence in himself as an interviewer of other men and a supreme belief that he could wheedle a secret out of anybody with whom he could procure an hour's quiet conversation.

As luck would have it, Bryce had no need to make a call upon the approachable and friendly Duke. Outside the little village at Saxonsteade, on the edge of the deep woods which fringed the ducal park, stood an old wayside inn, a relic of the coaching days, which bore on its sign the ducal arms. Into its old stone hall marched Bryce to refresh himself after his ride, and as he stood at the bow–windowed bar, he glanced into the garden beyond and there saw, comfortably smoking his pipe and reading the newspaper, the very man he was looking for.

Bryce had no spice of bashfulness, no want of confidence anywhere in his nature; he determined to attack Glassdale there and then. But he took a good look at his man before going out into the garden to him. A plain and ordinary sort of fellow, he thought; rather over middle age, with a tinge of grey in his hair and moustache; prosperous looking and well–dressed, and at that moment of the appearance of what he was probably taken for by the inn people—a tourist. Whether he was the sort who would be communicative or not, Bryce could not tell from outward signs, but he was going to try, and he presently found his card–case, took out a card, and strolling down the garden to the shady spot in which Glassdale sat, assumed his politest and suavest manner and presented himself.

"Allow me, sir," he said, carefully abstaining from any mention of names. "May I have the pleasure of a few minutes' conversation with you?"

Glassdale cast a swift glance of surprise, not unmingled with suspicion, at the intruder—the sort of glance that a man used to watchfulness would throw at anybody, thought Bryce. But his face cleared as he read the card, though it was still doubtful as he lifted it again.

"You've the advantage of me, sir," he said. "Dr. Bryce, I see. But—"

Bryce smiled and dropped into a garden chair at Glassdale's side.

"You needn't be afraid of talking to me," he answered. "I'm well known in Wrychester. The Duke," he went on, nodding his head in the direction of the great house which lay behind the woods at the foot of the garden, "knows me well enough—in fact, I was on my way to see his Grace now, to ask him if he could tell me where you could be found. The fact is, I'm aware of what happened last night—the jewel affair, you know —Mitchington told me—and of your friendship with Braden, and I want to ask you a question or two about Braden."

Glassdale, who had looked somewhat mystified at the beginning of this address, seemed to understand matters better by the end of it.

"Oh, well, of course, doctor," he said, "if that's it—but, of course—a word first!—these folk here at the inn don't know who I am or that I've any connection with the Duke on that affair. I'm Mr. Gordon here—just staying for a bit."

"That's all right," answered Bryce with a smile of understanding. "All this is between ourselves. I saw you with the Duke and the rest of them last night, and I recognized you just now. And all I want is a bit of talk about Braden. You knew him pretty well of late years?"

"Knew him for a good many years," replied Glassdale. He looked narrowly at his visitor. "I suppose you know his story—and mine?" he asked. "Bygone affairs, eh?"

"Yes, yes!" answered Bryce reassuringly. "No need to go into that—that's all done with."

"Aye—well, we both put things right," said Glassdale. "Made restitution—both of us, you understand. So that is done with? And you know, then, of course, who Braden really was?"

"John Brake, ex bank–manager," answered Bryce promptly. "I know all about it. I've been deeply interested and concerned in his death. And I'll tell you why. I want to marry his daughter."

Glassdale turned and stared at his companion.

"His daughter!" he exclaimed. "Brake's daughter! God bless my soul! I never knew he had a daughter!"

It was Bryce's turn to stare now. He looked at Glassdale incredulously.

"Do you mean to tell me that you knew Brake all those years and that he never mentioned his children?" he exclaimed.

"Never a word of 'em!" replied Glassdale. "Never knew he had any!"

"Did he never speak of his past?" asked Bryce.

"Not in that respect," answered Glassdale. "I'd no idea that he was—or had been—a married man. He certainly never mentioned wife nor children to me, sir, and yet I knew Brake about as intimately as two men can know each other for some years before we came back to England."

Bryce fell into one of his fits of musing. What could be the meaning of this extraordinary silence on Brake's part? Was there still some hidden secret, some other mystery at which he had not yet guessed?

"Odd!" he remarked at last after a long pause during which Glassdale had watched him curiously. "But, did he ever speak to you of an old friend of his named Ransford—a doctor?"

"Never!" said Glassdale. "Never mentioned such a man!"

Bryce reflected again, and suddenly determined to be explicit.

"John Brake, the bank manager," he said, "was married at a place called Braden Medworth, in Leicestershire, to a girl named Mary Bewery. He had two children, who would be, respectively, about four and one years of age when his—we'll call it misfortune—happened. That's a fact!"

"First I ever heard of it, then," said Glassdale. "And that's a fact, too!"

"He'd also a very close friend named Ransford—Mark Ransford," continued Bryce. "This Ransford was best man at Brake's wedding."

"Never heard him speak of Ransford, nor of any wedding!" affirmed Glassdale. "All news to me, doctor."

"This Ransford is now in practice in Wrychester," said Bryce. "And he has two young people living with him as his wards—a girl of twenty, a boy of seventeen—who are, without doubt, John Brake's children. It is the daughter that I want to marry."

Glassdale shook his head as if in sheer perplexity.

"Well, all I can say is, you surprise me!" he remarked. "I'd no idea of any such thing."

"Do you think Brake came to Wrychester because of that?" asked Brycc.

"How can I answer that, sir, when I tell you that I never heard him breathe one word of any children?" exclaimed 'Glassdale. "No! I know his reason for coming to Wrychester. It was wholly and solely—as far as I know—to tell the Duke here about that jewel business, the secret of which had been entrusted to Brake and me by a man on his death–bed in Australia. Brake came to Wrychester by himself—I was to join him next morning: we were then to go to see the Duke together. When I got to Wrychester, I heard of Brake's accident, and being upset by it, I went away again and waited some days until yesterday, when I made up my mind to tell the Duke myself, as I did, with very fortunate results. No, that's the only reason I know of why Brake came this way. I tell you I knew nothing at all of his family affairs! He was a very close man, Brake, and apart from his business matters, he'd only one idea in his head, and that was lodged there pretty firmly, I can assure you!"

"What was it?" asked Bryce.

"He wanted to find a certain man—or, rather, two men—who'd cruelly deceived and wronged him, but one of 'em in particular," answered Glassdale. "The particular one he believed to be in Australia, until near the end, when he got an idea that he'd left for England; as for the other, he didn't bother much about him. But the man that he did want! —ah, he wanted him badly!"

"Who was that man?" asked Bryce.

"A man of the name of Falkiner Wraye, answered Glassdale promptly. "A man he'd known in London. This Wraye, together with his partner, a man called Flood, tricked Brake into lending 'em several thousands pounds—bank's money, of course —for a couple of days—no more—and then clean disappeared, leaving him to pay the piper! He was a fool, no doubt, but he'd been mixed up with them; he'd done it before, and they'd always kept their promises, and he did it once too often. He let 'em have some thousands; they disappeared, and the bank inspector happened to call at Brake's bank and ask for his balances. And—there he was. And—that's why he'd Falkiner Wraye on his mind—as his one big idea. T'other man was a lesser consideration, Wraye was the chief offender."

"I wish you'd tell me all you know about Brake," said Bryce after a pause during which he had done some thinking. "Between ourselves, of course."

"Oh—I don't know that there's so much secrecy!" replied Glassdale almost indifferently. "Of course, I knew him first when we were both inmates of—you understand where; no need for particulars. But after we left that place, I never saw him again until we met in Australia a few years ago. We were both in the same trade—speculating in wool. We got pretty thick and used to see each other a great deal, and of course, grew confidential. He told me in time about his affair, and how he'd traced this Wraye to the United States, and then, I think, to New Zealand, and afterwards to Australia, and as I was knocking about the country a great deal buying up wool, he asked me to help him, and gave me a description of Wraye, of whom, he said, he'd certainly heard something when he first landed at Sydney, but had never been able to trace afterwards. But it was no good—I never either saw or heard of Wraye—and Brake came to the conclusion he'd left Australia. And I know he hoped to get news of him, somehow, when we returned to England."

"That description, now?—what was it?" asked Bryce.

"Oh!" said Glassdale. "I can't remember it all, now—big man, clean shaven, nothing very particular except one thing. Wraye, according to Brake, had a bad scar on his left jaw and had lost the middle finger of his left hand—all from a gun accident. He—what's the matter, sir?"

Bryce had suddenly let his pipe fall from his lips. He took some time in picking it up. When he raised himself again his face was calm if a little flushed from stooping.

"Bit my pipe on a bad tooth!" he muttered. "I must have that tooth seen to. So you never heard or saw anything of this man?"

"Never!" answered Glassdale. "But I've wondered since this Wrychester affair if Brake accidentally came across one or other of those men, and if his death arose out of it. Now, look here, doctor! I read the accounts of the inquest on Brake—I'd have gone to it if I'd dared, but just then I hadn't made up my mind about seeing the Duke; I didn't know what to do, so I kept away, and there's a thing has struck me that I don't believe the police have ever taken the slightest, notice of."

The Paradise Mystery

"What's that?" demanded Bryce.

"Why, this!" answered Glassdale. "That man who called himself Dellingham—who came with Brake to the Mitre Hotel at Wrychester—who is he? Where did Brake meet him? Where did he go? Seems to me the police have been strangely negligent about that! According to the accounts I've read, everybody just accepted this Dellingham's first statement, took his word, and let him—vanish! No one, as far as I know, ever verified his account of himself. A stranger!"

Bryce, who was already in one of his deep moods of reflection, got up from his chair as if to go.

"Yes," he said. "There maybe something in your suggestion. They certainly did take his word without inquiry. It's true —he mightn't be what he said he was."

"Aye, and from what I read, they never followed his movements that morning!" observed Glassdale. "Queer business altogether! Isn't there some reward offered, doctor? I heard of some placards or something, but I've never seen them; of course, I've only been here since yesterday morning."

Bryce silently drew some papers from his pocket. From them he extracted the two handbills which: Mitchington had given him and handed them over.

"Well, I must go," he said. "I shall no doubt see you again in Wrychester, over this affair. For the present, all this is between ourselves, of course?"

"Oh, of course, doctor!" answered Glassdale. "Quite so!" Bryce went off and got his bicycle and rode away in the direction of Wrychester. Had he remained in that garden he would have seen Glassdale, after reading both the handbills, go into the house and have heard him ask the landlady at the bar to get him a trap and a good horse in it as soon as possible; he, too, now wanted to go to Wrychester and at once. But Bryce was riding down the road, muttering certain words to himself over and over again.

"The left jaw—and the left hand!" he repeated. "Left hand —left jaw! Unmistakable!"

CHAPTER XXII. OTHER PEOPLE'S NOTIONS

The great towers of Wrychester Cathedral had come within Bryce's view before he had made up his mind as to the next step in this last stage of his campaign. He had ridden away from the Saxonsteade Arms feeling that he had got to do something at once, but he was not quite clear in his mind as to what that something exactly was. But now, as he topped a rise in the road, and saw Wrychester lying in its hollow beneath him, the summer sun shining on its red roofs and grey walls, he suddenly came to a decision, and instead of riding straight ahead into the old city he turned off at a by-road, made a line across the northern outskirts, and headed for the golf-links. He was almost certain to find Mary Bewery there at that hour, and he wanted to see her at once. The time for his great stroke had come.

But Mary Bewery was not there—had not been there that morning said the caddy-master. There were only a few players out. In one of them, coming towards the club-house, Bryce recognized Sackville Bonham. And at sight of Sackville, Bryce had an inspiration. Mary Bewery would not come up to the links now before afternoon; he, Bryce, would lunch there and then go towards Wrychester to meet her by the path across the fields on which he had waylaid her after his visit to Leicestershire. And meanwhile he would inveigle Sackville Bonham into conversation. Sackville fell readily into Bryce's trap. He was the sort of youth who loves to talk, especially in a hinting and mysterious fashion. And when Bryce, after treating him to an appetizer in the bar of the club-house, had suggested that they should lunch together and got him into a quiet corner of the diningroom, he launched forth at once on the pertinent matter of the day.

"Heard all about this discovery of those missing Saxonsteade diamonds?" he asked as he and Bryce picked up their knives and forks. "Queer business that, isn't it? Of course, it's got to do with those murders!"

"Think so?" asked Bryce.

"Can anybody think anything else?" said Sackville in his best dogmatic manner. "Why, the thing's plain. From what's been let out—not much, certainly, but enough—it's quite evident."

"What's your theory?" inquired Bryce.

"My stepfather—knowing old bird he is, too!—sums the whole thing up to a nicety," answered Sackville. "That old chap, Braden, you know, is in possession of that secret. He comes to Wrychester about it. But somebody else knows. That somebody gets rid of Braden. Why? So that the secret'll be known then only to one—the murderer! See! And why? Why?"

"Well, why?" repeated Bryce. "Don't see, so far."

"You must be dense, then," said Sackville with; the lofty superiority of youth. "Because of the reward, of course! Don't you know that there's been a standing offer—never withdrawn!—of five thousand pounds for news of those jewels?"

"No, I didn't," answered Bryce.

"Fact, sir—pure fact," continued Sackville. "Now, five thousand, divided in two, is two thousand five hundred each. But five thousand, undivided, is—what?"

"Five thousand—apparently," said Bryce.

"Just so! And," remarked Sackville knowingly, "a man'll do a lot for five thousand."

"Or–a–ccording to your argument—for half of it," said Bryce. "What you—or your stepfather's—aiming at comes to this, that suspicion rests on Braden's sharer in the secret. That it?"

"And why not?" asked Sackville. "Look at what we know—from the account in the paper this morning. This other chap, Glassdale, waits a bit until the first excitement about Braden is over, then he comes forward and tells the Duke where the Duchess's diamonds are planted. Why? So that he can get the five thousand pound reward! Plain as a pikestaff! Only, the police are such fools."

"And what about Collishaw?" asked Bryce, willing to absorb all his companion's ideas.

"Part of the game," declared Sackville. "Same man that got rid of Braden got rid of that chap! Probably Collishaw knew a bit and had to be silenced. But, whether that Glassdale did it all off his own bat or whether he's somebody in with him, that's where the guilt'll be fastened in the end, my stepfather says. And—it'll be so. Stands to reason!"

"Anybody come forward about that reward your stepfather offered?" asked Bryce.

"I'm not permitted to say," answered Sackville. "But," he added, leaning closer to his companion across the table, "I can tell you this—there's wheels within wheels! You understand! And things'll be coming out. Got to! We can't —as a family—let Ransford lie under that cloud, don't you know. We must clear him. That's precisely why Mr. Folliot offered his reward. Ransford, of course, you know, Bryce, is very much to blame—he ought to have done more himself. And, of course, as my mother and my stepfather say, if Ransford won't do things for himself, well, we must do 'em for him! We couldn't think of anything else."

"Very good of you all, I'm sure," assented Bryce. "Very thoughtful and kindly."

"Oh, well!" said Sackville, who was incapable of perceiving a sneer or of knowing when older men were laughing at him. "It's one of those things that one's got to do—under the circumstances. Of course, Miss Bewery isn't Dr. Ransford's daughter, but she's his ward, and we can't allow suspicion to rest on her guardian. You leave it to me, my boy, and you'll see how things will be cleared!"

"Doing a bit underground, eh?" asked Bryce.

"Wait a bit!" answered Sackville with a knowing wink. "It's the least expected that happens—what?"

Bryce replied that Sackville was no doubt right, and began to talk of other matters. He hung about the club–house until past three o'clock, and then, being well acquainted with Mary Bewery's movements from long observation of them, set out to walk down towards Wrychester, leaving his bicycle behind him. If he did not meet Mary on the way, he meant to go to the house. Ransford would be out on his afternoon round of calls; Dick Bewery would be at school; he would find Mary alone. And it was necessary that he should see her alone, and at once, for since morning an entirely new view of affairs had come to him, based on added knowledge, and he now saw a chance which he had never seen before. True, he said to himself, as he walked across the links and over the country which lay between their edge and Wrychester, he had not, even now, the accurate knowledge as to the actual murderer of either Braden or Collishaw that he would have liked, but he knew something that would enable him to ask Mary Bewery point–blank whether he was to be friend or enemy. And he was still considering the best way of putting his case to her when, having failed to meet her on the way, he at last turned into the Close, and as he approached Ransford's house, saw Mrs. Folliot leaving it.

Mary Bewery, like Bryce, had been having a day of events. To begin with, Ransford had received a wire from London, first thing in the morning, which had made him run, breakfastless, to catch the next express. He had left Mary to make arrangements about his day's work, for he had not yet replaced Bryce, and she had been obliged to seek out another practitioner who could find time from his own duties to attend to Ransford's urgent patients. Then she had had to see callers who came to the surgery expecting to find Ransford there; and in the middle of a busy morning, Mr. Folliot had dropped in, to bring her a bunch of roses, and, once admitted, had shown unmistakable signs of a desire to gossip.

"Ransford out?" he asked as he sat down in the dining–room. "Suppose he is, this time of day."

"He's away," replied Mary. "He went to town by the first express, and I have had a lot of bother arranging about his patients."

"Did he hear about this discovery of the Saxonsteade jewels before he went?" asked Folliot. "Suppose he wouldn't though —wasn't known until the weekly paper came out this morning. Queer business! You've heard, of course?"

"Dr. Short told me," answered Mary. "I don't know any details."

Folliot looked meditatively at her a moment.

"Got something to do with those other matters, you know," he remarked. "I say! What's Ransford doing about all that?"

169

"About all what, Mr. Folliot?" asked Mary, at once on her guard. "I don't understand you."

"You know—all that suspicion—and so on," said Folliot. "Bad position for a professional man, you know—ought to clear himself. Anybody been applying for that reward Ransford offered?"

"I don't know anything about it," replied Mary. "Dr. Ransford is very well able to take care of himself, I think. Has anybody applied for yours?"

Folliot rose from his chair again, as if he had changed his mind about lingering, and shook his head.

"Can't say what my solicitors may or may not have heard—or done," he answered. "But—queer business, you know—and ought to be settled. Bad for Ransford to have any sort of a cloud over him. Sorry to see it."

"Is that why you came forward with a reward?" asked Mary.

But to this direct question Folliot made no answer. He muttered something about the advisability of somebody doing something and went away, to Mary's relief. She had no desire to discuss the Paradise mysteries with anybody, especially after Ransford's assurance of the previous evening. But in the middle of the afternoon in walked Mrs. Folliot, a rare caller, and before she had been closeted with Mary five minutes brought up the subject again.

"I want to speak to you on a very serious matter, my dear Miss Bewery," she said. "You must allow me to speak plainly on account of—of several things. My—my superiority in—in age, you know, and all that!"

"What's the matter, Mrs. Folliot?" asked Mary, steeling herself against what she felt sure was coming. "Is it—very serious? And—pardon me—is it about what Mr. Folliot mentioned to me this morning? Because if it is, I'm not going to discuss that with you or with anybody!"

"I had no idea that my husband had been here this morning," answered Mrs. Folliot in genuine surprise. "What did he want to talk about?"

"In that case, what do you want to talk about?" asked Mary. "Though that doesn't mean that I'm going to talk about it with you."

Mrs. Folliot made an effort to understand this remark, and after inspecting her hostess critically for a moment, proceeded in her most judicial manner.

"You must see, my dear Miss Bewery, that it is highly necessary that some one should use the utmost persuasion on Dr. Ransford," she said. "He is placing all of you—himself, yourself, your young brother—in most invidious positions by his silence! In society such as—well, such as you get in a cathedral town, you know, no man of reputation can afford to keep silence when his—his character is affected."

Mary picked up some needlework and began to be much occupied with it.

"Is Dr. Ransford's character affected?" she asked. "I wasn't aware of it, Mrs. Folliot."

"Oh, my dear, you can't be quite so very—so very, shall we say ingenuous?—as all that!" exclaimed Mrs. Folliot. "These rumours!—of course, they are very wicked and cruel ones, but you know they have spread. Dear me!—why, they have been common talk!"

"I don't think my guardian cares twopence for common talk, Mrs. Folliot," answered Mary. "And I am quite sure I don't."

"None of us—especially people in our position—can afford to ignore rumours and common talk," said Mrs. Folliot in her loftiest manner. "If we are, unfortunately, talked about, then it is our solemn, bounden duty to put ourselves right in the eyes of our friends—and of society. If I for instance, my dear, heard anything affecting my—let me say, moral–character, I should take steps, the most stringent, drastic, and forceful steps, to put matters to the test. I would not remain under a stigma—no, not for one minute!"

"I hope you will never have occasion to rehabilitate your moral character, Mrs. Folliot," remarked Mary, bending closely over her work. "Such a necessity would indeed be dreadful."

"And yet you do not insist—yes, insist!—on Dr. Ransford's taking strong steps to clear himself!" exclaimed Mrs. Folliot. "Now that, indeed, is a dreadful necessity!"

"Dr. Ransford," answered Mary, "is quite able to defend and to take care of himself. It is not for me to tell him what to do, or even to advise him what to do. And—since you will talk of this matter, I tell you frankly, Mrs. Folliot, that I don't believe any decent person in Wrychester has the least suspicion or doubt of Dr. Ransford. His denial of any share or complicity in those sad affairs—the mere idea of it as ridiculous as it's wicked—was quite sufficient. You know very well that at that second inquest he said—on oath, too —that he knew nothing of these affairs. I repeat, there isn't a decent soul in the city doubts that!"

"Oh, but you're quite wrong!" said Mrs. Folliot, hurriedly. "Quite wrong, I assure you, my dear. Of course, everybody knows what Dr. Ransford said—very excitedly, poor man, I'm given to understand on the occasion you refer to, but then, what else could he have said in his own interest? What people want is the proof of his innocence. I could—but I won't —tell you of many of the very best people who are—well, very much exercised over the matter—I could indeed!"

"Do you count yourself among them?" asked Mary in a cold fashion which would have been a warning to any one but her visitor. "Am I to understand that, Mrs. Folliot?"

"Certainly not, my dear," answered Mrs. Folliot promptly. "Otherwise I should not have done what I have done towards establishing the foolish man's innocence!"

Mary dropped her work and turned a pair of astonished eyes on Mrs. Folliot's large countenance.

"You!" she exclaimed. "To establish—Dr. Ransford's innocence? Why, Mrs. Folliot, what have you done?"

Mrs. Folliot toyed a little with the jewelled head of her sunshade. Her expression became almost coy.

"Oh, well!" she answered after a brief spell of indecision. "Perhaps it is as well that you should know, Miss Bewery. Of course, when all this sad trouble was made far worse by that second affair—the working–man's death, you know, I said to my husband that really one must do something, seeing that Dr. Ransford was so very, very obdurate and wouldn't speak. And as money is nothing—at least as things go—to me or to Mr. Folliot, I insisted that he should offer a thousand pounds reward to have the thing cleared up. He's a generous and open–handed man, and he agreed with me entirely, and put the thing in hand through his solicitors. And nothing would please us more, my dear, than to have that thousand pounds claimed! For of course, if there is to be—as I suppose there is—a union between our families, it would be utterly impossible that any cloud could rest on Dr. Ransford, even if he is only your guardian. My son's future wife cannot, of course—"

Mary laid down her work again and for a full minute stared Mrs. Folliot in the face.

"Mrs. Folliot!" she said at last. "Are you under the impression that I'm thinking of marrying your son?"

"I think I've every good reason for believing it!" replied Mrs. Folliot.

"You've none!" retorted Mary, gathering up her work and moving towards the door. "I've no more intention of marrying Mr. Sackville Bonham than of eloping with the Bishop! The idea's too absurd to—even be thought of!"

Five minutes later Mrs. Folliot, heightened in colour, had gone. And presently Mary, glancing after her across the Close, saw Bryce approaching the gate of the garden.

CHAPTER XXIII. THE UNEXPECTED

Mary's first instinct on seeing the approach of Pemberton Bryce, the one man she least desired to see, was to retreat to the back of the house and send the parlourmaid to the door to say her mistress was not at home. But she had lately become aware of Bryce's curiously dogged persistence in following up whatever he had in view, and she reflected that if he were sent away then he would be sure to come back and come back until he had got whatever it was that he wanted. And after a moment's further consideration, she walked out of the front door and confronted him resolutely in the garden.

"Dr. Ransford is away," she said with almost unnecessary brusqueness. "He's away until evening."

"I don't want him," replied Bryce just as brusquely. "I came to see you."

Mary hesitated. She continued to regard Bryce steadily, and Bryce did not like the way in which she was looking at him. He made haste to speak before she could either leave or dismiss him.

"You'd better give me a few minutes," he said, with a note of warning. "I'm here in your interests—or in Ransford's. I may as well tell you, straight out, Ransford's in serious and imminent danger! That's a fact."

"Danger of—what?" she demanded.

"Arrest—instant arrest!" replied Bryce. "I'm telling you the truth. He'll probably be arrested tonight, on his return. There's no imagination in all this—I'm speaking of what I know. I've—curiously enough—got mixed up with these affairs, through no seeking of my own, and I know what's behind the scenes. If it were known that I'm letting out secrets to you, I should get into trouble. But, I want to warn you!"

Mary stood before him on the path, hesitating. She knew enough to know that Bryce was telling some sort of truth: it was plain that he had been mixed up in the recent mysteries, and there was a ring of conviction in his voice which impressed her. And suddenly she had visions of Ransford's arrest, of his being dragged off to prison to meet a cruel accusation, of the shame and disgrace, and she hesitated further.

"But if that's so," she said at last, "what's the good of coming to me? I can't do anything!"

"I can!" said Bryce significantly. "I know more—much more —than the police know—more than anybody knows. I can save Ransford. Understand that!"

"What do you want now?" she asked.

"To talk to you—to tell you how things are," answered Bryce. "What harm is there in that? To make you see how matters stand, and then to showy you what I can do to put things right."

The Paradise Mystery

Mary glanced at an open summer–house which stood beneath the beech trees on one side of the garden. She moved towards it and sat down there, and Bryce followed her and seated himself.

"Well—" she said.

Bryce realized that his moment had arrived. He paused, endeavouring to remember the careful preparations he had made for putting his case. Somehow, he was not so clear as to his line of attack as he had been ten minutes previously—he realized that he had to deal with a young woman who was not likely to be taken in nor easily deceived. And suddenly he plunged into what he felt to be the thick of things.

"Whether you, or whether Ransford—whether both or either of you, know it or not," he said, "the police have been on to Ransford ever since that Collishaw affair! Underground work, you know. Mitchington has been digging into things ever since then, and lately he's had a London detective helping him."

Mary, who had carried her work into the garden, had now resumed it, and as Bryce began to talk she bent over it steadily stitching.

"Well?" she said.

"Look here!" continued Bryce. "Has it never struck you—it must have done!—that there's considerable mystery about Ransford? But whether it has struck you or not, it's there, and it's struck the police forcibly. Mystery connected with him before—long before—he ever came here. And associated, in some way, with that man Braden. Not of late—in years past. And, naturally, the police have tried to find out what that was."

"What have they found out?" asked Mary quietly.

"That I'm not at liberty to tell," replied Bryce. "But I can tell you this—they know, Mitchington and the London man, that there were passages between Ransford and Braden years ago."

"How many years ago?" interrupted Mary.

Bryce hesitated a moment. He had a suspicion that this self—possessed young woman who was taking everything more quietly than he had anticipated, might possibly know more than he gave her credit for knowing. He had been watching her fingers since they sat down in the summer—house, and his sharp eyes saw that they were as steady as the spire of the cathedral above the trees—he knew from that that she was neither frightened nor anxious.

"Oh, well—seventeen to twenty years ago," he answered. "About that time. There were passages, I say, and they were of a nature which suggests that the re—appearance of Braden on Ransford's present stage of life would be, extremely unpleasant and unwelcome to Ransford."

"Vague!" murmured Mary. "Extremely vague!"

"But quite enough," retorted Bryce, "to give the police the suggestion of motive. I tell you the police know quite enough to know that Braden was, of all men in the world, the last man Ransford desired to see cross his path again. And—on that morning on which the Paradise affair occurred—Braden did cross his path. Therefore, in the conventional police way of thinking and looking at things, there's motive."

"Motive for what?" asked Mary.

Bryce arrived here at one of his critical stages, and he paused a moment in order to choose his words.

"Don't get any false ideas or impressions," he said at last. "I'm not accusing Ransford of anything. I'm only telling you what I know the police think and are on the very edge of accusing him of. To put it plainly—of murder. They say he'd a motive for murdering Braden—and with them motive is everything. It's the first thing they seem to think of; they first question they ask themselves. 'Why should this man have murdered that man?'—do you see! 'What motive had he?—that's the point. And they think—these chaps like Mitchington and the London man—that Ransford certainly had a motive for getting rid of Braden when they met."

"What was the motive?" asked Mary.

"They've found out something—perhaps a good deal—about what happened between Braden and Ransford some years ago," replied Bryce. "And their theory is—if you want to know the truth —that Ransford ran away with Braden's wife, and that Braden had been looking for him ever since."

Bryce had kept his eyes on Mary's hands, and now at last he saw the girl's fingers tremble. But her voice was steady enough when she spoke.

"Is that mere conjecture on their part, or is it based on any fact?" she asked.

"I'm not in full knowledge of all their secrets," answered Bryce, "but I've heard enough to know that there's a basis of undeniable fact on which they're going. I know for instance, beyond doubt, that Braden and Ransford were bosom friends, years ago, that Braden was married to a girl whom Ransford had wanted to marry, that Braden's wife suddenly left him, mysteriously, a few years later, and that, at the same time, Ransford made an equally mysterious disappearance. The police know all that. What is the inference to be drawn? What inference would any one—you yourself, for example—draw?"

"None, till I've heard what Dr. Ransford had to say," replied Mary.

Bryce disliked that ready retort. He was beginning to feel that he was being met by some force stronger that his own.

"That's all very well," he remarked. "I don't say that I wouldn't do the same. But I'm only explaining the police position, and showing you the danger likely to arise from it. The police theory is this, as far as I can make it out: Ransford, years ago, did Braden a wrong, and Braden certainly swore revenge when he could find him. Circumstances prevented Braden from seeking him closely for some time; at last they met here, by accident. Here the police aren't decided. One theory is that there was an altercation, blows, a struggle, in the course of which Braden met his death; the other is that Ransford deliberately took Braden up into the gallery and flung him through that open doorway—"

"That," observed Mary, with something very like a sneer, "seems so likely that I should think it would never occur to anybody but the sort of people you're telling me of! No man of any real sense would believe it for a minute!"

"Some people of plain common sense do believe it for all that!" retorted Bryce. "For it's quite possible. But as I say, I'm only repeating. And of course, the rest of it follows on that. The police theory is that Collishaw witnessed Braden's death at Ransford's hands, that Ransford got to know that Collishaw knew of that, and that he therefore quietly removed Collishaw. And it is on all that that they're going, and will go. Don't ask me if I think they're right or wrong! I'm only telling you what I know so as to show you what danger Ransford is in."

Mary made no immediate answer, and Bryce sat watching her. Somehow—he was at a loss to explain it to himself—things were not going as he had expected. He had confidently believed that the girl would be frightened, scared, upset, ready to do anything that he asked or suggested. But she was plainly not frightened. And the fingers which busied themselves with the fancy–work had become steady again, and her voice had been steady all along.

"Pray," she asked suddenly, and with a little satirical inflection of voice which Brice was quick to notice, "pray, how is it that you—not a policeman, not a detective!—come to know so much of all this? Since when were you taken into the confidence of Mitchington and the mysterious person from London?"

"You know as well as I do that I have been dragged into the case against my wishes," answered Bryce almost sullenly. "I was fetched to Braden—I saw him die. It was I who found Collishaw—dead. Of course, I've been mixed up, whether I would or not, and I've had to see a good deal of the police, and naturally I've learnt things."

Mary suddenly turned on him with a flash of the eye which might have warned Bryce that he had signally failed in the main feature of his adventure.

"And what have you learnt that makes you come here and tell me all this?" she exclaimed. "Do you think I'm a simpleton, Dr. Bryce? You set out by saying that Dr. Ransford is in danger from the police, and that you know more—much more than the police! what does that mean? Shall I tell you? It means that you—you!—know that the police are wrong, and that if you like you can prove to them that they are wrong! Now, then isn't that so?"

"I am in possession of certain facts," began Bryce. "I—"

Mary stopped him with a look.

"My turn!" she said. "You're in possession of certain facts. Now isn't it the truth that the facts you are in possession of are proof enough to you that Dr. Ransford is as innocent as I am? It's no use your trying to deceive me! Isn't that so?"

"I could certainly turn the police off his track," admitted Bryce, who was growing highly uncomfortable. "I could divert—"

Mary gave him another look and dropping her needlework continued to watch him steadily.

"Do you call yourself a gentleman?" she asked quietly. "Or we'll leave the term out. Do you call yourself even decently honest? For, if you do, how can you have the sheer impudence —more, insolence!—to come here and tell me all this when you know that the police are wrong and that you could—to use your own term, which is your way of putting it—turn them off the wrong track? Whatever sort of man are you? Do you want to know my opinion of you in plain words?"

"You seem very anxious to give it, anyway," retorted Bryce.

"I will give it, and it will perhaps put an end to this," answered Mary. "If you are in possession of anything in the way of evidence which would prove Dr. Ransford's innocence and you are wilfully suppressing it, you are bad, wicked, base, cruel, unfit for any decent being's society! And," she added, as she picked up her work and rose, "you're not going to have any more of mine!"

"A moment!" said Bryce. He was conscious that he had somehow played all his cards badly, and he wanted another opening. "You're misunderstanding me altogether! I never said—never inferred—that I wouldn't save Ransford."

"Then, if there's need, which I don't admit, you acknowledge that you could save him?" she exclaimed sharply. "Just as I thought. Then, if you're an honest man, a man with any pretensions to honour, why don't you at once! Any man who had such feelings as those I've just mentioned wouldn't hesitate one second. But you—you!—you come and—talk about it! As if it were a game! Dr. Bryce, you make me feel sick, mentally, morally sick."

179

Bryce had risen to his feet when Mary rose, and he now stood staring at her. Ever since his boyhood he had laughed and sneered at the mere idea of the finer feelings—he believed that every man has his price—and that honesty and honour are things useful as terms but of no real existence. And now he was wondering—really wondering—if this girl meant the things she said: if she really felt a mental loathing of such minds and purposes as he knew his own were, or if it were merely acting on her part. Before he could speak she turned on him again more fiercely than before.

"Shall I tell you something else in plain language?" she asked. "You evidently possess a very small and limited knowledge—if you have any at all!—of women, and you apparently don't rate their mental qualities at any high standard. Let me tell you that I am not quite such a fool as you seem to think me! You came here this afternoon to bargain with me! You happen to know how much I respect my guardian and what I owe him for the care he has taken of me and my brother. You thought to trade on that! You thought you could make a bargain with me; you were to save Dr. Ransford, and for reward you were to have me! You daren't deny it. Dr. Bryce —I can see through you!"

"I never said it, at any rate," answered Bryce.

"Once more, I say, I'm not a fool!" exclaimed Mary. "I saw through you all along. And you've failed! I'm not in the least frightened by what you've said. If the police arrest Dr. Ransford, Dr. Ransford knows how to defend himself. And you're not afraid for him! You know you aren't. It wouldn't matter twopence to you if he were hanged tomorrow, for you hate him. But look to yourself! Men who cheat, and scheme, and plot, and plan as you do come to bad ends. Mind yours! Mind the wheel doesn't come full circle. And now, if you please, go away and don't dare to come near me again!"

Bryce made no answer. He had listened, with an attempt at a smile, to all this fiery indignation, but as Mary spoke the last words he was suddenly aware of something that drew his attention from her and them. Through an opening in Ransford's garden hedge he could see the garden door of the Folliots' house across the Close. And at that moment out of it emerge Folliot himself in conversation with Glassdale!

Without a word, Bryce snatched up his hat from the table of the summer–house, and went swiftly away—a new scheme, a new idea in his mind.

CHAPTER XXIV. FINESSE

Glassdale, journeying into Wrychester half an hour after Bryce had left him at the Saxonsteade Arms, occupied himself during his ride across country in considering the merits of the two handbills which Bryce had given him. One announced an offer of five hundred pounds reward for information in the Braden–Collishaw matter; the other, of a thousand pounds. It struck him as a curious thing that two offers should be made —it suggested, at once, that more than one person was deeply interested in this affair. But who were they?—no answer to that question appeared on the handbills, which were, in each case, signed by Wrychester solicitors. To one of these Glassdale, on arriving in the old city, promptly proceeded —selecting the offerer of the larger reward. He presently found himself in the presence of an astute–looking man who, having had his visitor's name sent in to him, regarded Glassdale with very obvious curiosity.

"Mr. Glassdale?" he said inquiringly, as the caller took an offered chair. "Are you, by any chance, the Mr. Glassdale whose name is mentioned in connection with last night's remarkable affair?"

He pointed to a copy of the weekly newspaper, lying on his desk, and to a formal account of the discovery of the Saxonsteade jewels which had been furnished to the press, at the Duke's request, by Mitchington. Glassdale glanced at it —unconcernedly.

"The same," he answered. "But I didn't call here on that matter—though what I did call about is certainly relative to it. You've offered a reward for any information that would lead to the solution of that mystery about Braden—and the other man, Collishaw."

"Of a thousand pounds—yes!" replied the solicitor, looking at his visitor with still more curiosity, mingled with expectancy. "Can you give any?"

Glassdale pulled out the two handbills which he had obtained from Bryce.

"There are two rewards offered," he remarked. "Are they entirely independent of each other?"

"We know nothing of the other," answered the solicitor. "Except, of course, that it exists.

They're quite independent."

"Who's offering the five hundred pound one?" asked Glassdale.

The solicitor paused, looking his man over. He saw at once that Glassdale had, or believed he had, something to tell—and was disposed to be unusually cautious about telling it.

"Well," he replied, after a pause. "I believe—in fact, it's an open secret—that the offer of five hundred pounds is made by Dr. Ransford."

"And—yours?" inquired Glassdale. "Who's at the back of yours–a thousand?"

The solicitor smiled.

"You haven't answered my question, Mr. Glassdale," he observed. "Can you give any information?"

Glassdale threw his questioner a significant glance.

"Whatever information I might give," he said, "I'd only give to a principal—the principal. From what I've seen and known of all this, there's more in it than is on the surface. I can tell something. I knew John Braden—who, of course, was John Brake—very well, for some years. Naturally, I was in his confidence."

"About more than the Saxonsteade jewels, you mean?" asked the solicitor.

"About more than that," assented Glassdale. "Private matters. I've no doubt I can throw some light some!—on this Wrychester Paradise affair. But, as I said just now, I'll only deal with the principal. I wouldn't tell you, for instance—as your principal's solicitor."

The solicitor smiled again.

"Your ideas, Mr. Glassdale, appear to fit in with our principal's," he remarked. "His instructions—strict instructions—to us are that if anybody turns up who can give any information, it's not to be given to us, but to—himself!"

"Wise man!" observed Glassdale. "That's just what I feel about it. It's a mistake to share secrets with more than one person."

"There is a secret, then!" asked the solicitor, half slyly.

"Might be," replied Glassdale. "Who's your client?"

The solicitor pulled a scrap of paper towards him and wrote a few words on it. He pushed it towards his caller, and Glassdale picked it up and read what had been written—Mr. Stephen Folliot, The Close.

"You'd better go and see him," said the solicitor, suggestively. "You'll find him reserved enough."

Glassdale read and re-read the name—as if he were endeavouring to recollect it, or connect it with something.

"What particular reason has this man for wishing to find this out?" he inquired.

"Can't say, my good sir!" replied the solicitor, with a smile. "Perhaps he'll tell you. He hasn't told me."

Glassdale rose to take his leave. But with his hand on the door he turned.

"Is this gentleman a resident in the place?" he asked.

"A well-known townsman," replied the solicitor. "You'll easily find his house in the Close—everybody knows it."

Glassdale went away then—and walked slowly towards the Cathedral precincts. On his way he passed two places at which he was half inclined to call—one was the police-station; the other, the office of the solicitors who were acting on behalf of the offerer of five hundred pounds. He half glanced at. the solicitor's door—but on reflection went forward. A man who was walking across the Close pointed out the Folliot residence—Glassdale entered by the garden door, and in another minute came face to face with Folliot himself, busied, as usual, amongst his rose-trees.

The Paradise Mystery

Glassdale saw Folliot and took stock of him before Folliot knew that a stranger was within his gates. Folliot, in an old jacket which he kept for his horticultural labours, was taking slips from a standard; he looked as harmless and peaceful as his occupation. A quiet, inoffensive, somewhat benevolent elderly man, engaged in work, which suggested leisure and peace.

But Glassdale, after a first quick, searching glance, took another and longer one—and went nearer with a discreet laugh.

"Folliot turned quietly, and seeing the stranger, showed no surprise. He had a habit of looking over the top rims of his spectacles at people, and he looked in this way at Glassdale, glancing him up and down calmly. Glassdale lifted his slouch hat and advanced.

"Mr. Folliot, I believe, sir?" he said. "Mr. Stephen Folliot?"

"Aye, just so!" responded Folliot. "But I don't know you. Who may you be, now?"

"My name, sir, is Glassdale," answered the other. "I've just come from your solicitor's. I called to see him this afternoon—and he told me that the business I called about could only be dealt with—or discussed—with you. So—I came here."

Folliot, who had been cutting slips off a rose–tree, closed his knife and put it away in his old jacket. He turned and quietly inspected his visitor once more.

"Aye!" he said quietly. "So you're after that thousand pound reward, eh?"

"I should have no objection to it, Mr. Folliot," replied Glassdale.

"I dare say not," remarked Folliot, dryly. "I dare say not! And which are you, now?—one of those who think they can tell something, or one that really can tell? Eh?"

"You'll know that better when we've had a bit of talk, Mr. Folliot," answered Glassdale, accompanying his reply with a direct glance.

"Oh, well, now then, I've no objection to a bit of talk—none whatever!" said Folliot. "Here!—we'll sit down on that bench, amongst the roses. Quite private here—nobody about. And now," he continued, as Glassdale accompanied him to a rustic bench set beneath a pergola of rambler roses, "who are you, like? I read a queer account in this morning's local paper of what happened in the Cathedral grounds yonder last night, and there was a person of your name mentioned. Are you that Glassdale?"

"The same, Mr. Folliot," answered the visitor, promptly.

"Then you knew Braden—the man who lost his life here?" asked Folliot.

"Very well indeed," replied Glassdale.

"For how long?" demanded Folliot.

"Some years—as a mere acquaintance, seen now and then," said Glassdale. "A few years, recently, as what you might call a close friend."

"Tell you any of his secrets?" asked Folliot.

"Yes, he did!" answered Glassdale.

"Anything that seems to relate to his death—and the mystery about it?" inquired Folliot.

"I think so," said Glassdale. "Upon consideration, I think so!"

"Ah—and what might it be, now?" continued Folliot. He gave Glassdale a look which seemed to denote and imply several things. "It might be to your advantage to explain a bit, you know," he added. "One has to be a little—vague, eh?"

"There was a certain man that Braden was very anxious to find," said Glassdale. "He'd been looking for him for a good many years."

"A man?" asked Folliot. "One?"

"Well, as a matter of fact, there were two," admitted Glassdale, "but there was one in particular. The other—the second—so Braden said, didn't matter; he was or had been, only a sort of cat's–paw of the man he especially wanted."

"I see," said Folliot. He pulled out a cigar case and offered a cigar to his visitor, afterwards lighting one himself. "And what did Braden want that man for?" he asked.

Glassdale waited until his cigar was in full going order before he answered this question. Then he replied in one word.

"Revenge!"

Folliot put his thumbs in the armholes of his buff waistcoat and leaning back, seemed to be admiring his roses.

"Ah!" he said at last. "Revenge, now? A sort of vindictive man, was he? Wanted to get his knife into somebody, eh?"

"He wanted to get something of his own back from a man who'd done him," answered Glassdale, with a short laugh. "That's about it!"

For a minute or two both men smoked in silence. Then Folliot —still regarding his roses—put a leading question.

"Give you any details?" he asked.

"Enough," said Glassdale. "Braden had been done—over a money transaction—by these men—one especially, as head and front of the affair—and it had cost him—more than anybody would think! Naturally, he wanted—if he ever got the chance—his revenge. Who wouldn't?"

"And he'd tracked 'em down, eh?" asked Folliot.

"There are questions I can answer, and there are questions I can't answer," responded Glassdale. "That's one of the questions I've no reply to. For—I don't know! But—I can say this. He hadn't tracked 'em down the day before he came to Wrychester!"

"You're sure of that?" asked Folliot. "He—didn't come here on that account?"

"No, I'm sure he didn't!" answered Glassdale, readily. "If he had, I should have known. I was with him till noon the day he came here—in London—and when he took his ticket at Victoria for Wrychester, he'd no more idea than the man in the moon as to where those men had got to. He mentioned it as we were having a bit of lunch together before he got into the train. No—he didn't come to Wrychester for any such purpose as that! But—"

He paused and gave Folliot a meaning glance out of the corner of his eyes.

"Aye—what?" asked Folliot.

"I think he met at least one of 'em here," said Glassdale, quietly. "And—perhaps both."

"Leading to—misfortune for him?" suggested Folliot.

"If you like to put it that way—yes," assented Glassdale.

Folliot smoked a while in more reflective silence.

"Aye, well!" he said at last. "I suppose you haven't put these ideas of yours before anybody, now?"

"Present ideas?" asked Glassdale, sharply. "Not to a soul! I've not had 'em—very long."

"You're the sort of man that another man can do a deal with, I suppose?" suggested Folliot. "That is, if it's made worth your while, of course?"

"I shouldn't wonder," replied Glassdale. "And—if it is made worth my while."

Folliot mused a little. Then he tapped Glassdale's elbow.

"You see," he said, confidentially, "it might be, you know, that I had a little purpose of my own in, offering that reward. It might be that it was a very particular friend of mine that had the misfortune to have incurred this man Braden's hatred. And I might want to save him, d'ye see, from—well, from the consequence of what's happened, and to hear

187

about it first if anybody came forward, eh?"

"As I've done," said Glassdale.

"As—you've done," assented Folliot. "Now, perhaps it would be in the interest of this particular friend of mine if he made it worth your while to—say no more to anybody, eh?"

"Very much worth his while, Mr. Folliot," declared Glassdale.

"Aye, well," continued Folliot. "This very particular friend would just want to know, you know, how much you really, truly know! Now, for instance, about these two men—and one in particular—that Braden was after? Did—did he name 'em?"

Glassdale leaned a little nearer to his companion on the rose–screened bench.

"He named them—to me!" he said in a whisper. "One was a man called Falkiner Wraye, and the other man was a man named Flood. Is that enough?"

"I think you'd better come and see me this evening," answered Folliot. "Come just about dusk to that door—I'll meet you there. Fine roses these of mine, aren't they?" he continued, as they rose. "I occupy myself entirely with 'em."

He walked with Glassdale to the garden door, and stood there watching his visitor go away up the side of the high wall until he turned into the path across Paradise. And then, as Folliot was retreating to his roses, he saw Bryce coming over the Close—and Bryce beckoned to him.

CHAPTER XXV. THE OLD WELL HOUSE

When Bryce came hurrying up to him, Folliot was standing at his garden door with his hands thrust under his coat–tails —the very picture of a benevolent, leisured gentleman who has nothing to do and is disposed to give his time to anybody. He glanced at Bryce as he had glanced at Glassdale—over the tops of his spectacles, and the glance had no more than mild inquiry in it. But if Bryce had been less excited, he would have seen that

The Paradise Mystery

Folliot, as he beckoned him inside the garden, swept a sharp look over the Close and ascertained that there was no one about, that Bryce's entrance was unobserved. Save for a child or two, playing under the tall elms near one of the gates, and for a clerical figure that stalked a path in the far distance, the Close was empty of life. And there was no one about, either, in that part of Folliot's big garden.

"I want a bit of talk with you," said Bryce as Folliot closed the door and turned down a side-path to a still more retired region. "Private talk. Let's go where it's quiet."

Without replying in words to this suggestion, Folliot led the way through his rose-trees to a far corner of his grounds, where an old building of grey stone, covered with ivy, stood amongst high trees. He turned the key of a doorway and motioned Bryce to enter.

"Quiet enough in here, doctor," he observed. "You've never seen this place—bit of a fancy of mine."

Bryce, absorbed as he was in the thoughts of the moment, glanced cursorily at the place into which Folliot had led him. It was a square building of old stone, its walls unlined, unplastered; its floor paved with much worn flags of limestone, evidently set down in a long dead age and now polished to marble-like smoothness. In its midst, set flush with the floor, was what was evidently a trap-door, furnished with a heavy iron ring. To this Folliot pointed, with a glance of significant interest.

"Deepest well in all Wrychester under that," he remarked. "You'd never think it—it's a hundred feet deep—and more! Dry now—water gave out some years ago. Some people would have pulled this old well-house down—but not me! I did better—I turned it to good account." He raised a hand and pointed upward to an obviously modern ceiling of strong oak timbers. "Had that put in," he continued, "and turned the top of the building into a little snuggery. Come up!"

He led the way to a flight of steps in one corner of the lower room, pushed open a door at their head, and showed his companion into a small apartment arranged and furnished in something closely approaching to luxury. The walls were hung with thick fabrics; the carpeting was equally thick; there were pictures, books, and curiosities; the two or three chairs were deep and big enough to lie down in; the two windows commanded pleasant views of the Cathedral towers on one side and of the Close on the other.

"Nice little place to be alone in, d'ye see?" said Folliot. "Cool in summer—warm in winter—modern fire−grate, you notice. Come here when I want to do a bit of quiet thinking, what?"

"Good place for that—certainly," agreed Bryce.

Folliot pointed his visitor to one of the big chairs and turning to a cabinet brought out some glasses, a syphon of soda−water, and a heavy cut−glass decanter. He nodded at a box of cigars which lay open on a table at Bryce's elbow as he began to mix a couple of drinks.

"Help yourself," he said. "Good stuff, those."

Not until he had given Bryce a drink, and had carried his own glass to another easy chair did Folliot refer to any reason for Bryce's visit. But once settled down, he looked at him speculatively.

"What did you want to see me about?" he asked.

Bryce, who had lighted a cigar, looked across its smoke at the imperturbable face opposite.

"You've just had Glassdale here," he observed quietly. "I saw him leave you."

Folliot nodded—without any change of expression.

"Aye, doctor," he said. "And—what do you know about Glassdale, now?"

Bryce, who would have cheerfully hobnobbed with a man whom he was about to conduct to the scaffold, lifted his glass and drank.

"A good deal," he answered as he set the glass down. "The fact is—I came here to tell you so!—I know a good deal about everything."

"A wide term!" remarked Folliot. "You've got some limitation to it, I should think. What do you mean by—everything?"

"I mean about recent matters," replied Bryce. "I've interested myself in them—for reasons of my own. Ever since Braden was found at the foot of those stairs in Paradise, and I was fetched to him, I've interested myself. And—I've discovered a great deal—more, much more than's known to anybody."

Folliot threw one leg over the other and began to jog his foot.

"Oh!" he said after a pause. "Dear me! And—what might you know, now, doctor? Aught you can tell me eh?"

"Lots!" answered Bryce. "I came to tell you—on seeing that Glassdale had been with you. Because—I was with Glassdale this morning."

Folliot made no answer. But Bryce saw that his cool, almost indifferent manner was changing—he was beginning, under the surface, to get anxious.

"When I left Glassdale—at noon," continued Bryce, "I'd no idea—and I don't think he had—that he was coming to see you. But I know what put the notion into his head. I gave him copies of those two reward bills. He no doubt thought he might make a bit—and so he came in to town, and—to you."

"Well?" asked Folliot.

"I shouldn't wonder," remarked Bryce, reflectively, and almost as if speaking to himself, "I shouldn't at all wonder if Glassdale's the sort of man who can be bought. He, no doubt, has his price. But all that Glassdale knows is nothing—to what I know."

Folliot had allowed his cigar to go out. He threw it away, took a fresh one from the box, and slowly struck a match and lighted it.

"What might you know, now?" he asked after another pause.

"I've a bit of a faculty for finding things out," answered Bryce boldly. "And I've developed it. I wanted to know all about Braden—and about who killed him—and why. There's only one way of doing all that sort of thing, you know. You've got to go back—a long way back—to the very beginnings. I went back—to the time when Braden was

191

married. Not as Braden, of course—but as who he really was—John Brake. That was at a place called Braden Medworth, near Barthorpe, in Liecestershire."

He paused there, watching Folliot. But Folliot showed no more than close attention, and Bryce went on.

"Not much in that—for the really important part of the story," he continued. "But Brake had other associations with Barthorpe—a bit later. He got to know—got into close touch with a Barthorpe man who, about the time of Brake's marriage, left Barthorpe end settled in London. Brake and this man began to have some secret dealings together. There was another man in with them, too—a man who was a sort of partner of the Barthorpe man's. Brake had evidently a belief in these men, and he trusted them—unfortunately for himself he sometimes trusted the bank's money to them. I know what happened—he used to let them have money for short financial transactions—to be refunded within a very brief space. But —he went to the fire too often, and got his fingers burned in the end. The two men did him—one of them in particular—and cleared out. He had to stand the racket. He stood it—to the tune of ten years' penal servitude. And, naturally, when he'd finished his time, he wanted to find those two men—and began a long search for them. Like to know the names of the men, Mr. Folliot?"

"You might mention 'em—if you know 'em," answered Folliot.

"The name of the particular one was Wraye—Falkiner Wraye," replied Bryce promptly. "Of the other—the man of lesser importance—Flood."

The two men looked quietly at each other for a full moment's silence. And it was Bryce who first spoke with a ring of confidence in his tone which showed that he knew he had the whip hand.

"Shall I tell you something about Falkiner Wraye?" he asked. "I will!—it's deeply interesting. Mr. Falkiner Wraye, after cheating and deceiving Brake, and leaving him to pay the penalty of his over-trustfulness, cleared out of England and carried his money-making talents to foreign parts. He succeeded in doing well—he would!—and eventually he came back and married a rich widow and settled himself down in an out-of-the-world English town to grow roses. You're Falkiner Wraye, you know, Mr. Folliot!"

192

Bryce laughed as he made this direct accusation, and sitting forward in his chair, pointed first to Folliot's face and then to his left hand.

"Falkiner Wraye," he said, "had an unfortunate gun accident in his youth which marked him for life. He lost the middle finger of his left hand, and he got a bad scar on his left jaw. There they are, those marks! Fortunate for you, Mr. Folliot, that the police don't know all that I know, for if they did, those marks would have done for you days ago!" For a minute or two Folliot sat joggling his leg—a bad sign in him of rising temper if Bryce had but known it. While he remained silent he watched Bryce narrowly, and when he spoke, his voice was calm as ever.

"And what use do you intend to put your knowledge to, if one may ask?" he inquired, half sneeringly. "You said just now that you'd no doubt that man Glassdale could be bought, and I'm inclining to think that you're one of those men that have their price. What is it?"

"We've not come to that," retorted Bryce. "You're a bit mistaken. If I have my price, it's not in the same commodity that Glassdale would want. But before we do any talking about that sort of thing, I want to add to my stock of knowledge. Look here! We'll be candid. I don't care a snap of my fingers that Brake, or Braden's dead, or that Collishaw's dead, nor if one had his neck broken and the other was poisoned, but—whose hand was that which the mason, Varner, saw that morning, when Brake was flung out of that doorway? Come, now!—whose?"

"Not mine, my lad!" answered Folliot, confidently. "That's a fact?"

Bryce hesitated, giving Folliot a searching look. And Folliot nodded solemnly. "I tell you, not mine!" he repeated. "I'd naught to do with it!"

"Then who had?" demanded Bryce. "Was it the other man—Flood? And if so, who is Flood?"

Folliot got up from his chair and, cigar between his lips and hands under the tails of his old coat, walked silently about the quiet room for awhile. He was evidently thinking deeply, and Bryce made no attempt to disturb him. Some minutes went by before Folliot took the cigar from his lips and leaning against the chimneypiece looked fixedly at his visitor.

"Look here, my lad!" he said, earnestly. "You're no doubt, as you say, a good hand at finding things out, and you've doubtless done a good bit of ferreting, and done it well enough in your own opinion. But there's one thing you can't find out, and the police can't find out either, and that's the precise truth about Braden's death. I'd no hand in it—it couldn't be fastened on to me, anyhow."

Bryce looked up and interjected one word.

"Collishaw?"

"Nor that, neither," answered Folliot, hastily. "Maybe I know something about both, but neither you nor the police nor anybody could fasten me to either matter! Granting all you say to be true, where's the positive truth?"

"What about circumstantial evidence," asked Bryce.

"You'd have a job to get it," retorted Folliot. "Supposing that all you say is true about—about past matters? Nothing can prove—nothing!—that I ever met Braden that morning. On the other hand, I can prove, easily, that I never did meet him; I can account for every minute of my time that day. As to the other affair—not an ounce of direct evidence!"

"Then—it was the other man!" exclaimed Bryce. "Now then, who is he?"

Folliot replied with a shrewd glance.

"A man who by giving away another man gave himself away would be a damned fool!" he answered. "If there is another man—"

"As if there must be!" interrupted Bryce.

"Then he's safe!" concluded Folliot. "You'll get nothing from me about him!"

"And nobody can get at you except through him?" asked Bryce.

194

"That's about it," assented Folliot laconically.

Bryce laughed cynically.

"A pretty coil!" he said 4th a sneer. "Here! You talked about my price. I'm quite content to hold my tongue if you'd tell me something, about what happened seventeen years ago."

"What?" asked Folliot.

"You knew Brake, you must have known his family affairs," said Bryce. "What became of Brake's wife and children when he went to prison?"

Folliot shook his head, and it was plain to Bryce that his gesture of dissent was genuine.

"You're wrong," he answered. "I never at any time knew anything of Brake's family affairs. So little indeed, that I never even knew he was married."

Bryce rose to his feet and stood staring.

"What!" he exclaimed. "You mean to tell me that, even now, you don't know that Brake had two children, and that—that —oh, it's incredible!"

"What's incredible?" asked Folliot. "What are you talking about?"

Bryce in his eagerness and surprise grasped Folliot's arm and shook it.

"Good heavens, man!" he said. "Those two wards of Ransford's are Brake's girl and boy! Didn't you know that, didn't you?"

"Never!" answered Folliot. "Never! And who's Ransford, then? I never heard Brake speak of any Ransford! What game is all this? What—"

Before Bryce could reply, Folliot suddenly started, thrust his companion aside and went to one of the windows. A sharp exclamation from him took Bryce to his side. Folliot lifted a shaking hand and pointed into the garden.

"There!" he whispered. "Hell and—What's this mean?"

Bryce looked in the direction pointed out. Behind the pergola of rambler roses the figures of men were coming towards the old well–house led by one of Folliot's gardeners. Suddenly they emerged into full view, and in front of the rest was Mitchington and close behind him the detective, and behind him—Glassdale!

CHAPTER XXVI. THE OTHER MAN

It was close on five o'clock when Glassdale, leaving Folliot at his garden door, turned the corner into the quietness of the Precincts. He walked about there a while, staring at the queer old houses with eyes which saw neither fantastic gables nor twisted chimneys. Glassdale was thinking. And the result of his reflections was that he suddenly exchanged his idle sauntering for brisker steps and walked sharply round to the police station, where he asked to see Mitchington.

Mitchington and the detective were just about to walk down to the railway–station to meet Ransford, in accordance with his telegram. At sight of Glassdale they went back into the inspector's office. Glassdale closed the door and favoured them with a knowing smile.

"Something else for you, inspector!" he said. "Mixed up a bit with last night's affair, too. About these mysteries—Braden and Collishaw—I can tell you one man who's in them."

"Who, then?" demanded Mitchington.

Glassdale went a step nearer to the two officials and lowered his voice.

"The man who's known here as Stephen Folliot," he answered. "That's a fact!"

"Nonsense!" exclaimed Mitchington. Then he laughed incredulously. "Can't believe it!" he continued. "Mr. Folliot! Must be some mistake!"

"No mistake," replied Glassdale. "Besides, Folliot's only an assumed name. That man is really one Falkiner Wraye, the man Braden, or Brake, was seeking for many a year, the man who cheated Brake and got him into trouble. I tell you it's a fact! He's admitted it, or as good as done so, to me just now."

"To you? And—let you come away and spread it?" exclaimed Mitchington. "That's incredible! more astonishing than the other!"

Glassdale laughed.

"Ah, but I let him think I could be squared, do you see?" he said. "Hush—money, you know. He's under the impression that I'm to go back to him this evening to settle matters. I knew so much—identified him, as a matter of fact—that he'd no option. I tell you he's been in at both these affairs —certain! But—there's another man."

"Who's he?" demanded Mitchington.

"Can't say, for I don't know, though I've an idea he'll be a fellow that Brake was also wanting to find," replied Glassdale. "But anyhow, I know what I'm talking about when I tell you of Folliot. You'd better do something before he suspects me."

Mitchington glanced at the clock.

"Come with us down to the station," he said. "Dr. Ransford's coming in on this express from town; he's got news for us. We'd better hear that first. Folliot!—good Lord!—who'd have believed or even dreamed it!"

"You'll see," said Glassdale as they went out.

"Maybe Dr. Ransford's got the same information." Ransford was out of the train as soon as it ran in, and hurried to where Mitchington and his companions were standing. And behind him, to Mitchington's surprise, came old Simpson Harker, who had evidently travelled with him. With a silent gesture Mitchington beckoned the whole party into an empty waiting—room and closed its door on them.

"Now then, inspector," said Ransford without preface or ceremony, "you've got to act quickly! You got my wire—a few words will explain it. I went up to town this morning in answer to a message from the bank where Braden lodged his money when he returned to

England. To tell you the truth, the managers there and myself have, since Braden's death, been carrying to a conclusion an investigation which I began on Braden's behalf—though he never knew of it—years ago. At the bank I met Mr. Harker here, who had called to find something out for himself. Now I'll sum things up in a nutshell: for years Braden, or Brake, had been wanting to find two men who cheated him. The name of one is Wraye, of the other, Flood. I've been trying to trace them, too. At last we've got them. They're in this town, and without doubt the deaths of both Braden and Collishaw are at their door! You know both well enough. Wraye is—"

"Mr. Folliot!" interrupted Mitchington, pointing to Glassdale. "So he's just told us; he's identified him as Wraye. But the other—who's he, doctor?"

Ransford glanced at Glassdale as if he wished to question him, but instead he answered Mitchington's question.

"The other man," he said, "the man Flood, is also a well–known man to you. Fladgate!"

Mitchington started, evidently more astonished than by the first news.

"What!" he exclaimed. "The verger! You don't say!"

"Do you remember," continued Ransford, "that Folliot got Fladgate his appointment as verger not so very long after he himself came here? He did, anyway, and Fladgate is Flood. We've traced everything through Flood. Wraye has been a difficult man to trace, because of his residence abroad for a long time and his change of name, and so on, and it was only recently that my agents struck on a line through Flood. But there's the fact. And the probability is that when Braden came here he recognized and was recognized by these two, and that one or other of them is responsible for his death and for Collishaw's too. Circumstantial evidence, all of it, no doubt, but irresistible! Now, what do you propose to do?"

Mitchington considered matters for a moment.

"Fladgate first, certainly," he said. "He lives close by here; we'll go round to his cottage. If he sees he's in a tight place he may let things out. Let's go there at once."

The Paradise Mystery

He led the whole party out of the station and down the High Street until they came to a narrow lane of little houses which ran towards the Close. At its entrance a policeman was walking his beat. Mitchington stopped to exchange a few words with him.

"This man Fladgate," he said, rejoining the others, "lives alone—fifth cottage down here. He'll be about having his tea; we shall take him by surprise." Presently the group stood around a door at which Mitchington knocked gently, and it was on their grave and watchful faces that a tall, clean-shaven, very solemn-looking man gazed in astonishment as he opened the door, and started back. He went white to the lips and his hand fell trembling from the latch as Mitchington strode in and the rest crowded behind.

"Now then, Fladgate!" said Mitchington, going straight to the point and watching his man narrowly, while the detective approached him closely on the other side. "I want you and a word with you at once. Your real name is Flood! What have you to say to that? And—it's no use beating about the bush —what have you to say about this Braden affair, and your share with Folliot in it, whose real name is Wraye. It's all come out about the two of you. If you've anything to say, you'd better say it."

The verger, whose black gown lay thrown across the back of a chair, looked from one face to another with frightened eyes. It was very evident that the suddenness of the descent had completely unnerved him. Ransford's practised eyes saw that he was on the verge of a collapse.

"Give him time, Mitchington," he said. "Pull yourself together," he added, turning to the man. "Don't be frightened; answer these questions!"

"For God's sake, gentlemen!" grasped the verger. "What—what is it? What am I to answer? Before God, I'm as innocent as —as any of you—about Mr. Brake's death! Upon my soul and honour I am!"

"You know all about it;" insisted Mitchington.

"Come, now, isn't it true that you're Flood, and that Folliot's Wraye, the two men whose trick on him got Brake convicted years ago? Answer that!"

Flood looked from one side to the other. He was leaning against his tea–table, set in the middle of his tidy living room. From the hearth his kettle sent out a pleasant singing that sounded strangely in contrast with the grim situation.

"Yes, that's true," he said at last. "But in that affair I—I wasn't the principal. I was only—only Wraye's agent, as it were: I wasn't responsible. And when Mr. Brake came here, when I met him that morning—"

He paused, still looking from one to another of his audience as if entreating their belief.

"As sure as I'm a living man, gentlemen!" he suddenly burst out, "I'd no willing hand in Mr. Brake's death! I'll tell you the exact truth; I'll take my oath of it whenever you like. I'd have been thankful to tell, many a time, but for—for Wraye. He wouldn't let me at first, and afterwards it got complicated. It was this way That morning—when Mr. Brake was found dead—I had occasion to go up into that gallery under the clerestory. I suddenly came on him face to face. He recognized me. And—I'm telling you the solemn, absolute truth, gentlemen!—he'd no sooner recognized me than he attacked me, seizing me by the arm. I hadn't recognized him at first, I did when he laid hold of me. I tried to shake him off, tried to quiet him; he struggled—I don't know what he wanted to do—he began to cry out—it was a wonder he wasn't heard in the church below, and he would have been only the organ was being played rather loudly. And in the struggle he slipped—it was just by that open doorway—and before I could do more than grasp at him, he shot through the opening and fell! It was sheer, pure accident, gentlemen! Upon my soul, I hadn't the least intention of harming him."

"And after that?" asked Mitchington, at the end of a brief silence.

"I saw Mr. Folliot—Wraye," continued Flood. "Just afterwards, that was. I told him; he bade me keep silence until we saw how things went. Later he forced me to be silent. What could I do? As things were, Wraye could have disclaimed me—I shouldn't have had a chance. So I held my tongue."

"Now, then, Collishaw?" demanded Mitchington. "Give us the truth about that. Whatever the other was, that was murder!"

Flood lifted his hand and wiped away the perspiration that had gathered on his face.

"Before God, gentlemen!" he answered. "I know no more—at least, little more—about that than you do! I'll tell you all I do know. Wraye and I, of course, met now and then and talked about this. It got to our ears at last that Collishaw knew something. My own impression is that he saw what occurred between me and Mr. Brake—he was working somewhere up there. I wanted to speak to Collishaw. Wraye wouldn't let me, he bade me leave it to him. A bit later, he told me he'd squared Collishaw with fifty pounds—"

Mitchington and the detective exchanged looks.

Wraye—that's Folliot—paid Collishaw fifty pounds, did he?" asked the detective.

"He told me so," replied Flood. "To hold his tongue. But I'd scarcely heard that when I heard of Collishaw's sudden death. And as to how that happened, or who—who brought it about —upon my soul, gentlemen, I know nothing! Whatever I may have thought, I never mentioned it to Wraye—never! I—I daren't! You don't know what a man Wraye is! I've been under his thumb most of my life and—and what are you going to do with me, gentlemen?"

Mitchington exchanged a word or two with the detective, and then, putting his head out of the door beckoned to the policeman to whom he had spoken at the end of the lane and who now appeared in company with a fellow–constable. He brought both into the cottage.

"Get your tea," he said sharply to the verger. "These men will stop with you—you're not to leave this room." He gave some instructions to the two policemen in an undertone and motioned Ransford and the others to follow him. "It strikes me," he said, when they were outside in the narrow lane, "that what we've just heard is somewhere about the truth. And now we'll go on to Folliot's—there's a way to his house round here."

Mrs. Folliot was out, Sackville Bonham was still where Bryce had left him, at the golf–links, when the pursuers reached Folliot's. A parlourmaid directed them to the garden; a gardener volunteered the suggestion that his master might be in the old well–house and showed the way. And Folliot and Bryce saw them coming and looked at each other.

"Glassdale!" exclaimed Bryce. "By heaven, man!—he's told on you!"

Folliot was still staring through the window. He saw Ransford and Harker following the leading figures. And suddenly he turned to Bryce.

"You've no hand in this?" he demanded.

"I?" exclaimed Bryce. "I never knew till just now!"

Folliot pointed to the door.

"Go down!" he said. "Let 'em in, bid 'em come up! I'll—I'll settle with 'em. Go!"

Bryce hurried down to the lower apartment. He was filled with excitement—an unusual thing for him—but in the midst of it, as he made for the outer door, it suddenly struck him that all his schemings and plottings were going for nothing. The truth was at hand, and it was not going to benefit him in the slightest degree. He was beaten.

But that was no time for philosophic reflection; already those outside were beating at the door. He flung it open, and the foremost men started in surprise at the sight of him. But Bryce bent forward to Mitchington—anxious to play a part to the last.

"He's upstairs!" he whispered. "Up there! He'll bluff it out if he can, but he's just admitted to me—"

Mitchington thrust Bryce aside, almost roughly.

"We know all about that!" he said. "I shall have a word or two for you later! Come on, now—"

The men crowded up the stairway into Folliot's snuggery, Bryce, wondering at the inspector's words and manner, following closely behind him and the detective and Glassdale, who led the way. Folliot was standing in the middle of the room, one hand behind his back, the other in his pocket. And as the leading three entered the place he brought his concealed hand sharply round and presenting a revolver at Glassdale fired point–blank at him.

But it was not Glassdale who fell. He, wary and watching, started aside as he saw Folliot's movement, and the bullet, passing between his arm and body, found its billet in Bryce, who fell, with little more than a groan, shot through the heart. And as he fell, Folliot, scarcely looking at what he had done, drew his other hand from his pocket, slipped something into his mouth and sat down in the big chair behind him ... and within a moment the other men in the room were looking with horrified faces from one dead face to another.

CHAPTER XXVII. THE GUARDED SECRET

When Bryce had left her, Mary Bewery had gone into the house to await Ransford's return from town. She meant to tell him of all that Bryce had said and to beg him to take immediate steps to set matters right, not only that he himself might be cleared of suspicion but that Bryce's intrigues might be brought to an end. She had some hope that Ransford would bring back satisfactory news; she knew that his hurried visit to London had some connection with these affairs; and she also remembered what he had said on the previous night. And so, controlling her anger at Bryce and her impatience of the whole situation she waited as patiently as she could until the time drew near when Ransford might be expected to be seen coming across the Close. She knew from which direction he would come, and she remained near the dining–room window looking out for him. But six o'clock came and she had seen no sign of him; then, as she was beginning to think that he had missed the afternoon train she saw him, at the opposite side of the Close, talking earnestly to Dick, who presently came towards the house while Ransford turned back into Folliot's garden.

Dick Bewery came hurriedly in. His sister saw at once that he had just heard news which had had a sobering effect on his usually effervescent spirits. He looked at her as if he wondered exactly how to give her his message.

"I saw you with the doctor just now," she said, using the term by which she and her brother always spoke of their guardian. "Why hasn't he come home"

Dick came close to her, touching her arm.

"I say!" he said, almost whispering. "Don't be frightened —the doctor's all right—but there's something awful just happened. At Folliot's."

"What" she demanded. "Speak out, Dick! I'm not frightened. What is it?"

Dick shook his head as if he still scarcely realized the full significance of his news.

"It's all a licker to me yet!" he answered. "I don't understand it—I only know what the doctor told me—to come and tell you. Look here, it's pretty bad. Folliot and Bryce are both dead!"

In spite of herself Mary started back as from a great shock and clutched at the table by which they were standing.

"Dead!" she exclaimed. "Why—Bryce was here, speaking to me, not an hour ago!"

"Maybe," said Dick. "But he's dead now. The fact is, Folliot shot him with a revolver—killed him on the spot. And then Folliot poisoned himself—took the same stuff, the doctor said, that finished that chap Collishaw, and died instantly. It was in Folliot's old well–house. The doctor was there and the police."

"What does it all mean?" asked Mary.

"Don't know. Except this," added Dick; "they've found out about those other affairs—the Braden and the Collishaw affairs. Folliot was concerned in them; and who do you think the other was? You'd never guess! That man Fladgate, the verger. Only that isn't his proper name at all. He and Folliot finished Braden and Collishaw, anyway. The police have got Fladgate, and Folliot shot Bryce and killed himself just when they were going to take him."

"The doctor told you all this?" asked Mary.

"Yes," replied Dick. "Just that and no more. He called me in as I was passing Folliot's door. He's coming over as soon as he can. Whew! I say, won't there be some fine talk in the town! Anyway, things'll be cleared up now. What did Bryce want here?"

"Never mind; I can't talk of it, now," answered Mary. She was already thinking of how Bryce had stood before her, active and alive, only an hour earlier; she was thinking, too, of her warning to him. "It's all too dreadful! too awful to understand!"

"Here's the doctor coming now," said Dick, turning to the window. "He'll tell more."

Mary looked anxiously at Ransford as he came hastening in. He looked like a man who has just gone through a crisis and yet she was somehow conscious that there was a certain atmosphere of relief about him, as though some great weight had suddenly been lifted. He closed the door and looked straight at her.

"Dick has told you?" he asked.

"All that you told me," said Dick.

Ransford pulled off his gloves and flung them on the table with something of a gesture of weariness. And at that Mary hastened to speak.

"Don't tell any more—don't say anything—until you feel able," she said. "You're tired."

"No!" answered Ransford. "I'd rather say what I have to say now—just now! I've wanted to tell both of you what all this was, what it meant, everything about it, and until today, until within the last few hours, it was impossible, because I didn't know everything. Now I do! I even know more than I did an hour ago. Let me tell you now and have done with it. Sit down there, both of you, and listen."

He pointed to a sofa near the hearth, and the brother and sister sat down, looking at him wonderingly. Instead of sitting down himself he leaned against the edge of the table, looking down at them.

"I shall have to tell you some sad things," he said diffidently. "The only consolation is that it's all over now, and certain matters are, or can be, cleared and you'll have no more secrets. Nor shall I! I've had to keep this one jealously guarded for seventeen years! And I never thought it could be released as it has been, in this miserable and terrible fashion! But that's done now, and nothing can help it. And now, to make everything plain, just prepare yourselves to hear something that, at first, sounds very trying. The man whom

205

you've heard of as John Braden, who came to his death—by accident, as I now firmly believe—there in Paradise, was, in reality, John Brake—your father!"

Ransford looked at his two listeners anxiously as he told this. But he met no sign of undue surprise or emotion. Dick looked down at his toes with a little frown, as if he were trying to puzzle something out; Mary continued to watch Ransford with steady eyes.

"Your father—John Brake," repeated Ransford, breathing more freely now that he had got the worst news out. "I must go back to the beginning to make things clear to you about him and your mother. He was a close friend of mine when we were young men in London; he a bank manager; I, just beginning my work. We used to spend our holidays together in Leicestershire. There we met your mother, whose name was Mary Bewery. He married her; I was his best man. They went to live in London, and from that time I did not see so much of them, only now and then. During those first years of his married life Brake made the acquaintance of a man who came from the same part of Leicestershire that we had met your mother in—a man named Falkiner Wraye. I may as well tell you that Falkiner Wraye and Stephen Folliot were one and the same person."

Ransford paused, observing that Mary wished to ask a question.

"How long have you known that?" she asked.

"Not until today," replied Ransford promptly. "Never had the ghost of a notion of it! If I only had known—but, I hadn't! However, to go back—this man Wraye, who appears always to have been a perfect master of plausibility, able to twist people round his little finger, somehow got into close touch with your father about financial matters. Wraye was at that time a sort of financial agent in London, engaging in various doings which, I should imagine, were in the nature of gambles. He was assisted in these by a man who was either a partner with him or a very confidential clerk or agent, one Flood, who is identical with the man you have known lately as Fladgate, the verger. Between them, these two appear to have cajoled or persuaded your father at times to do very foolish and injudicious things which were, to put it briefly and plainly, the lendings of various sums of money as short loans for their transactions. For some time they invariably kept their word to him, and the advances were always repaid promptly. But eventually, when they had borrowed from him a considerable sum—some thousands of pounds—for a deal which was to be carried through within a couple of days, they decamped with the money, and completely disappeared, leaving your father to bear the consequences. You may easily understand what followed. The money which Brake had lent them was the bank's money. The bank unexpectedly came down on him for his balance, the whole thing was found out, and he was prosecuted. He had no defence—he was, of course, technically guilty—and he was sent to penal servitude."

Ransford had dreaded the telling of this but Mary made no sign, and Dick only rapped out a sharp question.

"He hadn't meant to rob the bank for himself, anyway, had he?" he asked.

"No, no! not at all!" replied Ransford hastily. "It was a bad error of judgment on his part, Dick, but he—he'd relied on these men, more particularly on Wraye, who'd been the leading spirit. Well, that was your father's sad fate. Now we come to what happened to your mother and yourselves. Just before your father's arrest, when he knew that all was lost, and that he was helpless, he sent hurriedly for me and told me everything in your mother's presence. He begged me to get her and you two children right away at once. She was against it; he insisted. I took you all to a quiet place in the country, where your mother assumed her maiden name. There, within a year, she died. She wasn't a strong woman at any time. After that—well, you both know pretty well what has been the run of things since you began to know anything. We'll leave that, it's nothing to do with the story. I want to go back to your father. I saw him after his conviction. When I had satisfied him that you and your mother were safe, he begged me to do my best to find the two men who had ruined him. I began that search at once. But there was not a trace of them—they had disappeared as completely as if they were dead. I used all sorts of means to trace them—without effect. And when at last your father's term of imprisonment was over and I went to see him on his release, I had to tell him that up to that point all my efforts had been useless. I urged him to let the thing drop, and to start life afresh. But he was determined. Find both men, but particularly Wraye, he would! He refused point–blank to even see his children until he had found these men and had forced them to acknowledge their misdeeds as regards him, for that, of course, would have cleared him to a certain extent. And in spite of everything I could say, he there and then went off abroad in search of them—he had got some clue, faint and indefinite, but still there, as to Wraye's presence in America, and he went after him. From that time until the morning of his death here in Wrychester I never saw him again!"

The Paradise Mystery

"You did see him that morning" asked Mary.

"I saw him, of course, unexpectedly," answered Ransford. "I had been across the Close—I came back through the south aisle of the Cathedral. Just before I left the west porch I saw Brake going up the stairs to the galleries. I knew him at once. He did not see me, and I hurried home much upset. Unfortunately, I think, Bryce came in upon me in that state of agitation. I have reason to believe that he began to suspect and to plot from that moment. And immediately on hearing of Brake's death, and its circumstances, I was placed in a terrible dilemma. For I had made up my mind never to tell you two of your father's history until I had been able to trace these two men and wring out of them a confession which would have cleared him of all but the technical commission of the crime of which he was convicted. Now I had not the least idea that the two men were close at hand, nor that they had had any hand in his death, and so I kept silence, and let him be buried under the name he had taken   John Braden."

Ransford paused and looked at his two listeners as if inviting question or comment. But neither spoke, and he went on.

"You know what happened after that," he continued. "It soon became evident to me that sinister and secret things were going on. There was the death of the labourer—Collishaw. There were other matters. But even then I had no suspicion of the real truth—the fact is, I began to have some strange suspicions about Bryce and that old man Harker—based upon certain evidence which I got by chance. But, all this time, I had never ceased my investigations about Wraye and Flood, and when the bank–manager on whom Brake had called in London was here at the inquest, I privately told him the whole story and invited his co–operation in a certain line which I was then following. That line suddenly ran up against the man Flood —otherwise Fladgate. It was not until this very week, however, that my agents definitely discovered Fladgate to be Flood, and that—through the investigations about Flood —Folliot was found to be Wraye. Today, in London, where I met old Harker at the bank at which Brake had lodged the money he had brought from Australia, the whole thing was made clear by the last agent of mine who has had the searching in hand. And it shows how men may easily disappear from a certain round of life, and turn up in another years after! When those two men cheated your father out of that money, they disappeared and separated—each, no doubt, with his share. Flood went off to some obscure place in the North of England; Wraye went over to America. He evidently made a fortune there; knocked about the world for awhile; changed his name to

208

Folliot, and under that name married a wealthy widow, and settled down here in Wrychester to grow roses! How and where he came across Flood again is not exactly clear, but we knew that a few years ago Flood was in London, in very poor circumstances, and the probability is that it was then when the two men met again. What we do know is that Folliot, as an influential man here, got Flood the post which he has held, and that things have resulted as they have. And that's all!—all that I need tell you at present. There are details, but they're of no importance."

Mary remained silent, but Dick got up with his hands in his pockets.

"There's one thing I want to know," he said. "Which of those two chaps killed my father? You said it was accident—but was it? I want to know about that! Are you saying it was accident just to let things down a bit? Don't! I want to know the truth."

"I believe it was accident," answered Ransford. "I listened most carefully just now to Fladgate's account of what happened. I firmly believe the man was telling the truth. But I haven't the least doubt that Folliot poisoned Collishaw —not the least. Folliot knew that if the least thing came out about Fladgate, everything would come out about himself."

Dick turned away to leave the room.

"Well, Folliot's done for!" he remarked. "I don't care about him, but I wanted to know for certain about the other."

* * * * *

When Dick had gone, and Ransford and Mary were left alone, a deep silence fell on the room. Mary was apparently deep in thought, and Ransford, after a glance at her, turned away and looked out of the window at the sunlit Close, thinking of the tragedy he had just witnessed. And he had become so absorbed in his thoughts of it that he started at feeling a touch on his arm and looking round saw Mary standing at his side.

"I don't want to say anything now," she said, "about what you have just told us. Some of it I had half-guessed, some of it I had conjectured. But why didn't you tell me! Before! It wasn't that you hadn't confidence?"

"Confidence!" he exclaimed. "There was only one reason—I wanted to get your father's memory cleared—as far as possible—before ever telling you anything. I've been wanting to tell you! Hadn't you seen that I hated to keep silent?"

"Hadn't you seen that I wanted to share all your trouble about it?" she asked. "That was what hurt me—because I couldn't!"

Ransford drew a long breath and looked at her. Then he put his hands on her shoulders.

"Mary!" he said. "You—you don't mean to say—be plain!—you don't mean that you can care for an old fellow like me?"

He was holding her away from him, but she suddenly smiled and came closer to him.

"You must have been very blind not to have seen that for a long time!" she answered.

Printed in the United States
24945LVS00002BA/80

9 781419 176630